ForeTold

"Survivor Stories of the

Prophetic End of the World"

Book One

Library of Congress Info

ISBN-13: 978-0-9830844-5-7
Control Number: 2018933863

Published in the United States of America by:
The Plan Bible™
10026-A S. Mingo Rd. #324
Tulsa, OK 74133

Publisher's Contact: www.PlanBible.com

Mark 13:23b

…behold, I have foretold you all things.

(KJV)

Dedications

I dedicate this book to my lovely wife who has walked this journey with me in a manner that has passionately inspired faith. Her patience has been a true stabilizer while traveling life together.

I would also like to give extra special thanks to Dr. Cheryl Swanson for the numerous hours of editing necessary to shape the work into its final version.

The legacy of this book is devoted to those who find themselves in need of a savior after the disappearance of countless millions who have gone home to be with their Lord and Savior Jesus Christ. God is merciful and desires that all come to repentance and the knowledge of His Son Jesus Christ.

~Jeff Swanson

I would like to dedicate this book to my wife and son without whom my confidence would not be possible to accomplish much in life. As I have wrestled with the concept of Eschatology (the study of End Times from a Biblical standpoint) and have nearly eliminated comments from non-Biblical sources that pontificate regarding the End Times, my focus has been upon what the truth of the Scripture says about itself. Jesus states in John 3 "Surely, I say to you," which is a legal determination that since no one else can really verify what He is saying, He must do what He does with the Father's authority. I believe that that is the best way to consider the Scripture that is yet to be fulfilled. To Him do I dedicate my life and study. Finally, I would like to thank April Scharpf for cleverly providing us with the title for the book series.

~Dr. Scott Young

Prologue

Every eye was intensely focused on the Judge, the King of kings, the Lord of lords, as He sat upon His throne. His countenance was as lightning. His eyes were as burning fire, yet his face was full of mercy and compassion. Nathan never thought it would come to this, an appeal before the highest court in the Kingdom, but he knew his future business would depend on the verdict.

The onlookers waited outside the Temple's sanctuary building with anticipation as they could sense someone's life was going to change forever. The focus was on Jesus Christ, who, as it had been prophesied, rules the earth with an iron rod. Nathan briefly glanced about seeing that the entire inside of the throne room where the court was held was gold of the finest purity. Every light glistened intensely as if emanating from the gold itself.

Next to the alabaster throne was the Tree of Life. The natural onlookers knew that one bite from this Tree, and they would be able to live forever. However, it had been foretold that they would not be able to eat of it until the completion of the 1,000-year reign of Christ on earth. The fruit, which resembled a cluster of dates from a palm tree, beckoned but was only available to the Resurrecteds who are now ruling and reigning with Jesus Christ on earth. Nothing like it had been seen on earth since the original Garden of Eden. The Tree was reproduced from the one in heaven where the loving heavenly Father still resides. The fragrance permeated the Throne room and caused every physical sense to tingle.

A spring of crystal clear living water started as a trickle, originating from under the Master's throne. It grew in size, seemingly by itself, as it traversed through the massive Temple complex before it exited the outer courtyard's eastern gate a half-mile away. This river gave life to the New Jerusalem that was the capital of planet earth.

Jesus raised His right hand just slightly, but it served to gather the audience's attention. Light beams could be seen through the holes in His hands that existed as a memorial of His love for all humanity, when He removed their sins forever.

"Nathan, you are in the right." Condensed verdicts were often the norm from this highest courtroom. Nathan's architecture business would be vindicated for all to see. This verdict meant that his business would grow exponentially, and he would be able to bless more people than he ever imagined. Nathan glanced over to see his legal opponent's head slumped down, looking somber but knowing that justice had been served.

Part One

ForeTold

CHAPTER 1

200 Years Later...

Nathan Covington's bones were beginning to ache. The hours upon hours of leaning over his architecture drawings were being felt, but the older method allowed him to see the buildings better than the three-dimensional images currently being created. The younger generations, who were born long after him, were always pushing the boundaries of advanced technologies. He realized the technological advances in architecture were no different than those which had occurred in communication devices throughout the centuries, but he had trouble keeping up with the rapid pace of technology advancement.

He stood up and stretched. As he thought about the *Kingdom Generation* workers he had in his company, his mind began to wander and reflect on the changes that had occurred since Jesus had set up His earthly reign.

The *Kingdom Generations* - those born during what the Bible called the Thousand Year Reign - would never realize how new technologies were continually challenging the minds of the *Survivor Nations* - those natural people who survived what the Bible called the Great Tribulation. The *Survivor Nations* and their descendants are now called Naturals.

The *Kingdom Generations* Naturals and the *Survivor Nation* Naturals are a separate group of people. They are not the ruling class which is comprised of a select group known as Resurrecteds – who rule and reign over the earth as the Bride of the Bridegroom, Jesus Christ the Lord of lords and King of kings.

The original *Survivor Nations* had passed through the *Judgment of the Living* after the Great Tribulation. They could not forget the time when Jesus separated them out to partake of the Kingdom on earth. The grace of God had given them life beyond human expression.

Nathan was one of those survivors. Good-natured catcalls of *"grampa"* had been tossed his way over the years in reference to his antiquated methods of organizing and working. Now, his back was paying the price for his old-fashioned ways of leaning into his work.

Nathan was the founder of the architectural firm known as Covington International. His partner was his Kingdom son, Alexander, who was born after Jesus' return to earth. They had first begun to dream about opening a firm two hundred and fifty years ago as the two of them sat on the lawn of his son's University, hours after he had graduated with his doctoral degree in architecture. Through the succeeding years, Alexander would prove to be much more visionary than Nathan about the direction the company should go. But one thing they had agreed on from the first was that they wanted their firm to be a place for training young architects using the standard twenty-five year apprenticeship model.

Both Nathan and Alexander enjoyed it when an employee had finished his or her apprenticeship. That is, when the apprentice made "The Choice" as they called it: to either open his or her own branch of the company or open up a new company.

How far Nathan had come in his Christ-likeness! It was quite a contrast to his old competitive nature, which used to rise up in the beginning of this new era. If an apprentice would make the choice to launch out and start his own company, Nathan would try to convince them to stay on, not wanting to lose their experience. The Kingdom needed creative geniuses to flourish but, at the time, Nathan selfishly wanted them to remain under his corporate roof. Momentary flashes of anger would rise inside, until Nathan remembered the King of king's ways and the anger would quickly subside.

Now, at his advanced age of 347, all those old ways of thinking were long forgotten, and internal peace was the only thing that mattered. Perfect contentment brought joy to each new day.

Nathan paused from his wandering thoughts and gazed out the window. Gleaming new structures made of the finest cut stone rose around him. Prosperity for all people under the rule of Jesus Christ was evident everywhere he looked. His business had flourished in the new economy, so much so that he now resided at the palace, as Nathan liked to think of his huge estate. It was a place of aesthetic beauty on a scale that cultivated his imagination and allowed him to perform at the highest level. His diligent business efforts had led to this reward, and no one could take it away from him. Everything about it was a memorial to how the King had given him a new chance for life in the Kingdom. What great grace God had given to one who did not deserve such as this.

His garden was vast; it could only be strolled through when measured in hours. It contained varieties of flowers from all over the Kingdom. Every brilliant color and hue imaginable was arrayed like a tapestry that made his heart soar every time he saw it. Since the curse of the land was removed, gardens seemed to display themselves in perfection that made the eye scan endlessly without finding a flaw or a weed in sight. The aroma of hundreds of thousands of blooming flowers delighted all who entered. In the distance Nathan's pet grizzly bear and caribou could be seen grazing on the vibrant green grass. They grazed in harmony with each other displaying the Master's complete reversal of all adverse effects that the fall of humanity had had on the animal kingdom. The harmony once found in the Garden of Eden at the beginning of creation was now restored for all to enjoy.

Nathan and his wife, Julia, had celebrated their 295th wedding anniversary under the large sprawling oak tree behind the home on their estate. Nathan's first wife,

Kathryn, celebrated with them, which felt a little odd. However, Kathryn was a Resurrected and marriage was no longer necessary or desired by the Resurrecteds, for they were married to the King – not in the physical sense experienced before the Return, but married in a whole-hearted, devotional way. The Resurrecteds experienced incomparable joy that was absolutely unwavering. This constant state of joy exceeded any earthly pleasure. In her was no jealousy or envy. Her whole being emanated the character of Jesus Christ, and she was delighted the two were enjoying the Kingdom together. It was now 300 years *After the Return,* and Kathryn did not look a day over 30. Her resurrected body had been transfigured into the glory of the Master. It was as if God's glory shone forth from her spirit and emanated for all to see.

Over the years, Julia and Nathan had raised twelve children. Inside, their estate home was adorned with photos from hundreds of events and travels throughout the entire Kingdom. There were no travel restrictions and every place on earth was eager to serve vacationing families, granting them a magical experience at every destination. Each place was an amazing display of creativity endowed by the Father of heaven. Every wall was a monument to another family event that made them shout for joy, thanking God for what they had been given.

One day as Nathan was traversing the main hallway, praising God for his family, he noticed a particular envelope like none he had ever seen. He paused as he reached for the ornate envelope, and his hands began to shake as he read the word "Jerusalem". His favorite place in the entire Kingdom: Jerusalem, which was the capital of the planet. It was the hallowed center of the Kingdom. Slowly, he opened the envelope and read the words that it contained:

You are hereby requested by the Maker of the Universe to attend our annual festival in the Holy City on this year's Feast of Tabernacles in the year 300 After His Return. The King will announce you to His Father in heaven and to the Naturals of the earth along with four other invitees. All will tell their testimonies of the grace bestowed upon them in the years Before His Return. A special vehicle will arrive five days before the event, brought by a Resurrected to escort you to Jerusalem in preparation for your Testimony. Consider your words prayerfully as the Master prepares the Kingdom's heart to hear what you have to say. He is always with you.

Farewell...Gabriel

Nathan had never seen more authentic calligraphy than that which was penned by the hand of the angel Gabriel. Time seemed to stand still as he absorbed what the letter said. His heart raced. He was being honored by the King to be one of the Holy Testifiers such as those he had heard over the years. He had never imagined this honor would come to him.

He stood still for several long moments trying to absorb the magnitude of what this meant. Finally, he carefully and thoughtfully tucked the letter into the envelope and went in search of Julia. He found her, busy as usual, in the kitchen.

"Julia, would you go to Jerusalem with me?"

"Jerusalem?" she questioned, surprise lighting her face as she looked up from the vegetables she was dicing at the kitchen island. Setting down the knife and wiping her hands, she turned to give Nathan her full attention.

Nathan slowly shared the contents of the invitation with her and the meaning of the words that were penned.

9

Julia thought quietly about what Nathan had told her for a moment and then said, "I think it would be better if I stayed home and interceded for you. I also think if I'm not there it will allow you to focus on this monumental task you have been given." She softly touched his chin.

"I trust your insight," Nathan replied. "I will miss having you by my side, but I know from the years we've spent together, your prayers will help me immensely and I feel I can use all the help I can get at this point."

"Oh, Nathan, I am so excited that you have been chosen. The Master thinks so highly of you. Your testimony will be recorded for the next generations to come!" Julia beamed.

"But what will I say?" Nathan asked, feeling overwhelmed as he turned and gazed out the window, his brow furrowed in contemplation as the weight of the responsibility of the request settled on him.

"Preparation for that day must come with prayer," Julia answered softly.

"He is expecting me to be great," Nathan muttered.

"Actually, I am too."

"What do you mean?" he asked.

"I know it is difficult to even think back to the days *Before the Return*." Julia paused for a moment to gather her thoughts.

She continued, "Life is so different now, and it is painful to force the mind to think about times that we were not in the Master's will. However, these *Kingdom Generations* need guidance and wisdom. The wisdom that comes from experiencing what we could have escaped, if we had only believed. One day, at the end of the Lord's thousand years, these *Kingdom Generations* will have their hearts tested. They must be found pure and obedient to the Lord or Satan, the deceiver who will be released from his prison in the *Abyss*, will come and steal them away forever. Your testimony reveals the magnitude of God's grace, by which he has given you the Kingdom. It is an honor to plant this seed in those who hear. The seed you plant could ultimately save them from eternal separation. I can see them now in eternity thanking you, even though you might never get a chance to meet them in this age."

Julia then asked, "Do you remember when I told you about owning that accounting business *Before the Return*? Monthly, I would worry about finances. New software and updated servers were always needed to keep the doors open, and payroll was constantly in the back of my mind," she paused as she reached into the refrigerator resuming her meal preparations.

"I know, honey. We never trusted the Master in those days. We both had our professions which consumed us to the detriment of our families."

"Yes, exactly...but the *Kingdom Generations* have never had to experience that kind of fear and anxiety because they have grown up under the abundant provision in this Kingdom," Julia replied. "They need to hear about what it is like to be separated from the Master."

"But, I will be on stage in front of the whole Kingdom. I fear that I will utter a message that is not pleasing," Nathan said as he looked away.

"What did Moses say to the burning bush?" Julia queried.

"Sounds like the beginning of a joke..."

Julia ignored his comment, picked up the knife again and went thoughtfully on, "Moses complained about being slow of speech, but you are not slow of speech, and the Lord wants your authentic testimony." Then she playfully pointed the knife toward the study and waved it in encouragement for him to get started as she said, "You have some work ahead of you, young man."

Over the next few days, Nathan communicated with his office that he would not be available to work on the Holmann building project. The Holmann's were notified of the delay, but they were already aware of Nathan's invitation and knew that their project would be on hold for a time. Nathan's name had been broadcast on the Kingdom airwaves as one of this year's Testifiers; therefore, no one questioned his need for solitude.

Solitude in the Kingdom was a time for introspective reflection on the King, His will, and His ways. Living in a place like the Garden of Eden, which was spreading to encompass the whole planet, created the perfect motivational environment to encourage both Naturals and the *Kingdom Generations* to grow in God's eternal love.

As Nathan mused about these *Kingdom Generations*, it never ceased to amaze him that in such a place as this, there still could be secret sins of the heart. Nathan thoughts drifted to one of his rising apprentices employed at his office ten years ago. Alexander had appointed this apprentice, Helen Proctor, to handle the Bodenstein estate project, which was located near a new mountain range. Due to the massive earthquake that had occurred on the last day of the Great Tribulation, all the old mountain ranges were gone and new ones had risen in different places causing geography to no longer be the same as the *old world*. The Bodenstein's had survived the Great Tribulation. As direct descendants of the tribe of Issachar, God's Chosen people of Israel, they were given the honor of ruling over the non-Hebrew Naturals on earth. They spent most of the year in Israel, but from time to time wished to travel back to their new estate in the mountains.

Helen Proctor had been one of the fifth *Kingdom Generations* (called 5ths) born since the return of Christ. She was young and eager to learn all the intricacies of art and science necessary for effective building techniques. In the beginning, she was the best listener of the eight new apprentices that Nathan and Alexander had taken on. She followed requests closely and asked some of the best questions. She didn't really concern herself with the politics that affect large companies. The Resurrecteds overseeing their city were not a concern to her at first. However, in time she started to resent being one of the *Kingdom Generations*. She began questioning the Lord's choice for her to be alive now, rather than in the *old world* where she would have been given the opportunity to receive Christ and live in a resurrected body. She was slowly pulling away from the peace that the entire society so bountifully lived in. Inwardly, the resentment was starting to swell.

One day Helen approached Alexander. "I need more than my parent's view of the Kingdom. Jesus has rewarded those who work hard, so I want to earn my own way in this life and achieve more."

If Nathan had heard that comment, he would have addressed his concerns instantly by confronting the issue. Alexander, however, did not give it much thought at the time. The younger generations were always willing to step out and accomplish tasks that were either deemed too dangerous or unwise in the eyes of their elders. Alexander assumed this was one of those instances.

Another issue of which Nathan was unaware was that Helen's mother had died at the tender age of 84 signifying the existence of an unrighteous issue for which she had refused to repent. Normally, such an occurrence marked the children for significant counseling from Jerusalem no matter what their age; however, Helen had refused to cooperate and complete the counseling.

She began to work longer hours on the Bodenstein project with Alexander's interspersed oversight. When she asked a coworker to help her understand what Alexander was requesting for the third floor of the building, the father and son should have seen it coming. She had enlisted the help of Thulan, who was also young and still within his own apprenticeship. They stayed night after night busily creating and recreating the levels that the Bodenstein's had asked for. Thulan shared the same sentiment as Helen; he should have been given the chance to be a Resurrected ruler. Alexander's love for the project being done with excellence blinded him to the resentment that was building in the two young lives.

Thulan and Helen didn't renew their minds to Kingdom thinking through daily meditation on the words and teachings of Jesus. Instead, they allowed their sinful nature to become engrafted deep in their hearts and dreamed of having more power than what was given to them by God's grace and providence.

The apostle Peter was the top magistrate for that sector of the Kingdom. When word came forward of the unrest, he summoned them to his throne. He listened to each of them when they arrived. He found them unrepentant of their inward sin and unwilling to consider a change of heart. Helen's hot tears of anger fell to the floor before her. As Peter dismissed them from the building he was deeply saddened, because he knew what would come next. Due to their pride, greed and unrepentance, both would perish before ever reaching the young age of one hundred.

Nathan knew that these were the types of people he would need to reach with his testimony. He needed to inspire them to seek the Master's ways and obey them, not because it was expected of them but because they loved the Master and wanted to express great appreciation for what He had done for them. He needed to encourage them to run their race, so that they would one day be able to partake of the Tree of Life in the New Jerusalem to come. He knew once they ate just one bite of the Tree of Life, they would live forever and sin would have no hold on them. They would still have natural bodies, but they would be like the Resurrecteds in the sense that they would never be able to die!

Nathan spent time praying that God would give him the right words to say and humbly offered his testimony to accomplish these ends. As he prayed, He felt a peace beyond his understanding encompass him and knew he had been heard.

A grandfather clock began to chime in the hallway, signaling to Nathan that it was time to rest.

ForeTold

CHAPTER 2

The next morning, Julia was already showering before Nathan opened his eyes. A beautiful worship tune permeated the air drawing him out of sleep. It was a familiar song as it had recently been sung by their worship leader, a Resurrected, during a fellowship gathering at the local house of worship.

Nathan stretched and gingerly rose to his feet. His plantar fasciitis was back in his left foot and both knees screamed for relief as he reached for the ornate bedpost to steady himself. Stretching a little more to ease the ache in his back, he thought of the benefits that awaited him in Jerusalem. Once there he would be able to avail himself of the leaves from the Fruit Trees flourishing along the River of Living Water, which streamed from the Temple. Those leaves would bring healing to his physical body and welcome relief from his continual discomfort.

Once dressed, Nathan moved to his study and closed the door. With the impending weight of his testimony, there could be no distractions. He lowered himself into his chair and picked up his worn Bible. How long he spent reading he did not know, but he read until peace rose up from within and he could formulate his thoughts regarding his experiences during the Tribulation and seeing his Lord and Master face to face for the first time. As the words of life infiltrated his heart and mind, the pieces began to fall into place. He was now finally ready to write.

He found his favorite pen and lined notepad, imprinted with the Kingdom University's logo upon the cover. This logo was adorned with the Lion and Lamb gently butting heads underneath a Cross. Most of the *Kingdom Generations* didn't use pen and paper, but Nathan still preferred it. He was grateful that a few retailers still catered to the old-timers and carried their archaic ink pens and paper notepads. The *Kingdom Generations* favored the digital means; pens that had a memory bank that transcribed and stored their words electronically allowing them to securely record their deepest thoughts and personal revelations for future use.

Nathan sensed the Lord's presence as he began to record his testimony. Each word and phrase was carefully thought through; his testimony would contain no idle words. He knew the power of words in the Kingdom and the power of testimony. He could no longer suppress the pain of his past knowing that sharing his experiences would benefit these new *Kingdom Generations* and perhaps save them from a needless shortened life and eternal destruction.

Nathan wanted the Master to be pleased. This would be his one opportunity to express his deep gratitude for being part of the Kingdom. He wanted his words to penetrate deep into the hearts of the listeners. He looked down at what he had written. It was good, he thought, but was it what the Master wanted him to share?

He lowered himself onto his aching knees and prayed once again, "Lord of heaven and earth, I honor Your name as the Creator, the Redeemer and now my King. Please open my heart to the events of the past, so that I can reveal them in a way that glorifies You in all that I say as well as in the way that I say them. Give me utterance without fear so that none in the sound of my voice will be lost at the end of the thousand years when Satan is released to deceive. Let my testimony be one of Your grace and Your faithfulness to never give up on me even when I was wandering so far from You."

Instantaneously, Nathan received the answer. He saw it in the form of a picture. He saw his sinful life from a young age until Jesus came into his heart, when he made Him the Lord of his life forever. He could see when he had made poor choices and repeatedly spurned God's love. However, his eyes were opened to all of God's patience and all of His faithfulness as He kept knocking at the door of Nathan's heart. He also remembered when all else was no longer of any value, and there was nothing left to live for, God was there. God met him right where he needed Him. And looking back now, he was able to discern the many times angels aided him when he did not deserve it. This had only been revealed to him after he entered the Kingdom.

He returned to his desk, but instead of picking up his pen he reached for an electronic tablet which would do the writing for him, sensing the words of his testimony urgently clamoring for release from within him. So he began to speak forth his testimony.

Fourteen pages of words came forth in what seemed like an unstoppable flood of compassion for those who were going to hear this message. It flowed without effort. The testimony burst forth as if it could hardly wait to be heard. He was not even aware of the time as the hours flew by. The only thing that mattered was getting this right. People's eternity could be at stake, based on what he shared and the way he shared it.

Eventually Nathan glanced at the time, which now read seven o'clock. Nathan understood the significance of that number. Seven represented spiritual perfection in the Lord's language. It was as if the Lord said, "*It is finished.*"

Nathan's soul felt extreme satisfaction and he sensed the joy of the Master in what had been accomplished. He paused and gave thanks for the work of the day, taking some precious moments to glorify the One who had brought him through so much. He sighed with relief as he felt the assurance that the Master had prepared him to say just what needed to be said.

ForeTold

CHAPTER 3

Nathan reveled in his time spent in the presence of the Master preparing his testimony, but the time had come to search through the house for Julia. He found her relaxing quietly on the back porch swing. Joining her, they watched the beautiful display of red-orange color as the sun began its descent over the horizon. The flagrant artistry of the sky as the sun set gave Nathan one more reason to marvel at the awesomeness of the Master.

Nathan heard Julia sigh with pleasure at the scene and turned his gaze in her direction. She was beautiful. Her long black hair gleamed with the rays of the sinking sun and her dark eyelashes framed her big brown eyes. Her true age was impossible to discern by outward appearance, she didn't look a day over 55.

"You are the prettiest 345 year old woman I have ever seen," he smiled.

Julia returned the smile with a mischievous one of her own.

Nathan continued, "No one would guess your age, but with me, they can see signs of old age creeping in."

"Thank you," Julia replied as she squeezed his arm, "but contrary to what you believe or feel, you are still my handsome husband."

"I don't feel...," Nathan began, but she interrupted him before he could finish his sentence.

"The healing leaves on the Fruit Trees in Jerusalem are going to do wonders for you. After this visit you will be good to go for another 350 years."

"By the way, since you are going to Jerusalem, I made a list of a few items that I would like you to bring home," Julia added.

"I will be glad to," he replied. "Maybe I could also learn how to lose a little weight while I'm there," he stated as he jovially patted his belly.

"I love you just the way you are," Julia retorted. "You will feel better once you see the doctors there."

"They certainly helped me when I went before," Nathan mused in agreement.

They fell back into the quiet hush of the evening as the last rays of the sun disappeared and the air grew noticeably cooler. As Nathan's thoughts drifted to the coming days, his eyes began to grow heavy. Julia, sensing his weariness, pulled him up from the swing and led him inside.

Five in the morning seemed to arrive quickly. The alarm, set to play music, went off with a chorus of a worship song that gave praise and gratitude to the Author of life. How great it was to be in the Kingdom, Nathan marveled as he contemplated the words of the chorus. As the music concluded, he reached to turn off the alarm and knelt beside the bed to spend a few more moments in worship and prayer before allowing his mind to fill with the many details of the coming day.

The doorbell rang. Julia opened the door and greeted Kathryn warmly. The two exchanged small talk and caught up with the details of their daily lives. The support and acceptance that Kathryn freely extended to both Nathan and Julia never ceased to amaze them. Those who were resurrected with or without their spouses didn't seem to be concerned about marriage anymore. The pervading feeling seemed to be an all-consuming love for the Master which translated into greater peace and joy than any earthly marriage could offer. While it was difficult for the Resurrecteds to describe to the Naturals just how much fulfillment their lives contained, it was evident to any who observed them.

"Are you sure you would prefer to stay home and watch the broadcasts of the Feast of Tabernacles this year rather than accompanying your husband?" Kathryn asked.

Julia looked down, "It still seems strange to hear you say that to me."

"What did I say that seems so strange?" Kathryn stepped back in bewilderment.

"Husband," Julia confessed.

Kathryn's eyes filled with tenderness and she grasped Julia's hands, "I love you both. The two of you are serving the Master together and building His Kingdom, and it fills me with great joy."

"That's what I love about you! Pure sincerity because the Master's love emanates out of you." Julia's thoughts turned inward and she said to herself, "I made some bad choices *Before the Return,* or I too would be a Resurrected."

Kathryn responded to Julia's unspoken thought, "Remember, you were forgiven for those choices long ago, when Jesus Himself took all of your sins upon His body on the Cross, and then cast them into the heart of the earth." This heightened perception and sensitivity by the Holy Spirit is characteristic of all Resurrecteds.

Julia looked stunned and repentantly said, "You speak the truth. Thank you for reminding me of God's mercy and grace." She moved forward and embraced her saying, "I have so much to be thankful for."

It was at that instant that Nathan came around the corner with a shoulder bag for his journey. He stopped in midstride as he watched his earthly wife hugging his former wife. His initial inclination was to turn back the way he had come so as not to intrude. However, he was held in place as feelings of gratitude overcame him as he witnessed the display of true acceptance. The revealing nature of the Spirit of Love was evident in this one moment in time.

Nathan regained his composure as he entered the room and greeted Kathryn. Turning to Julia he said, "I love you and will call when we arrive." Nathan kissed her tenderly.

"I love you too," Julia replied and then turned toward Kathryn once more. "To answer your earlier question, I am content staying here and watching the broadcasts. Nathan and I have discussed this and feel he will be less distracted if I stay home and support him in prayer from here."

"I understand," Kathryn replied. She turned to Nathan and asked, "Are you ready?"

Nathan drew in a deep breath and nodded.

They stepped out onto the front porch and approached the small vehicle parked in front of the house. With a wave of Kathryn's hand the trunk of the car opened automatically. As she took Nathan's bag, he thought to protest that it might be too heavy. Nevertheless, Kathryn easily lifted it and gently deposited it in the trunk, casting a mischievous grin his way since she knew what he was thinking. He smiled sheepishly at her as she then, with another wave of hand, the trunk shut itself. Shaking his head, Nathan proceeded to enter the vehicle on the right as Kathryn slid into the driver's seat.

Still shaking his head, Nathan commented, "This is weird. You don't even need a vehicle. Just like the Master all you have to do is picture in your mind where you want to be and you are there. But I appreciate you escorting me in this aero-car."

Kathryn turned the engine on and prepared to lift off. Within seconds they were moving through the air at Mach speeds. Nathan marveled a little as he thought about how advanced transportation – and everything else - had become since Jesus had set up the Kingdom. What was once just for movies and the imagination had become reality. He didn't often avail himself of the aerial modes of transportation preferring the slower pace of ground transports unless traveling to the Holy City, so it had been a while since he had experienced the sensation of traveling at such speeds.

"I haven't gone this slowly for some time," Kathryn joked.

"So sorry to slow you down," Nathan retorted.

"Oh, there is no need to apologize," Kathryn responded. "In all seriousness, I requested this assignment. I am so pleased with who you have become. I see you as the Lord does: finished. The race is not completed, but you have won in many ways."

"That is amazing."

"What?"

"How Resurrecteds can discern the heart of a person," Nathan commented.

"The Scripture states, *'Man looks on the outer appearance, but God looks upon the heart.'* Only by the Holy Spirit living within us can this be done." Kathryn briefly glanced in his direction.

"I think I know that Scriptural reference...," Nathan began.

Kathryn went on as if he had not spoken, "It is as if there is a marathon that you are running. At this point, you are a good portion of the way through.

"Before I was resurrected, I often felt fearful and anxious anticipating future events that I could not control. I didn't really start my race or keep my eyes on the prize until our son was caught up into heaven, leaving us behind. After that I became extremely focused, and once my race was completed, I realized that Jesus was running it with me all the way. It was as if He was cheering me on and then watching with joy as I broke the tape at the end.

"Having run my race, I now have insight into the journey you are on. I instantly see your battles and many of the struggles you are facing. I pray the Lord gives you the vision to see yourself victoriously crossing the finish line," she said with sincerity. After a brief pause she concluded, "I love the insight with which the Master has blessed me. There is a peace that comes with the knowledge I've been given, but also a certainty that the work we do is important for eternity."

Nathan grew quiet as he thought deeply about all Kathryn had said. She understood his need to process, and did not break the silence. She continued to navigate toward the Holy City and soon noticed Nathan recline and stretch out in his seat. She glanced his way briefly and saw that while he stared thoughtfully out the window, his eyes were growing heavy. Before long, Nathan dozed off much like he had on past road trips.

CHAPTER 4

Kathryn spoke softly, "Nathan, wake up," as she gently nudged him and pointed out the window of the aero-car. Nathan opened his eyes and looked in the direction she was pointing. His eyes slowly focused on the city coming into view.

This wasn't just any city; it was The City, Jerusalem, the jewel of the Kingdom. It had a glory canopy that gave the impression the city was engulfed in the presence of the Almighty, even though the Father still resided in heaven awaiting the day when He would dwell amongst all His people. At this time, the glory beamed in all directions like a fire surrounding the city. There was no doubt this was where Jesus Christ resided and dwelled among His people. The glory of the Lord shone forth creating a sense of safety and security for all. Even just looking upon the city, Nathan could feel the comforting presence of the Master. He felt the unconditional love and warmth, surrounding and encompassing him. It was as if he was submersed in the embraced of the arms of the One who had come to save him.

The walls surrounding the city were made of precious stones like rubies. The ever-open gates of jewels sparkled as an unending stream of people came bearing gifts of wealth honoring the King of kings. They came bearing great gifts out of humble gratitude for the prosperity they enjoyed in His Kingdom. Their faces were radiant with joy as they walked down streets that glistened like a reflection of the glory shining through the city.

In the distance Nathan could see the River of Living Water flowing towards the North side of the city from the Holy Temple, where it divided into two. One branch

27

curved to the East, flowing down to the Living Sea, once known as the Dead Sea, but now restored to life by the presence of the Master. The other side flowed to the West, emptying into the Mediterranean Sea. On both banks of the river grew magnificent Fruit Trees, whose leaves never withered. Every month they bore new fruit, because the water from the River gave them continual life. The trees also produced leaves with properties for the healing of the Naturals. The grandeur was almost impossible to comprehend!

The highways leading into the city were the widest of any in the Kingdom, but that did not distract from the beauty of the surrounding countryside which seemed like just an extension of the grandeur of the city itself. The grass was a brilliant emerald green, carpeting hills and valleys alike. Groves of trees and gardens possessing all manner of lush vegetation could be seen from every vantage point in the city. It was like the Garden of Eden had been restored and was expanding out from this central location.

Ground vehicles could be seen moving rapidly along the roadways, many of the occupants arriving for the Feast of Tabernacles, a most holy time for the City. Nathan and Kathryn continued along above the highways, which afforded them a panoramic view of Jerusalem.

Nathan, being a long-time architect, was filled with awe and wonder as he looked on the beautiful city.

The buildings, designed by the Resurrecteds, were famous throughout the entire Kingdom for their innovation and graceful lines. Heavenly-based technologies were used to create building materials strong enough to hold the intricate angles, and decorate the most important city on earth.

Kathryn pulled up outside of the Habakkuk Hotel just south of the city center. The ride had been smooth and even though they had traveled at speeds that were impossible in the *old world*, Nathan's back had become stiff from the position he had been in for the three-hour journey.

"Let me help you check in," Kathryn said as she gracefully got out of the car and moved toward the trunk to retrieve his bag and swing it over her shoulder. Stepping to the passenger side where Nathan had opened his door, she offered him a supporting hand as he climbed out. "I will take you up on that," Nathan replied as they stepped through the entrance and into the plaza lobby, which was adorned with the most ornate furnishings and wall hangings that he had ever seen. It was almost too much for him to take in.

A bellman, dressed in the elegant livery of the hotel staff, graciously removed Nathan's bag from Kathryn's shoulder and escorted them to the registration desk, where Nathan thought to introduce himself to the attendant.

Before he could say a word, "Welcome, Mr. Covington. We have been expecting you. We hope you will find your room to your satisfaction. Your wife called ahead for you and requested that your bed and pillows be programmed with your preferred degree of firmness. She also asked that we have your Jacuzzi waiting at a perfect temperature for you."

"Thank you," said Nathan as he pulled his payer-unit out of his wallet.

"May I remind you, sir that no one pays for hotels in Israel. You are our honored guest. It is a pleasure to meet you. I have been reading on the Kingdom airwaves about the work you have done. I admire your architecture; your buildings are brilliant."

Nathan looked up in surprise, "Why, thank you. They pale in comparison to anything created by the Resurrecteds. They are capable of designs that our minds are not even able to fathom." Nathan offered his thumbprint to determine the location of his room inside the massive 170-story hotel.

"The Resurrecteds create immense beauty, but they speak of your designs with admiration that would elevate any Natural's self-esteem. So, please enjoy your stay with us, Mr. Covington, and be sure and let us know if you need anything at all. We are honored to serve you."

"Thank you," Nathan replied as he turned to follow Gene, the front desk bellman, to the elevator where Kathryn bid him goodnight. He was quiet as he tried to internalize the overwhelming idea that his work was valued by the Resurrecteds on the earth, whom he thought of as being perfect. It was another humbling reminder of all that he had received from the Master since entering the Kingdom.

Gene escorted Nathan to his room on the 150th floor. After Gene opened his door, Nathan made his way inside and was drawn to the window that looked out at the breathtaking picturesque view of the City with a glimpse of the Temple and the River of Living Water in the distance. He paused a moment, taking it all in.

"May I remind you the windows have a privacy dimming system, which can be activated on the touch screen of your personal control panel," Gene also pushed a button near the light switch to illuminate the flowing white valances and curtains.

"Would you allow me to hang your clothing in the closet, place your toiletries on the vanity, and then check the temperature on your Jacuzzi?"

"That isn't necessary..."

"I would be happy to do this for you for all you have done in service to the Kingdom," Gene busied himself with placing Nathan's belongings in their proper place. After less than ten minutes he was finished and bid Nathan goodnight with a handshake.

CHAPTER 5

Nathan spent most of that first night in his hotel room in quiet reflection, exactly how he wished it. He envisioned himself stepping up to the podium to deliver his speech with Jesus behind him on His throne. Not that he was sure there would be a podium, he was just assuming based on the celebrations he had seen in the past. However, each year Jesus seemed to uniquely design the setting to reflect those who were to testify. This year, Nathan knew that regardless of how it looked in the past, speaking onstage would be completely different from watching the proceedings from the comfort of his home. He squared his shoulders as the realization that the presence of the Lord would give him the confidence and ability he needed.

As he continued to quiet his soul, Nathan began to think about Samuel, his first son who was caught up in the Rapture before the Tribulation. He eagerly anticipated being reunited with his son in the morning. He pondered how nervous the thought of speaking before a large crowd made him feel, while his son had the ability to be on stage and sing in front of huge crowds. Then he remembered Samuel's word to him that it almost worried him if he didn't get nervous before a performance. He felt the nerves actually kept him sharp, on key and performing well. Nathan relaxed and smiled to himself as he began to feel more positive that his nervousness would be an asset, peaking at the right time.

Nathan brought his thoughts back to the present. As he made himself comfortable on the sofa he became enthralled with just how magnificent his room really was. Like the rest of the Holy City and many other parts of the Master's Kingdom, it reflected the goodness of God. His room was adorned with a fifteen-foot vaulted, arched

31

ceiling of cherry wood carved into a relief of the gates of Jerusalem. Every metallic fixture imaginable in the room, from the doorknobs to the bathroom faucets, was gleaming twenty-four carat gold. The light fixtures were adorned with precious crystals which cut the light into a magnificent display of the full spectrum of vibrant colors.

His eyes scanned down to the richly polished marble floor, on which was etched a representation of the River of Living Water which seemingly sparkled aqua blue. Ornate rugs of the finest silk lay under hand-carved exotic wood furnishings upholstered in opulent fabrics Louis XIV ball and claw furniture, overlaid in pure gold. On the walls, hand painted murals depicting the miracles of Jesus as recorded in the Bible served as memorials to God's power to heal and deliver His people.

As he considered his magnificent room, he realized that it did not differ from most hotel rooms in Jerusalem. The wealth of the Kingdom was for all to enjoy. Theft was a thing of the past, as were the vaults once used to lock up one's valuables. What a contrast to the petty covetousness that propelled the economy of the *old world* that he was about to give testimony to. He thought about the failures of his life *Before the Return.* They were many and he, as many who testified before him at the Feast of Tabernacles, were not proud of what they had done outside the Lord's will.

Nathan now understood the significance of I Corinthians 3:13-17, where it contained examples of different motives of Christians who had wasted their lives upon the "wood, hay and stubble." In the previous age these people indulged in luxury cars and homes as status symbols of financial success, and sought the affections of people who never truly loved them. Too much of his life had been filled with this nonsense; of not loving his family well enough and working too many hours. He had long ago realized that he had made a god of what used to be displayed upon old world TV screens - like the Lexus LS 980 he once drove – his beloved car. The best the *old world* had to offer was nothing but a mere Ford Pinto compared to what the least enjoyed in the Kingdom. He smiled to himself as he realized the things he took for granted in this Kingdom caused the things he had once thought important in his old life to slip into insignificance. With a sigh of appreciation, Nathan decided to call it a night.

At seven the next morning, the alarm awakened him from a deep sleep. Though it was a weekday, he could hardly wait to get to the Worship Center and hear today's message from the Master. One of the benefits to being in the Holy City was to attend the teaching sessions Jesus held each day. In anticipation, he rolled out of bed, stretched to relieve the aches in his back and went to shower and start his day. He had thirty minutes before he was to meet Kathryn and his son Samuel downstairs to go to the Worship Center.

Through the years, Nathan, often accompanied by Julia, had made a practice of meeting Kathryn and Samuel for most High Holy Days and attending worship services. On those occasions, they, being Resurrecteds, would transport themselves to the place of worship with a thought and save seats for Nathan and Julia. This time, however, he assumed they would meet him in the lobby and take him to the Jerusalem Worship Center in the same vehicle Kathryn had used for his trip to Jerusalem.

His eyes scanned the lobby as he stepped off of the elevator. He noticed them standing in a corner, inspecting the hotel. It was fascinating for Nathan to watch the two of them - both appearing to be around the age of 30 years old. It also amazed him how interested they were in the smallest details of the environment in which they found themselves. The Resurrecteds were beings who could travel to any portion of the universe to discover such things as exoplanets or distant star systems, and yet could also live in the moment and take the time to appreciate every aspect of the Master's Kingdom. In this moment, Samuel was pointing out the lines within a painting on the wall, while Kathryn hung on every word her son spoke. Nathan was not creative enough to be considered an artist because he was more of a "color within the lines" sort, but lines and colors in the work of others could delight him for hours. Samuel's fascination with the painting seemed to be an inheritance of art appreciation from his dad, while his musical abilities were from Kathryn. Nathan smiled to himself at the thought.

"Hey, Dad!" Samuel exclaimed as he ran towards him, embracing in a bear hug.

Nathan stepped back and looked at Samuel. "Son, you haven't aged a day!" he joked while Samuel chuckled.

"We thought you might be hungry, so we will be stopping by this wonderful café and bakery that makes the best breakfast specialties on earth. How does that sound?" Kathryn asked.

"That'd be great," Nathan moved towards the door.

As they approached the café, Nathans senses were delighted by the sights, sounds, and aromas that surrounded him. There were no longer walls around the Old City of Jerusalem. In fact, since Jesus had come to rule and reign, there was no need for fortified walls anywhere in the world. But in spite of the missing structures, there were still glimpses of the old next to the new. The streets were still cobbled in places and the buildings were close with narrow twisting streets that suddenly opened to parks and expanses of olive groves and pomegranate trees. Small courtyards and garden spaces were tucked here and there.

The sounds of Resurrecteds and Naturals going about their daily tasks could be heard while the wafting of fresh baked goods and exotic meats and vegetables filled the air.

Ten minutes later, they all stepped into Ardon's Delights, which happened to be just down the street from the Jerusalem Worship Center. They were seated at a table in the courtyard surrounded by arbors covered with bougainvillea and large pots of geraniums that provided shade while giving a framed view of the neighborhood surrounding the café.

They spent a few moments looking over the extensive menu. The two Resurrecteds settled on the traditional sesame bagels with cream cheese and coffee while Nathan indulged in a sampler plate of pastries, smoked lox, yogurt and fruit. There was just something about being in the Holy City that awakened a desire for such traditional fare and Nathan was happy to savor each of the unique flavors.

As they waited for their orders to arrive to the table, conversation flowed easily between them.

"It is such a joy to see you both again," Nathan remarked. "Tell me what you have been up to since I last saw you. It seems like you Resurrecteds are always about the Master's most important business."

Samuel and Kathryn looked at each other and Samuel motioned for her to speak first. "My new assignment from the Master is to address future transportation needs for Naturals. The growth of the Master's government will have no end and one day the earth will fill to capacity. As He promised Abraham, *'Count the stars in the sky if you can, so too, you will have as many descendants.'* We know there are over 70 sextillion stars out there."

"Wow, that's a lot of kids," Nathan interjected with wonder.

"Ever since being caught up to heaven in the rapture, my knowledge has increased in countless ways. The potential of what can be done when the Spirit is involved is many times more powerful than the greatest inventions man has ever known.

35

"I began to realize that the stars are not only within the reach of Naturals, but possible, because the understanding of the laws of interstellar flight are becoming more well known. For the Resurrecteds, power for spiritual flying comes from our spirit connected to the Master's power. Our faith activates our soul to believe it is possible. It is a matter of getting our will, our thoughts, and our emotions lined up with what our spirit is already capable. The soul governs the body to simply perform the Spirit's power. I only began to realize this after I was released from the constraints of an earthly body," Kathryn explained.

"I am trying to understand what you are saying," Nathan struggled to conceptualize these things that the mind was designed to know but was limited by the constraints of being inside a natural body. Unfortunately, he truly felt that he was failing to grasp her technological know-how.

"I realize the desires you Naturals have to travel among the stars are from the Master. We are all designed to explore and expand. Don't be concerned with understanding the science behind how the Spirit can protect the body and the soul in space travel. We have drawn up the plans, with the help of the Lord, to create the first experience of travel beyond light-speed for Naturals. However, it is a process to bring the plans into manifestation. The Lord is wonderful. Our minds have been expanded many times in comparison to what they once were before our resurrection. The Lord doesn't do all the mental work for us. We work together as co-creators to bring His plans to pass."

"How has technology progressed in this area?" Samuel asked Kathryn, encouraging her to go on.

"A group of us first reviewed all that we knew about nuclear fusion engine technology and the hazards that were posed to the environment as well as to the bodies who operated them. Now, we are moving into studying the warping of space in a controlled manner with experiments in quantum tunnel travel."

"OK, you really *are* talking over my head. Do you really believe that Naturals will be able to travel to the many planets we know are orbiting stars?" Nathan pushed his plate aside and leaned his elbows on the table as he tried to process what Kathryn was saying.

"Yes, we will have to in order to fulfill the Master's purpose for the universe, which was built for all of us to enjoy." Kathryn explained.

"Wait," Nathan interrupted as he suddenly realized how much time had gone by. "Aren't we going to miss the worship service?"

"No, we will go to the late service at eleven," Samuel assured him. "We wanted time to talk with you about some of these advances. We were told by the Lord that you needed to hear these things, because some of what we discuss today could spur you and your team, back at your architecture firm, to new creative designs. He also communicated that my story and Mom's would help you gain perspective for your testimony topics that are to come at the Monday assembly."

Nathan's eyes widened, "Right! I hadn't thought about either my speech or the plan the Lord had for me." With that he settled back, preparing to listen more intently to Kathryn. "I'm sorry, you were saying?"

"We are now on our way to discovering interstellar travel for Naturals. Once the great judgment occurs at the end of this 1,000-year reign, you Naturals will be able to eat of the Tree of Life and live forever. Then, you will need transportation in order to expand the Kingdom to the many stars throughout the galaxies. The Scriptures state that His blessings will go down to the thousandth generation, and we have had just 250 since Adam and Eve. Each of the Resurrecteds has a part in pulling humanity forward to experience the wonders of dwelling with God throughout the universe. The Lord has created everything, from the subatomic particles to the ends of the vast universe, for use in His plan," Kathryn rested her hand upon Samuel's shoulder.

"So now part of your job is to design engines in order to travel to the stars at faster than light speeds?" Samuel asked.

"That's right!" Kathryn gesticulated excitedly. "I began to realize that current astrophysics research would not be sufficient to handle those complexities. Many Resurrecteds, like myself, are sitting under the Lord's mentorship to find out how to accomplish this. It isn't that He tells us what to do, but His instruction upon growing knowledge allows us to open our minds to unrealized possibilities. Since humans will exist forever in the Lord's kingdom, there is so much that we need to explore," she stopped with the realization that Nathan had heard all he was capable of receiving at the moment.

They thanked their server for breakfast and moved out into the busy street.

"I hope you don't mind walking the few blocks to the Worship Center. I have a command from the Lord to share my testimony with you before the service," Samuel paused and looked at his Dad.

"That would be fine," Nathan agreed. "It would feel good to walk off some of that wonderful breakfast we just enjoyed."

Samuel began, "In the previous age, before the return, when I was about seven or eight years old, I first became aware that my sin separated me from the Creator. I lied to my teacher to cover up an inappropriate action and wound up getting my best friend in trouble with the principal and his parents. All along I knew I did it, but I could not bring myself to confess the truth and disappoint both you and mom. I thought had I gotten away with it, but deep down inside I knew that I was wrong in the eyes of God, and there was nothing I could do to fix the problem.

"In time, I developed a habit of blaming others for my bad choices, which seared my conscience to the point where I doubted God even existed. After all, school was teaching us that science had all the answers, and that we evolved from a single cell, and the universe created itself by a big-bang, as if adding enough time could create all things. There seemed no need to correct my problem, until one day, Jamal, a friend for whom I am eternally grateful, shared the truth with me.

"Jamal said, 'I believe what the Bible says. In chapter one of the Book of Romans, it states that since there is a Creation, there must be a Creator.

"The word science is actually from the Latin word meaning *to know*, but the Bible states the fear or reverence of God is the beginning of knowledge. And who better to know all things but the One who created all things? Could those He created, people who call themselves a scientist, be all knowing? When I thought about it, he logical pointed out the impossibility of my belief!

"Scientists even contradict themselves by believing in the big-bang, for it contradicts the first law of thermodynamics which states that energy, which all matter is made of, cannot be created or destroyed; only transformed. Since that is a scientific law, to believe something contrary to it is to believe contra-science. However, the Creation account does not contradict this law. God spoke all things into existence. It was His energy or power that was transformed into all matter that we see today. The amazing thing is that His Word also holds all creation together forever!"

Nathan listened and marveled at his first son's ability to put the creation story into words that anyone could understand.

39

"That removed my doubts about whether or not God existed; however, there was still this issue in my heart. I was not right with God. And if He existed, then He is the One who sets the standard for what is right and wrong, not I. But how could I fix the problems of my past? I could not relive them and redo them! How many good deeds could I do to make up for them?

"Then Jamal answered that question stating, 'There is nothing that you can do to fix your sin problem. No amount of good deeds, or giving money or time will relinquish the sin in your life. The good news is you do not have to! Someone had to pay the price for that sin. And no human is eligible to do it. Jesus, God's only Son, paid the price by taking all your sin into His body. Then after dying left my sins and everyone else's, in the heart of the earth forever! Your requirement is to believe in Him, as the Son of God, whom God raised from the dead and confess Him as Lord.' I further learned that the evidence of His lordship is found in obeying Him, by doing His will."

As Nathan contemplated what Samuel was saying, he failed to realize that the beauty they encountered as they turned another corner in their walk seemed to enhance the words that had been spoken.

Samuel continued, "That night I went to my bedroom, knelt down on my knees and did exactly that. I confessed Jesus as Lord. Things did not change immediately. But, the Holy Spirit began to help me recognize when I would begin to think of blaming others for something I had actually done and I would instantly repent. The Lord also showed me that demonic spirits were causing me to be offended. So, I began to forgive others even for the smallest things. I was determined not to be offended because Jesus, who was rejected by His own chosen people, never got offended. He simply trusted the Father all the way to the cross, even unto death!

"I came to realize it was God's grace, His amazing power that was transforming my life. The more I focused on His Word, and the fact that His Holy Spirit was living inside of me, the more my thoughts began to line up with the nature of Christ. I received my heavenly prayer language as spoken in the second chapter of Acts. Then my ability to walk in the love of God really took off. I could hear His voice. It was as if before I even would call upon Him, He would answer and talk to me in the early hours of the morning. My desires to please Him grew beyond any earthly desire. He would remind me that *'to him who has been given much, much is required.'* I said, anything Lord, not my will be done, but Your will be done in my life." They continued walking to the last corner where the Worship Center was in sight.

Samuel went on, "At that point in my life, it was as if He deposited this incredible seed in my heart; a seed of desire to sing and worship, not to bring glory to myself but to give glory to Him alone.

"Before I went up in the Rapture, I enjoyed studying eschatology. From those studies, I learned that eternal life was so much more than just going to heaven. My eyes were opened to the completion of God's magnificent plan. That plan is not comprehendible without the help of the Holy Spirit revealing the truth of things to come. But oh, Dad, once I got that picture of the age to come, the one we live in now, I never lost hope. It was the anchor of my soul that pulled me through all the hard things the enemy threw at me. I could see the rewards of being Resurrected, the joy of being with Jesus forever. Nothing seemed to matter anymore except His plan for me to walk with Him until the end of the Church age.

"My favorite praise song had always been *'Between the Cherubim'* by Jesus Culture. When I was Raptured up into heaven, I heard that song playing very loudly. It was just for me. It fulfilled the Scripture, Psalms 37:4 – *'Delight yourself in the Lord and He will give you the desires of your heart.*' It was so personal and yet I knew I was among vast multitudes that were being taken to heaven in the twinkling of an eye.

"Later, I found out that others seemed also to hear songs that specifically ministered to them."

Samuel looked over to see Nathan looking less than delighted. He instantly realized that his Dad was fighting regret that he had not given his life to the Lord before the Tribulation period, thus saving himself a lot of heartache. In wisdom Samuel stated, "I know sometimes you wish you were a Resurrected, but the Lord has a mighty work for you to do as a Natural. Your testimony will be powerful for these *Kingdom Generations*. They need to appreciate what the Lord has given them, and the things they will never have to go through. Your testimony of His grace is incredible!"

Nathan responded with genuine appreciation, "Thanks, son. The Lord was gracious enough to bless me with you. He has seen me this far, and I know He will be with me and see me through the rest of the way."

The door to the Worship Center now stood in front of them. The rest of Samuel's testimony would have to wait until later.

CHAPTER 6

The family stepped into the one of the most magnificent building imaginable. The architecture of the Worship Center was beyond comprehension. The rounded shape of the walls seamlessly followed the contours of the room giving it the perspective that it went on endlessly. Everything glistened, reflecting the glory of the Master. The walls appeared to be made of sapphires in various hues, reflecting the modest lighting. It all created a peaceful and serene setting that did not distract from the focal point of the stage. It was designed with Christ as the center with seating arranged in such a way that it allowed the people to sit as closely to Him as possible.

Because of Nathan's esteemed place in the Festival, he was given a front row seat. He understood this was an incredible honor. Although anyone could attend the message anywhere in the world through highly developed communication technology, it made his nerves tingle with anticipation of being in the presence of the Master as He delivered His message.

The crowd fell silent in humble awe as Jesus walked with authority to the center of the stage to decree His blessing and begin teaching. The magnificence of His countenance was breathtaking. His eyes were as burning fire, seeing and knowing all things, and yet His face was full of mercy and compassion. Although Jesus had the ability to look into the hearts of all present, Nathan felt as if Jesus was looking only at him, confirming that He understood Nathan's deepest and most intimate needs. Tears rolled down Nathan's face without reservation while spontaneous worship broke out all around him as each individual recognized they were in the presence of the One, true God. Nathan joined in without hesitation, his heart full and overflowing with love for Jesus.

As the worship ebbed to a more reverent hush, Jesus began to teach the crowd, "You have heard it said that faith operating by love is all that matters. I tell you there are many here today wearing the rewards of obeying My commands of operating in faith by love. You see the robes of righteousness on the Resurrecteds. Though righteousness was placed in their spirits the moment they made Me Lord of their lives, each gem you see glistening on their robes and in their crowns is a memorial of obedience to the Father's will as they walked in love, all the time believing that what they did was pleasing to Him, even if they did not see an immediate reward."

This mention of the clothes of the righteous caused Nathan to look over at Kathryn and Samuel's robes as a reference point to what Jesus was saying.

He went on, "I wrote, *Be perfect as I am perfect.* Perfection is the maturing process which begins by receiving righteousness by faith. There is nothing you can do to earn the Father's righteousness. It is a free gift received by faith in Him. It means you are in right standing with the Father." Jesus held out his arms with his palms clearly visible and continued, "See the holes in My hands. They were the price of your righteousness. All sin - past, present and future - was laid upon this body of mine, and I took it and disposed of it in the heart of the earth forever, so that you could reside in the Kingdom today. You Naturals who are currently running your race know that one day, if you continue in obedience inside of My grace, will be rewarded with an outer robe of righteousness just as the Resurrecteds have today. After the Great Judgment, you will be given the privilege of eating of the Tree of Life and living forever. In that day, all of heaven and earth will be unified, and I will hand the Kingdom over to the Father and He Himself will dwell among you forever.

Be encouraged by the Resurrecteds. Their acts of obedience glisten on their robes. They were not saved by them, but they are honored with them. They wear them as fine linens illuminating them as royalty."

The Lord continued His message, stating, "I wrote, in Psalms 98:2 – *I have made My salvation known and revealed My righteousness to the nations.* Follow My ways and you too will fulfill your destiny as the Resurrecteds have. Finish your race and you will fulfill what is written in Revelation 22:14 – *Blessed are those who wash their robes, that they may have the right to the tree of life and may go through the gates into the city.*"

The audience listened intently. Each word that came forth from Jesus was powerful and brought life with it; each syllable was absorbed as if life itself depended upon it.

Jesus knew He had given the message that this audience needed for this day. As those present began to file past Jesus, He touched each one giving them a special impartation that they needed.

While others filed past, Nathan sat, unable to move yet, as the afterglow of the words permeated his soul. Kathryn and Samuel understood and said nothing, patiently allowing Nathan the time he needed.

Nathan could not help but to reevaluate his own destiny. He understood that his salvation was a gift from God. God's grace was the only reason he was still alive. His testimony would be a powerful witness to those like him still running a race that would not end until the completion of the 1,000 years. Then, he too would partake of the Tree of Life that is only available now to the Resurrecteds. *What a glorious day that will be,* he thought to himself, *All things are possible to those who believe.*

Nathan slowly rose from his chair, and looked toward Samuel and Kathryn. Without speaking a word, they too filed past Jesus receiving their blessings from Him and then proceeded out of the auditorium.

They turned to look at Nathan. "Wow", was all he could say.

"It's mesmerizing to be in the presence of Jesus, isn't it, Dad?" Samuel asked.

"Yes. His message has renewed and empowered my heart for the mission of the message I must give..." Nathan said as he lowered his head and wiped away a tear.

They turned and began to maneuver their way down the crowded sidewalk towards the clinic where Nathan had an appointment to address any physical needs he had. They walked in silence, each meditating on Jesus' message.

After a few minutes, Samuel broke the silence. "Dad, I know as a Natural, you will not see heaven as it is today. However, my intention is to encourage you to finish your race and to see the *new heaven and new earth* come after the renovation by fire. The Resurrecteds have passed through the fire that judged our works and we made it just fine. When that great finish line is crossed you too will fulfill the Scripture of Isaiah 43:2 -*When you walk through the fire, you will not be burned.* Would you like to hear the rest of my testimony?"

Nathan nodded.

Samuel began where he had left off. "When the trumpet blast blew at the Rapture, everything instantly changed. I rode that amazing journey to heaven with my eyes wide-open, traveling at an immense rate of speed, even faster than the speed of light! I noticed that my body felt completely whole with no defect anywhere. It was pure energy traveling through my insides making my mind much sharper.

"As I entered the outer reaches of heaven, I realized that life would never be the same. I was in such a state of anticipation and joy that all I wanted to do was to get into the Master's presence.

"Once in heaven, everyone was headed toward the highest point – the Heavenly Temple crowning Mount Zion. I came to the gates of the outer court of the Temple. Massive entryways adorned with every kind of jewel sparkled with the back lighting of God's illuminating presence.

"I turned to see the angel who then took my hand and swiftly walked me, along with many others, towards the throne room. He motioned to me, and I recognized grandma and great grandpa Beau who were welcoming me home.

"Pressing onward, we came to the inner court where the presence of God was so strong I felt I would buckle under the purity of holiness. As we moved further into the Temple, I could see the Throne Room of God, where the power of love, the Creator of heaven and earth, the One who resurrected Jesus Christ, the Ancient of Days, dwelled. Eager anticipation consumed me, as I knew I would see the Father soon. However, first my works must be judged.

"The angel brought me to the entrance of a room next to the Great Throne Room. More light than I had ever seen emanated from it. He left me before the Bema Seat – the judgment place - where Jesus sat. I watched as another angel took a measuring device and measured out all the deeds of my life. It was as if all the motives of every deed I had done for the Kingdom were on one side, and my reward was on the other. I could feel a burning sensation that did not really hurt, as all my works were sent through the judgment fire. My mind raced to the Scripture that states the only thing that counts is what is done in faith expressed through love, and I eagerly awaited the outcome. As the burning sensation faded, the angel placed a beautiful crown of jewels upon my head. Jesus looked over and beamed, *Well done, my good and faithful servant,* and then hugged me. It was a moment I will remember throughout all eternity. Then Jesus took me to the Throne Room of the Father," Samuel stopped to wipe a tear from his right eye.

"Dad, I saw every color available in the universe. The Father's robe flowed with the hues of a rainbow, but as I started to look to His face, I suddenly looked away remembering that on earth, Moses was not allowed to see the face of Yahweh, the Father. Jesus knowing my reaction turned my chin to the throne and proudly pronounced, 'Father, this is Samuel, whom I am pleased to announce has finished his race. He overcame by obediently trusting in Me and did not waiver in his faith. He boasted in My name for Your sake and taught others to worship in Spirit and in Truth.'"

At this revelation, Nathan found a bench of acacia wood that was conveniently along the path. As he sat, his mind raced with his heart overwhelmed by everything that Samuel was describing. Nathan was hearing Revelation chapters four and five played out in his son's recitation, because his son had been faithfully obedient to do the Master's bidding.

"Jesus spoke the most beautiful words over me that cannot be put into any language in heaven or on earth. I was given my assignment: I was placed in the worship band. I picked up the finest guitar I had ever seen and reflexively began to tune it, but suddenly realized that it was tuned. The other band members held instruments poised for my first melody in heaven. As I reached for a B flat on the first fret, I fell to my knees and began to weep tears of joy and gratitude. This was my dream - that I would play in heaven and write more songs. The bassist took the guitar from my hands knowing that I needed to bow to the One who made me," Samuel paused before he could continue.

After wiping the tears away, he went on, "I reached up to feel the crown upon my head and flung it toward the throne, knowing that instead I deserved a crown of thorns for my inadequacies. I didn't deserve any of this. I heard my crown ping against the ornate carvings upon the Seat of Mercy, and quickly more of the same pinging noises surrounded me. All of those around, who had tasted from the heavenly River of Life flowing from the Throne were reacting in the same fashion that I was. I quickly stepped to my feet and led a large following of people in a song that the Lamb had written upon my heart long ago. It felt like a song I had written. I realized in that moment, it actually had all come from Him, and He would receive all the glory for it.

"Since then I have had the opportunity to lead worship with some of those same band members. Our continual mission is that our music will fill heaven and earth glorifying the Lord."

They made their way in silence toward the entrance of the clinic that had come into view, contemplating Samuel's place among the Resurrecteds. It was all so far beyond Nathan's understanding. He could not travel to heaven with his physical body, but he couldn't wait for the day after the renovation by fire when the *new heaven and new earth* would come into being and he would be able to see for himself what Samuel had described.

"Dad, Mom and I know that you want to be alone at the clinic, and we would love to have a light dinner with you later on. Do you mind if we take off and meet you here at the end of your appointment?" Samuel asked.

"Of course! Do I get to see you disappear?" Nathan asked, his eyes twinkling, because it was fascinating to see someone vanish before one's eyes, which is exactly what happened after he received a brief hug from each of them.

ForeTold

CHAPTER 7

Nathan was excited to enter the clinic. He could hardly wait to have the leaves from those special Fruit Trees applied like a healing salve to restore and prevent further deterioration to his joints. It would remove the pain he had been experiencing in no time. Healing salves, made from different combinations of the leaves from the various Fruit Trees, were effective in curing whatever ailments were in his body. Those trees were given life from the River of Living Water that flowed from the throne of the Master, the Author of life. He created life with His words. By His words He maintains life for all. Healing occurred when faith accompanied the application of the natural leaves.

The staff members of the clinic, some of which were Naturals and others Resurrecteds, administered a balanced symphony of healing power for the whole person including the body, the thoughts, and emotions.

All of the Naturals marveled at how effectively these offices were run. The waiting rooms had digital forms which catalogued the patient's needs. Once the form was filled out the staff assessed each ailment, some of which came from natural deterioration over time and others that came from wrong thinking, bitterness or resentment. Then the Resurrecteds started the treatment by praying with the patient; speaking healing words over each need.

The process took a good two hours, so each appointment was set with that amount of time in mind. After the patient's needs were addressed, the patient sealed the healing with confessions of agreement and praises to the Master. This walking by faith pleased God.

Nathan stepped up to the reception desk and introduced himself.

"Oh, you are Nathan Covington. We have been expecting you! We have cleared our schedule for those who will be speaking from the *Survivor Nations*. The chosen Testifiers need to be totally restored before they speak so no afflictions will hinder their ability to deliver their testimony. Would you mind filling in what your needs are?" The receptionist handed him a virtual form. Nathan sat down and filled it out.

After returning the tablet to the receptionist, Nathan remembered the note from Julia and handed it to her to be filled while he was at the appointment. Nathan was then instructed on what would occur next.

"You will find a locker with your name on it. Please change into the robe you will find there. And on a personal side note: thank you so much for coming to testify. Each of you has encouraged me already and you haven't even spoken yet. I love this job, because I meet other Survivor Naturals that I can relate to from all over the Kingdom!" The red-haired receptionist shook his hand and pointed out the room in which he could change.

As he removed his clothes and donned the robe as instructed, he again marveled at the fact there was no charge for these amazing health clinics. Another staff member then led him to a room where he proceeded to immerse into a luxurious tub of Living Water from the River. It also contained the proper oils from the leaves of the Fruit Trees needed for Nathan's particular physical ailments. Nathan's whole body relaxed as he soaked in the Living Water.

After Nathan had soaked for a time, a Resurrected physician entered the room and asked Nathan if he was ready to pray. "We are going to heal your issues today. Remember all healing starts by believing the Master has already healed you, when He took those stripes upon Himself." He then laid hands on Nathan's shoulders and began to pray healing Scriptures over him.

"Heavenly Father, we come to You and honor Your name as the Creator, Redeemer, and Healer of all who believe on Your Son, Jesus. We worship You and receive from You the power to heal Nathan everywhere there is a need. We speak Your Word that states by the stripes Jesus took on His back, Nathan is healed right now. We speak to Nathan's body and command it to be whole and function as designed for Your glory. In Jesus' mighty name we pray." The physician started to walk away and then turned back, being led by the Holy Spirit within.

"Nathan, before I leave, I must tell you something. My name is Seth, and I was a physician *Before the Return*. I lived and died in a beautiful mountain town only a few miles from an underground facility called *The Ground* in Silverton, Colorado."

"Really? I was working, as an architect, on that facility before the Mark was mandated. I haven't met anyone who lived in that place. Did you know I designed much of that complex?"

"No, I didn't! Well, I think that God has brought you full circle by introducing us today. What you did kept hundreds of us alive. That was no accident, my friend!" Dr. Seth grasped Nathan's arm, "Your work saved more than you know. Take solace in that fact." Nathan settled back into a deep calm as he let the physician's words permeate his whole body.

"It's time to get out of the tub, sir," proclaimed a staff member as he scurried into the room to assist Nathan to the next session.

Nathan's whole body felt so much better as he climbed out of the tub.

A massage therapist spent the next hour using various techniques upon his back, shoulders, knees and shins to loosen the areas affected by his advancing age. He brought in blended salves made from the Fruit Tree leaves available to heal the Nations and applied them throughout the session. These oils were only named by

53

what they cured: Knee, Shin, Spine, Sole, and Deltoid. He hadn't even mentioned that his deltoids were bothering him but that didn't make them any less sore. Then Nathan, and the clinic staff working with him, in unity and agreement, prayed over each area of the body, commanding it to be healed as the salve was applied. Each area, after it was slathered with the oil, tingled for several minutes. It wasn't the same feeling as a burn from a stove, but as if the cells were excited into an earlier - younger - stage of existence, wherever the essential oil had been applied. Each area of his body, once treated, felt a renewed sense of life he hadn't felt in more than a hundred years, since he had last been here at the clinic.

The last physician came in with vials of oils that filled the room with aromas Nathan had not smelled in a long time. Each one was announced by the physician: Frankincense, Myrrh, and Cedar. Each of the oils was prescribed by the physician to complete the healing process. As the session concluded, Nathan felt an increase of peace in his soul and tranquility in his mind.

"You guys are better than you were a century ago!" Nathan exclaimed.

"Thank you. Being a physician for the Master is so rewarding, to Him be all the glory! Now for today, as the oils continue to absorb, keep your focus on the healing power of God the Father and you will reach a state of calm and assurance as your faith increases and then you will sleep very soundly.

"Your physician back home will have my electronic notes when you return. Thank you for your service to the Kingdom. I will be listening to the entire broadcast! Oh, and the oils your wife requested have been delivered to your hotel room." The dark-headed female physician shook his hand with vigor and Nathan returned it as he felt renewed energy flowing throughout his body.

The ortho tech returned with a perfect custom set of fitted shoes. Handing them to Nathan, he explained, "They might feel a little unusual at first, like walking on water, but within a few days you will notice that sensation start to ease."

Back at the locker, Nathan changed into his clothes. He felt as if he almost floated out of the treatment area and over to his family, who were seated in a corner of the waiting room.

"Are you ready to go, Dad?" Samuel asked as Nathan appeared.

"Yes, I think I am," Nathan replied

They walked out to the street and then spent much of the late afternoon looking at the sites around the beautiful city as they visited with one another. The art and the architecture were spectacular to behold, and the city buzzed with visitors from all the lands who had flocked to the city for the Feast of Tabernacles.

Nathan suddenly understood that he was not celebrating the Feast in the exact way that the Lord intended it to be done. It was designed to be spent with the family. All were the family of God, but his new family was back home. His remembered this was his original family and it was a joy to be together.

"I am sorry you have to move so slowly with me in tow," Nathan said as he noticed a group of Resurrecteds gliding by so quickly he almost didn't see them.

"Oh Dad, it's nice to move at your speed once in a while," Samuel joked and Nathan punched him in the shoulder. The fun and visiting continued as the family stopped in for an early dinner at a French restaurant one block from the hotel. After a quick bite, they arrived back at the hotel and hugged each other goodnight.

"I'll see you Monday morning. I will pick you up at 6:00. They want you there early," Kathryn explained.

"I can walk."

"Not this time," Kathryn retorted. "You will need escorts to guide you and drop you off, or you won't reach the Temple gates before the crowds begin to make it virtually impassable."

"Ok, see you then," Nathan agreed as he waved goodbye and turned toward the elevator. Making his way back to his room, he was still enjoying the renewed vigor he was experiencing from the treatments he had had earlier in the day. He spent the rest of the evening in thanksgiving and worship for the healing he had received.

CHAPTER 8

Nathan arrived downstairs Monday morning to the view of a crowd of people bustling in the streets. A limo, the likes of which he had never seen, was waiting to take him to his destination. The luminescent finish of the exterior matched the color of the robes that the Resurrecteds wear, and the interior seats had the ability to swivel giving the passengers panoramic views in comfort. The complete breakfast bar simmered, giving an aroma outside the vehicle.

As he opened the door himself, waving the limo driver away from doing the job for him, people shouted joyfully that they were looking forward to his testimony. At first, Nathan could only stare and raise his hand in a friendly gesture. It was at that moment that the discomfort with being the center of attention collided with the reality of being in the Kingdom of Christ. In those times *Before the Return*, he avoided the limelight at all costs. At times, he didn't even want his own family's attention. He was content to duck his head and quietly and unobtrusively go about his daily tasks.

"It should only be a twenty-minute drive even with the traffic, sir," the driver stated over his shoulder as he prepared to pull onto the thoroughfare.

"Thank you for the ride. I really didn't need it..." Nathan trailed off as his hand brushed over the seat upon which he sat, made of the finest leather he had ever encountered.

"Nothing's too good for the King," the driver replied.

"But I am not the King," a startled Nathan corrected.

"You are in the King's direct service today, and that makes you one of the select few to receive this treatment. We will be picking up one of the others in a minute."

The limo moved swiftly in and out of traffic zones, mostly clogged with pedestrians moving toward the Temple, and the elevated amphitheater-seating that overlooked the Temple area. Nathan stared out the window, fascinated to see angels serving as traffic officers for the event. In times of old, the angels' seven to ten foot heights would have frightened people off the streets. But in this Kingdom age, they assisted with orchestrating the flow of people and transports to their mutual destination: the Temple.

Soon they pulled up to the front of another building and picked up a woman with flowing blonde hair and a silk blue dress that brought out the color of her eyes.

"How are you today?" Nathan asked in greeting as he scooted over, allowing her entrance to the vehicle.

"Were you prepared for this?" the woman asked, gesturing to the stirring crowds outside of the door.

"Not at all," Nathan shook his head.

"I am Othellia, and I know you are Nathan from the news coverage of the event. It is nice to meet you," Othellia extended her hand with a smile.

"Thank you, it's nice to meet you too. You know, I didn't watch the transmissions. I was too busy, first with my current projects and then preparing for my testimony," Nathan admitted.

"I know...the newscasts mentioned that your wife had declined any interviews for you."

"She did? She didn't even tell me. I am blessed to have such a great and thoughtful wife. I don't know about you, but the closer we get to the Temple the more nervous I become, as if I just drank four cups of java. But, you don't seem that nervous, why is that?" Nathan asked as he clasped his hands together to still the shaking that had come upon him during the ride in the limo.

"I have sung in front of thousands, although I have never spoken in front of millions. Or billions. So I will admit that this does make me a little nervous," Othellia replied.

"Billions? That's not helping," he retorted with a grin.

Overhearing their conversation, the driver suddenly spoke up from the front seat. "The King in His foreknowledge knew you two would speak before the foundation of time. He only desires the truth. Your testimony will change the lives of younger generations like myself and will encourage us to see how blessed we are in this age. It will also show how important it is to keep obeying the Master inside of His incredible mercy. I have taken many Survivor Naturals to the annual events and to drive the two of you is a great honor and privilege."

The two passengers glanced at each other neither knowing how to respond to the compliment.

They stopped in front of the VIP entrance at the back of the amphitheater and were quietly whisked inside where they were to be briefed on the proceedings of the day. As they reached the lowest level of the amphitheater, the security angels opened a red door that led into a huge conference room. A *V*-shaped set of tables with chairs around the outside were arranged toward the front of the room and allowed for the five of them to sit comfortably. The other three, who had arrived only a few minutes earlier, turned as Othellia and Nathan walked into the room. Each introduced him or herself to the others and proceeded to speak in hushed and humbled tones about the honor that had been bestowed on them.

All conversation ceased the moment that the King of kings stepped into the room. The moderator brought the meeting to order, "Please be seated. Greetings to you honored Testifiers. Now hear the words of the Son of the great God Jehovah. "

"Blessings to each of you from the Father of heaven and earth. This is a momentous day in your lives. Fear not. Do not allow any thought to steal the message that is inside your heart today. God is with you and I speak this into you: nerves of steel and the power of My Spirit to rise up inside you aiding every word you utter." Suddenly, all of them felt the word preside inside, calming their nerves.

"The younger generations need to hear your testimony, so they can understand My Father's plan and walk it out. Today, the children of your youth have not seen the consequences of a world that obeyed the devil. They have not seen the result of his demons continually tempting flesh to do evil. Hearing your testimonies will help them understand the culmination of rebellion at the end of the previous age. You will encourage them to follow the 'I Am'." As Jesus whispered the last comment, the power in His words propelled their chairs back from the table. All five Testifiers fell prostrate on the floor at the feet of Jesus and began to worship. After a brief interlude, Jesus asked them to return to their seats around the table so He could continue with His instructions.

"We will walk out of this room and proceed down the corridors to the amphitheater pathway outside, where the people will see you enter. We will then make our way through the Temple's western gate and wind through the outer court's colonnades. The procession will finish when we pass into the inner courtyard, where the sacrifices will cease for a time during your messages.

"I will be with you throughout your entire testimony, so that you won't feel as if you are losing track by getting stuck on a past thought. It is best for each of you to think of the audience; allow your heart to paint the depictions for them in love and in faith. The crowd will listen, picturing and understanding in their own way how you lived and survived through the most troubled time in human history. Focus your mind's eyes on Me when you speak, because I AM the author and the finisher of your faith and all that I do is for the glory of the Father. Because I see the beginning from the end, I see your words taking root and coming to full fruition," Jesus concluded. Once again when Jesus had spoken the *'I Am'* portion of His name, each was moved to worship Him.

As their worship wound down, the King of kings motioned for them to follow Him through another red door and into a corridor. Nathan was only vaguely aware of the beauty which surrounded him, as his mind was transfixed on the message he would soon deliver. Jesus led them down numerous halls until finally they stepped out of the amphitheater recesses onto the pathway. The amphitheater adjacent to the Temple allowed millions to see the proceedings in person. Cheering throngs stood to their feet in adoration of the King of kings, as they waited for the event of the year to begin.

Seated high above the amphitheater's furthest reaches were two seats of honor reserved for the King of Israel and this year's herald who would commentate on the day's events to the entire kingdom.

Earlier that morning, King David opened the ceremony commanding the attention of the whole kingdom. "Welcome! Today, on this 300th anniversary of our Lord's great Kingdom, in celebration of the Feast of Tabernacles, I greet you in the name of the King of kings and Lord of lords, Jesus Christ." David paused while the crowd cheered their approval of their Lord. "I give the honor of the herald of this festival to a prophet that is well known throughout the kingdom for his wisdom. He foretold of this day, giving hope to God's chosen people when our people had fallen away and needed correction by king Nebuchadnezzar. Please help me welcome the author, prophet and inspired one by the Holy Spirit who bears the name of his book: Ezekiel."

Then Ezekiel rose from his seat stating, "We are celebrating our 300th year of peace on earth with gratitude to the One that made that possible: the Prince of peace. We thank Jesus, the Creator and Redeemer, for bringing justice to earth by ruling with an iron rod for the

61

past three centuries in a time where peace has empowered prosperity beyond what any of us could have imagined. Let the Nations enter the presence of our Lord!"

The Festival opens each year with the entrance of all the Nations of the earth, with representatives from every tribe and every land. Each Nation entered the amphitheater carrying flags of their country waving in the breeze. The procession of each group followed like the opening ceremonies of the 20th Century Olympic Games; however, those ceremonies paled in comparison to the gala and pageantry that came with the Kingdom proceedings.

Ezekiel commented, "Israel, as always, is the first to open the ceremonies as the host nation of the Kingdom. Her flag is flying over a delegation led by none other than Ruth. This princess delighted Boaz as testified in the book titled after her name several millennia ago. She still looks as young as the Bible described," Ezekiel continually prompted the crowd to remember the Scriptural references as a memorial of God's goodness.

"And her contingent is beset by the best of God's chosen people with Elijah and Enoch following right behind along with the rest of those honorable prophets who spoke during dark times centuries before. Seeing them in resurrected bodies is a testimony to the great power of our God. Their magnificent robes are washed white from the blood of the Lamb that had been shed for their sins.

"The Persian nation is following along behind as they have done every year since the ceremonies began. They haven't missed a Feast and have always accorded themselves with respect to their gracious King."

Each nation strode by represented by their brightest group of skilled workers such as cooks and carpenters which indicated how each group of people contributed to the Kingdom. Nations that specialized in a certain product or invention were represented by those responsible for those items, allowing them to showcase their talent. The representatives in the Feast of Tabernacles opening procession were ordinary, everyday citizens of the Kingdom.

Ezekiel observed, "Do not the people of the Kingdom fully grasp that we have the *peace that passes all understanding* reigning in Jerusalem in this day and age? The words of the Lord are to be followed without question. Last year, the Venezuelans and the Tibetans were the only ones who didn't participate with representation for the Feast of Tabernacles. Each of those lands had to import food because the Lord had warned that there would be no rain for the countries who failed to attend the Feast.

"This year a nation is not represented as indicated by an angel stepping out from the amphitheater recesses. It looks like the Egyptians have failed to celebrate the Feast at Jerusalem, thus their land will drink no rain in the coming year," Ezekiel proclaimed as an agitation he could not quell rose up from within him.

"Yes," he continued, "We have been hearing rumblings from the Egyptians for the past nine months regarding those who have fallen astray due to their lack of a pursuit of Christ. The Egyptians have seen the highest number of young people not reach the age of 100 in the past dozen years. Sin will most assuredly manifest if they do not worship Jesus and seek Him with a pure heart. He desires to heal their land if they will humble themselves as the Scripture admonishes."

The succeeding nations continued entering the amphitheater to a recitation that proceeded for the next three hours. They were arrayed in all of their beautiful colors.

There were reports interspersed throughout the hours of the *Five Honored Testifiers* as they were called by the media. Camera views had displayed them leaving their hotels and limos to enter the amphitheater while crowds roared, and sideline reporters caught the highlights of the event.

"We have now come to the time for which we have all been waiting: Jesus, in His infinite wisdom, chose to bring about the Testifiers for a time such as this," stated Ezekiel.

"Many descendants of the *Survivor Nations* have grown up on the testimonies of men and women like these. Each has spoken of the temptations and fallen nature of people at the time of the Tribulation, and how by the grace of God they came into the Kingdom, contrasting to today's reconstructed earth where people live in harmony with one another.

"We honor these five Testifiers this year. Each was a survivor, or Survivor Natural as called by some, who lived through the Great Tribulation. That Tribulation was planned to awaken people to make a decision for Christ, or against Him. Each had to make the choice before *The Great Day of the Lord* when He returned. Their testimonies are riveting, and this group has been specially chosen on this hollowed day for you to hear." Ezekiel exclaimed.

"Please direct your attention to the center platform on the porch of the opening of the Temple Building's Sanctuary where the Throne of Jesus resides. From this platform our Testifiers will share their testimonies. The Nations will hear of the trials of the *old world* testifying to the Lord's grace. The five have been given opportunities over the next two days to recite their testimonies during our Feast of Tabernacles, as Jesus established.

"We celebrate this feast in tents around the city. Our amphitheater is filled with people who are willing to sleep under the stars in eager anticipation of hearing the testimonies of events that transpired before many of them were born."

64

Ezekiel went on to describe what the viewers at home could not see, "Jesus is orienting each of the Testifiers, explaining that He has prayed for them. He has removed all shame, and the testimony is richer for the sharing."

With that, King David rose to stand next to the prophet Ezekiel in honor of Jesus, and the five started around the amphitheater pathway as the cheering throngs remained on their feet until they reached the Temple outer gate.

ForeTold

CHAPTER 9

The Temple outer court gate was magnificent. The polished white marble threshold glistened in the sunshine. The gatekeepers stood beside the doors covered in bronze so pure they looked like gold. The five Testifiers led by Jesus walked through it with ease, as the audience roared their appreciation. Each felt a combination of humility mixed with gratitude for being chosen for such an honor. It was a moment that uplifted the individual but also brought him or her face to face with the reality of how blessed one was to be in God's Kingdom.

The Testifiers slowly made their way through the colonnades of the Temple's outer court coming to the inner court gate. The crowd waved palm branches in raised hands and offered praise offerings on this special occasion to the One who had created them.

As soon as they entered the inner court gate the quiet of the people could be felt. One didn't dare cheer in the presence of the holiness that occurred inside the inner court area. The sacrifices had finished early for the day in anticipation of the beginning of the Feast. The area around the altar where the sacrifices were performed had been washed clean from the blood.

As the Testifiers approached the platform on the Sanctuary porch, they saw five golden chairs covered in upholstery embroidered with palm trees and cherubim. They were arranged in front of the open doors of the Temple Building Sanctuary. This was the place of honor for the Testifiers.

Each stood by their chair. As the minutes passed by, Nathan felt his anticipation rise because he was slated to be the first Testifier. For most of the day his nerves had risen and fallen with each new event. But, since Jesus had prayed over him, he was no longer nervous, just feeling a great desire to please his Lord. Then the King of kings, standing at the podium at the side of the doors, addressed the people. He raised His hands to pray.

"My Father, I thank You that we celebrate this festival each year to remember all that You have done to deliver us into the safety of Your Kingdom. In this Age when peace reigns, Your children share their testimonies of Your grace for all to hear. Their testimonies are an example of Your kindness, and Your love to bring them into the Kingdom. I pray for each Testifier to have clarity of thought, steadfastness of heart, and understanding of the things they have seen in times past." As Jesus concluded His prayer, He motioned with His hands for the crowd to be seated.

"The testimony custom was instituted 300 years ago when the Millennium Kingdom clock began and will continue each year until the end of the 1,000 years," Jesus continued. "We gather at the capital of Jerusalem to unite all humanity in harmony with one hope, one vision, one Kingdom. Our heavenly Father ordained this time of the Feast of Tabernacles as a reminder of God's power of deliverance. Deliverance from the enemy in the past established with the Exodus from Egypt. This Festival is so named because of the booths or temporary dwellings My chosen children lived in during their deliverance from Egypt.

"Today, we celebrate those who have been delivered from the Great Tribulation and graced with the Kingdom. Five courageous souls survived the end of the world. Their testimonies were written within the heavenly book of remembrance. Those of you who did not live when the enemy dwelled upon this planet and tempted the hearts of mankind should consider yourself blessed. These are my beloved who have walked through the trial," Jesus paused indicating it was Nathan's time to rise and come near the podium.

"Nathan, My son, was born 349 years ago. He experienced his earthly son being caught away in the first phase of the First Resurrection when My Faithful Church was raptured. He then witnessed his wife go in the second harvest. Son," Jesus said turning toward Nathan, "Go back to the time before the Tribulation that My servant Daniel referred to as the seventieth week. Tell your testimony of My grace and forgiveness in your life." Jesus motioned with His right hand, palm up, inviting Nathan to step up to the podium and bring forth his testimony. Then Jesus took His seat inside the sanctuary on His throne.

"My Lord, my God, Creator of heaven and earth, it is such an honor and privilege to be here this morning," Nathan began. I have spent a long time praying and contemplating the words to describe the gratitude of my heart, not just to be here sharing today, but for the amazing gift to be in Your kingdom. I so thank You for allowing me to live in it.

"Fellow citizens of the Kingdom, do not take it lightly if you have been born during this age. God planned for you to live during this time and in this place before He ever spoke a single molecule into existence.

"My testimony is one of God's forgiveness, His patience toward me, and His loving compassion that never gave up. He planned for me to live just prior to the Tribulation period and for that I am now grateful. However, it was not always as such for me. I was once selfish and wanted to rule my own life. My testimony is that of a man coming out of the Babylonian System that had a strangle hold on humanity until Jesus broke its power.

"My testimony begins when I was sixteen. I thought I was a Christian. I was passionate about my church youth group - or at least the cute girls in it. We sang

69

songs and discussed current events. I would sit and hang on to every word the pastor spoke until one night I became offended and everything changed for the worse. The pastor preached a message called 'The Real Place of Hell.' He spoke about a place 1800 miles below the surface of the earth where those who refuse to choose Jesus would be sent as a final punishment. I could not fathom a God who would do this. That was when I started making a god of my own choosing rather than the God of the Bible, the Creator of heaven and earth." Nathan paused in humility as he looked back over his shoulder to focus on the Master. Jesus encouraged him to continue with a look of confident assurance that could only come from the radiant face of the Savior, the Christ.

"Time passed quickly as I became more interested in solving life's problems on my own. Yet, God did not give up on me. He was continually reaching out to me. Nathan's voice rang with joy as he once more glanced back at Jesus whose eyes blazed with love and compassion that cultivated courage and peace inside his heart.

In a flash, Nathan thought about an article he read as a boy explaining how mountain climbers could focus better than most. When exposed high on a cliff where death is only one mistake away, the climber's entire being became laser focused in the moment, spirit, soul and body all in unison. So too, Nathan flowed with intense concentration.

Then Nathan's testimony came forth like a stream...

Part Two

ForeTold

CHAPTER 10

Long Ago, before the Tribulation...

Nathan had not known what to say to his wife and son on Saturday night when they asked him if he was going with them to see the new Disney movie. He mumbled an excuse as he looked over his reading glasses from the easel holding the next major project that would help him scale the ladder of Warner and Associates. A partnership in an architectural firm was all he had ever dreamed of, but he only had mediocre abilities when compared with some of the giants in the Denver market. Yet he felt that he was better than Doug Warner, who was the owner, or even some of the snot-noses the firm hired just out of the University of Colorado. After all, he had the experience the younger associates lacked and Doug was a salesman more than an architect.

It was more than twenty years earlier when Nathan had gone to Wichita State and met his wife, Kathryn. She was an elementary education major, commonly known as the El. Ed. easy degree by his college buddies. However, it helped his standing with the frat house because she was considered one of the hotties. The problem for Nathan was that even though she was very attractive, he had a wandering eye. He was careful not to do so in her presence but, since he was an architect, he felt beauty was only in the eye of the beholder, and that his artistic bent gave him an eye to appreciate beauty more than others. He rationalized to himself that it was just part of his innate nature, almost a duty, to appreciate how a woman might look.

Before either of them had finished their courses of study, Kathryn found out that she was pregnant with a son. Since neither would consider an abortion even though they weren't married, they made plans to rectify the situation and become a family. He surmised that she could support him if she quit pursuing her degree to allow him to focus full time on school, at times taking 21 hours per semester. To that end, they stayed in a cheap housing unit in Wichita, Kansas with her working at Wal-Mart during the day and TGI Friday's most nights. Nathan doubled up on the class load to finish as quickly as possible with the baby on the way.

After his graduation, they moved to Aurora, Colorado, where he found his first position as an architect designing backyards for Doug Warner's large landscaping firm. He hated the idea of conceptualizing what in his mind only amounted to porches and small rose patches for people who were spending more money on their backyard than he had spent on his wife's Toyota Corolla that was 10 years old when he bought it.

The baby came in the month after they arrived. At that point they were living in a small rented townhome near Mississippi and Alameda avenues in Aurora. It was definitely not the nicest part of the city, but he had always dreamed of living in Denver and had finally dragged Kathryn across Kansas to do so.

Nathan was also secretly obsessed with the Lexus that he felt he would never own. He found himself at the Lexus dealership on Fridays after five looking at a maroon GS 450 sedan. As his dream car, it had to have navigation and tan leather for him to even want to sit in it. There was a hope of a cheaper model he had seen in the pamphlets called an IS 250. The problem was that the 980 was three times the car that the IS 250 was, which was probably why it had the higher price tag, but the 450 was the model that he really wanted. It had all of the latest technologies that contributed to pushing the price tag well beyond what his modest budget could afford. In spite of that, he took one or two of them out for a test drive down I-225 only to circle back toward home in his wife's old Civic.

Arriving home, he walked through the front door to a world that never quite lived up to his standards. While Kathryn worked hard to make the place a home, all Nathan could focus on were the faint smells of baby vomit and used diapers, the clutter of toys on the floor and the ceaseless sounds of a whirling, old washing machine.

His wife, with an amazing figure, still looked beautiful but now had a new type of muffin top stuck upon her hips - their son. No longer was Friday nights a time for him to quietly enjoy Kathryn's company or even be able to go out on a date with her. Instead, the evenings were spent with a crying baby whose tears stained his Denver Bronco jumper which had been purchased at Wal-Mart. Almost every night when Nathan would return home from work; Kathryn would deposit Samuel in his lap within minutes of his arrival. He tried to make the best of it by playing patty cake, but the boy would only play for a short time before something would inevitably upset him, causing Nathan to thrust him in frustration back into Kathryn's arms.

Nathan never seemed to understand that his annoyed tone of voice and hushed cuss words drew the attention of his son as he grew older. Many times those invectives would so distress Samuel that he would burst into tears or retreat to another room in the house, causing a distance to develop between father and son. But, frustrations and discontent would get the best of him and Nathan could not seem to help himself. He felt that he couldn't receive the breaks that the other men and women at the office easily acquired.

Being married to Kathryn would have been fine if they weren't tied down with a child. Of course, he loved Samuel, but it cramped the lifestyle that was supposed to come with a hot young wife. And to make matters worse, Nathan felt that Kathryn's affections were more and more reserved for the baby rather than for him. He longed for weekends in Breckenridge in a luxury cabin like the owner of the landscaping firm. It seemed like every Monday morning he would watch as the owner gleefully bounced into the office sporting a sunburned face and sunglass-indentations around his eyes.

"Can't we do something this weekend?" Nathan asked plaintively.

"Like what? Oh, I know...we could take Samuel to the Denver Zoo. He would love to see the new cubs that have been born this spring!" His rolling eyes did not deter her plans or packing of the baby stroller in preparation for early Sunday morning.

He found the NFL Network late on Saturday night and turned it on low to serve as background noise as he worked on his backyard creations for some Highlands Ranch home. He figured it would keep him occupied for a while and give him a good excuse not to participate in the evening bedtime rituals that seemed to take forever. He wouldn't admit it to himself, but he also figured it would keep him occupied through the night hours, knowing that by Sunday morning he would be too groggy to keep his promise to tote the child to the zoo. If he did manage to drag himself along, a nap on a park bench with the metal slats digging into his back would be his perceived lot while Kathryn and Samuel spent endless hours viewing every single animal. Nathan, however, imagined that the animals distained the zoo as much as he did.

As time went on, Kathryn began to leave him out of her Sunday morning plans. The solace of the Sunday mornings, which should have led to productive work hours, instead provided Nathan with more time for feeding one temptation or another. Feeling trapped in a marriage that was dominated by a young child, and having a wife whose attentions were focused more in Samuel's direction than his, Nathan rationalized that indulging in pornography on these Sunday mornings was only fair in order to meet his physical needs. After all, his marriage wasn't living up to his expectations. Every time Kathryn mentioned the idea of having more children, Nathan balked at the idea. Those early years were not his idea of marital bliss and, in his opinion; one child was definitely more than enough. To add insult to injury, the Broncos had been losing for the past three years and were continually rebuilding the team, causing Nathan's temper over their mounting losses to carry over into his creations on Sunday nights.

As his son grew into a teenager, he was much more fun to be around, especially when throwing a baseball or football, but there was a definite lack of relational depth and Nathan failed to see that Samuel longed to spend time with him. The only attention that Samuel received from Nathan was when the computer or the car needed repaired, because his father refused to have another individual repair either. This required Samuel to assist Nathan by handing him the correct tool at the right time. If the tool was not anticipated, then a tongue lashing would commence that was proportional to the level of frustration that had built up within Nathan that week. Unfortunately, being a typical teenager, Samuel's mind would invariably wander to a song that he was playing in his head or a girl's face that had captured his attention. This would inevitably lead to him failing to hand his father the correct 5/8" socket wrench with the extender at the right time.

These types of interactions only further served to drive the wedge deeper between Nathan and Samuel. The ensuing distance continued to grow until one pivotal point in Samuel's life.

Samuel was driving an old Ford subcompact that was so ugly his friends immediately recognized him on the streets of Aurora. One day, at the last turn before entering their driveway, his mother was stopped at the side of the road. Samuel had not even noticed as he passed her and drove up to the garage, but once he started walking away from his car, he caught the glint of his mother's green Honda Civic. He curiously hoofed his way toward the car when he noticed his mother kneeling by the back left tire where she was clearly struggling with a lug nut. Arriving by her side, he reached to help her out, but she looked up with an expression that stopped him and he noticed a tear escaping from the corner of her eye. *I'll do it myself* was her attitude accompanied by a muttered curse to leave her be. He apologized and abided by her desire to accomplish the task on her own and quietly made his way back to the house.

Within thirty minutes, his father had driven by and stopped to help his wife with the finishing touches of the spare tire and the tightening of the lug nuts. Samuel could see them through the window of his bedroom as he played another chord progression on his guitar that had danced about in his thoughts all day. Not giving the incident another thought, he remained absorbed in the music until his bedroom door suddenly slammed against the wall. Samuel's head jerked up in surprise and he saw his father standing there in a towering rage.

"Why didn't you help your mother? All you do is sit in here and sulk over your music. You must be the laziest son on the planet!" Nathan yelled, striding across the room to shake his fist in Samuel's face. Samuel stared at his father's fist and, as if from a distance, listened to the rest of the tirade wisely keeping his mouth shut. He began to pray silently that he would shrivel away and die, so that he could make his father feel really bad for berating him so unjustly. He had learned that no explanation was allowed when his father reached the fevered heights of his temper.

Kathryn stepped into the doorway and stopped Nathan with a scream, "What are you *doing?*!!! I told him not to help me. I wanted to do it myself, and I knew he was here if I needed him. This was a perfect opportunity to test my tire changing skills which I absolutely failed. Don't you get it?!!" Tears then streamed down her reddened face. Kathryn's humiliation and frustration coupled with regret for being in another fight over nothing of consequence only added to her sorrow.

"Well, you shoulda helped!" Nathan directed to Samuel, trying to keep his own dignity intact.

From this point on, Nathan continually tried to rationalize and justify his response, never quite letting go of the feelings of anger and bitterness towards his son. He realized that this was the first time he had ever wanted to hit his own child. Nathan kept those feelings bottled up inside, fearing that if he ever let them loose he would not be able to control them. He didn't even really know why he experienced such feelings. He actually loved his son, but was inept at being able to show it.

Over the succeeding months, Nathan knew that he had truly lost any hope of connecting with his boy. His son was polite at the correct times, such as when they were out in public together, although that was very rare indeed, but the desire to be around his father was gone. Samuel, having recently rededicated his life to Jesus, had begun to see Nathan for what he was. He knew his father was not the despot he often acted like, but he recognized that Nathan had stopped believing in the Lord a long time ago in order to accomplish what he had wanted to in life. Although he continued to hold his father at a distance, Samuel also began to pray for him, exchanging resentment for a love that was beyond his own ability.

As Samuel was getting closer to graduating from high school in Aurora, the ache to connect even on a small level was pounding upon Nathan's hardened heart. With his son planning to leave for Colorado State in Fort Collins, Nathan dreaded being left with the nothingness of his marriage. His marriage had had very little intimacy for the past several years because he was working so often on the next project for the firm or catering to the needs of his ego to get ahead. Rather, he should have been building a lasting relationship with the woman he had married.

His job continued to leave him unfulfilled as well. Sure, there were a few raises over the years, but none of them meant true partnership within the company. Nathan still could not afford to buy that Lexus he wanted and instead had gotten a red Honda Accord - used of course. Nathan lacked the confidence needed to go searching for another job, because he believed that there was no one that would hire him if he could not make it as a partner in a nothing landscaping company, until he met Carmen Luongo.

Carmen was a client who asked for some truly strange designs in his backyard. He wanted some of the usual barbecue pits and walkways to and from to please his wife, but Carmen also wanted an underground shelter. He was an engineer for the Lockheed-Martin facility located on the edge of the Front Range. He was also one odd duck, and even though Nathan's judgment of character was not his most honed sense, even he felt it.

Carmen wanted a shelter which rivaled any below-ground creation Nathan had ever heard of. He wanted a canned food dispensary and storage, along with a living space for him and his wife, neither of who wanted to bring kids into this dying world. Carmen was determined to survive in a world that only Mel Gibson's ex-cop character *Mad Max* could appreciate. Nathan was given special bonuses for completing phases of this project, one of the biggest designs that his landscaping company had ever undertaken.

Unfortunately, the project was the final nail in the coffin when it came to Carmen's marriage. Due to his end of the world eccentricities, the relationship between

Carmen and his wife had suffered irreparable damage. Nathan saw what was happening in Carmen's marriage and noted the same telltale signs in his own, but neither Nathan nor Kathryn would take the time to admit the truth of it and continued on as casual roommates.

ForeTold

CHAPTER 11

With Samuel transitioning from high school to college, Kathryn had chosen to return to college herself, taking accelerated courses to finish her own degree in education. At this point Samuel needed her so much less for any driving activities, she was able to apply for and receive a grant to finish her schooling. Some of the courses were online at Metro State College, and they did accept many of her basic course credits from many years ago. However, the teaching courses she had taken were not accepted, Kathryn realized she would have some ground to make up.

The lectures, mostly online with a few in the classroom, challenged her faith in God. They never jived well with the little she had learned in her youth about Christ's teachings in the Bible. The educational lectures centered upon concepts rooted in humanistic themes. They seemed to fling Scriptural caution to the wind with their unabashed acceptance of all types of alternative lifestyles as being normal for a child to experience. She was taught in her classes that the adolescent must be exposed to all manner of role choices in the family and supported in choosing any as acceptable. Slowly, the need to find her professors' approval in her spoken and written communications reshaped her beliefs to the point where her faith was not enough to stand upon.

She hadn't ever spent much time reading the Bible, but she did know that God wouldn't approve of the test answers she was regurgitating. Her son kept bringing up the Scriptures of Jesus returning to the earth to which she politely nodded in agreement, even though she believed that it was Samuel's own spiritual escapism she was listening to. As Samuel read to her about Jesus instantly rapturing those who walked with Him. She found herself dismissing the idea as absurd, but that did little to dissuade his theological discourse. Samuel's preaching was meant to encourage her toward truth, but in reality only drove her from the Biblical view toward her professors' opinions. These professors' views were based on natural evidence that, in her mind, appeared more plausible than that of a dusty old black King James Bible.

"I heard this kid the other day that spoke before a class about something that might resonate with you," Kathryn offered while helping Samuel with his laundry on one of his weekends home as a freshman from CSU.

"Yeah, what's that?" Samuel didn't look at her, but folded his jeans, placing them back into his empty hamper, in preparation for going back to school later that day.

Kathryn continued, "Well, this kid talked about the concept that we can delay Jesus coming back. He said he felt the need to preach the message of Jesus throughout the world *first* and *then* the end will come. He mentioned that talk about Jesus coming back imminently actually creates laziness in people and lulls them to sleep. In addition, it makes them inactive to where they do nothing but stand by and wait to 'escape' from this awful world we live in. You know that 'snatching away' stuff you write about on your Facebook page promotes a sense of this escapism?" Kathryn asked, although she really didn't believe in any of what she had heard but was trying to connect with Samuel.

"But what do you think about what the kid was saying?" Samuel asked.

Kathryn explained, "Jesus probably can't come back for a long time. I don't know, maybe I believe that God helps them who help others...or maybe he who helps himself helps others," now she could not look at her son fearing the verbal exchange might make him angry.

"That isn't even in the Bible, Mom," Samuel replied sadly.

"How do you know? You can't know all the words in the Bible," she retorted, but then began to doubt her own words. "Can you?"

"Can I memorize all the Scripture? No, but did you know that little children in ancient Hebraic times were required to recite whole passages of the Torah before they were allowed to enter the Temple? So too, we can know a lot of it and be familiar with the rest. I also know that we do not have the power to delay the timing of anything that God has ordained. God's foreknowledge knows the time of every event before it happens. Sorry, Mom. I don't believe that teaching you heard is correct," Samuel concluded, knowing he needed to speak the truth but also knowing what he was saying was not helping his mother accept anything.

He was quiet for a minute as he continued to fold his clothes and then added thoughtfully, "In Revelation 9:15 it mentions that He holds back the four angels for *this year, month, day and hour.* It is the only time in Scripture that this is mentioned. It is such a unique verse that it is rarely talked about. But, if Jesus was chosen before the foundation of the earth to be slain, as Revelation 13:8 states, it means that He has foreseen all that will ever happen, before it happens. If He has foreseen everything, then God has an absolute time that things will be accomplished, including Jesus' return."

"I don't get that," his mother said turning to him.

"Well, I saw this lawyer guy's program on www.BethlehemStar.com that talked about the exact time that Jesus was born. It was based upon astronomical charts and pinpointed the time of His birth to around 3 BC, during the Feast of Trumpets in September. In fact, interestingly enough, the date corresponded to September 11th on our current calendar. He used computer software to locate the constellations that would have occurred in the area during that time. It is so exact that he also showed the time that Jesus was killed on the cross to be April 3, 33 AD on the Julian calendar.

"Now, think about this: If the God of the universe had an exact time assigned for Jesus to come the first time, and the stars were perfectly positioned to announce the birth of the Messiah to all who could understand the meanings, and if a blood moon occurred at exactly the time of His death, don't you think that God has a schedule for all things? Since Revelation 9:15 are an exact moment on God's timetable, doesn't it make sense that the timing for the return of Jesus is up to Him and not us, Mom?" He paused thoughtfully. "I think that the Maker of all things knows the end and the beginning."

"I don't know. So many of the teachings I have heard don't even support the existence of God. How can they all be wrong?" she asked, although in the face of Samuel's arguments, her response sounded hollow, even to her own ears.

"I wish I could explain to you why those who believe in other religions and other doctrines believe like they do. But, I can't. I do know that I want to study more about the events that have taken place and those that have been prophesied in relation to astronomical events. I believe they will provide support for the answers to our questions about the timing of God's plan as it is outlined in the Scriptures," Samuel ended.

Kathryn had no rebuttal but she had a hard time believing her young son was smarter than the professors she had been listening to. He was an intelligent kid, no doubt, but how could he possibly be right on this one? After all, he was only 19.

Over the next couple of years, Kathryn avoided initiating conversations with Samuel about spiritual things, because he seemed to win them all. She still clung to her professors' teachings based on humanism as the way to understand matters of the soul. She had read part of that book called *Left Behind* but found it difficult to believe and barely finished the first one in the series. The topics in that particular collection stirred up controversy among those in her college circles anyway.

Kathryn continued to struggle, however, as the memories of the conversations with Samuel seemed to incessantly re-play themselves in her mind. As a result, she began to listen to a few Bible teachers on the radio as she drove to school each day at Metro State. In spite of her previous arguments against the existence of God, her heart was being stirred and she began to learn about Biblical principles in a way she never had before. She realized that her marriage was not all as it should be. Nathan and her had drifted very far apart, although he would sometimes listen to her ideas about schooling. She learned not to discuss teachings she heard on the radio with him or the spiritual conversations she had with Samuel, because he would completely shut down.

She believed that Nathan heard her but wasn't the least interested in those ideas. Kathryn frankly wasn't sure that Nathan was even a Christian anymore. If she hadn't heard about his church experience when he was younger, she would never believe he had been saved. Maybe he never had any faith, but at this point Kathryn was realizing that she didn't either.

After listening to Kathryn prattle on about the concepts of teaching she was learning, Nathan would tell her about the projects that he was working on. He told her of the strange designs that Carmen was requesting and that piqued her interest. Kathryn latched onto the topic as a means to open up conversation with Nathan and bridge the ever widening gap between them.

"So why does he ask you to design these fantastic underground man-caves?" Kathryn asked.

"I don't think that they are man-caves. I think these are the shelters we see in those stupid Armageddon-type movies," he took off his shirt and reached for a magazine as he slipped under the covers.

"Yeah, I agree. I don't think things are going to get as bad as Samuel thinks they are."

"I used to hear you guys talk about that religious stuff for hours. I wish he would focus on his school with the same vigor that he devotes to his God," Nathan muttered as he reached for his reading glasses.

"Don't worry about Samuel, he gets great grades, but I do wish he'd spend a little more time developing a social life. Did you know that he is almost 21 right now and still hasn't had a serious girlfriend?" Kathryn asked.

"No I didn't. Shouldn't he have been through a few girls by now?" he asked as he peered over the top of his reading glasses at Kathryn.

"I am not really wanting him to do the rounds. It just seems a little strange that he doesn't care about girls that much," Kathryn replied.

"Is he gay then?" Nathan asked.

"No! Why would you ask that? I think that he just wants to devote all of his spare time to God. I guess that's a good thing if he is going to be a pastor like he plans. But, he is so into the end time stuff like your guy Carmen," Kathryn said, shaking her head in perplexity.

"Carmen doesn't believe the same way that Samuel does, but I think he does believe in something. Hey, can I catch the ten o'clock sports to see who the Broncos drafted?" Nathan slyly changed the subject as he raised the volume on the TV, effectively dodging the God-talk that made him so uncomfortable.

Kathryn, for her part, continued to look for opportunities to engage Nathan in conversation and put into practice some of the teachings she heard on the radio in order to improve their marriage while there was still hope.

CHAPTER 12

A few months later, Nathan needed to replace some slats along his fence line due to a series of severe hailstorms that had damaged parts of the old privacy fence. He found he did not have the correct type of screws, so he headed to a nearby Lowe's store to pick up the screws and lumber he needed. Down aisle 16 beside the two inch wood screws which would complete his job he ran into Carmen, who was searching for nails.

"Hi Carmen, how are you?" Nathan asked as he reached to shake his hand.

"Wow, Nathan. Great to see you!! It seems like I haven't seen you in forever. I have so many business projects going on that I've had no time to even come here and browse or enjoy the smells of the freshly cut lumber. What are you here for?" Carmen asked as he grabbed a huge box of nails and threw them into his cart with a thud.

"Working on a fence project, hail damage, you know," Nathan replied."

"Me too! You haven't picked your lumber yet, have you? We can talk while we go do that," Carmen stated and the two men walked on and began to talk about his underground project's foreman. The foreman kept changing little points of the design from what Carmen required and from the exact specs that Nathan had designed, which caused mounting labor costs.

"Hey," Carmen began as he lifted a slat that seemed straight to both of them and placed it in his cart. Nathan waited silently and let Carmen continue choosing slats for both of them since he seemed to be on a roll. "Do you really like your job?" Carmen asked.

"Uh, well yeah, it's fine," Nathan responded.

"Doesn't sound that convincing to me" Carmen retorted. "I've got a friend who would really love you, and your design abilities. I mean he is building an underground castle for the super-rich. He has a website that will blow your mind. Each apartment in the castle costs upwards of three mill for 900 square feet and includes every amenity one could ask for. They have storerooms stocked with food and you can bring as many guns as you like which are then stored in an armory. If I hadn't wanted to be on my own and already built my underground man-cave I woulda gone in with them. As it stands, I have quick access to more food stuffs that I think we are gonna need down the road. Oh, and I just purchased two sub-Uzis for $1500 each...state of the art designs with 2000 rounds per minute for medium range. Combine those with my sniper rifle when they are far away and my nine millimeters, for when they come too close, I am all set up. How 'bout you? You gotta stock up at that gun show coming in November. They've got the best stuff there. My dream..." Carmen's voice faded as he placed the last of the slats for the both of them in their respective carts.

"Thanks for finding cedar ones for me. It would have taken me much longer. Ya hate to have them with imperfections in the wood. I can design anything, but I suck at buying the materials," Nathan admitted as he and Carmen moved toward the checkout lines.

"Hey, I still have your cell; ya want me to send you his contact info? He loves architects! The interesting part is that he wants me to head up these projects for him. I don't have anyone for the job, but I was thinkin' you might be perfect!"

"Yeah, you know, I would like to hear from him...or I guess you...about that," Nathan replied realizing that sounding too eager might get back to his boss. So, he added a little less enthusiastically, "Ya know, to keep the options open."

"Done and done," Carmen said already reaching for his phone to send the information to Nathan who then heard his iPhone ping with the incoming text.

The rest of the day, he couldn't stop thinking about the possibilities of working on a real building even though it might be underground. The complexities would be a fantastic challenge that would bring him wealth and prestige in the architectural world just as he had always dreamed. He was already working over 55 hours per week and was making a paltry salary in his estimation. The landscape company could not afford the rates that many of his other architectural classmates were making in the big industrial firms. He figured the increase in income that should come with such a job would warrant any number of hours. He began to think disdainfully about his job at Warner and Associates, diminishing it to nothing more than a two-bit landscape job.

At home, as Nathan looked up on-line information about the very impressive company Carmen had spoken about, his imagination conjured up dollar signs accumulating in his checkbook register. He started to ask himself if he had dry cleaned his suit recently, in case he needed it for an interview. Then he realized the man creating this opportunity, who probably had hundreds of millions was portrayed to be in jeans all the time. He would not want a suit man.

Time flew as he worked on his fence conjuring potential drawings in his head and leaving him feeling as if no time had passed.
As he finished the work on the fence and headed to the shower, he debated with himself about telling Kathryn now or waiting until he had the job in hand in case they had to relocate. He concluded that he had to tell her now. Once he finished his shower and had changed, he went to find Kathryn and inform her of his need for an updated

resume. He explained the potential job with some of the details embellished to make it sound more appealing.

"Well, if you think it could be better for you, then that might be great. But I am not up for moving. Also, would you have to spend more hours working?" she asked almost plaintively.

"Nah, I don't think so," Nathan flinched inwardly as he spoke the lie. "I think I can get along with about the same number of hours. But, I won't really know anything until I talk to them. They may not even be hiring or looking for someone more skilled. I don't want to get my hopes up," Nathan said, playing for sympathy by throwing the *I'm probably not good enough* theme to arouse her compassion and distract from the lie.

"How can you say that? They'd be stupid not to hire you," Kathryn replied, swallowing her own initial negative reaction to the news in order to support Nathan as she continued to work on strengthening their marriage.

"I sure hope so. I will let you know more, if I get the interview," he stated as he turned and walked off, ending the conversation.

By Monday he had updated his resume with all the needed relevant information. He realized that he had worked for the landscaping firm for so long that his recent work experience was not very impressive. He spent much of his lunch hour chewing on a protein bar and thinking of other achievements which might make him seem more marketable. This was the aspect of his resume that made him the most nervous. His life reduced to two pages which could make or break a career and a potential six figure income.

He was so pre-occupied with the fantasy of a new career that he missed several opportunities to argue with the sales staff throughout the rest of the day. They usually ticked him off strutting around the office with their high fives for closed deals. It also usually bothered him that he wasn't even called an architect most of the time by any of the staff, including those in the design department, even though he had more experience and education than all of them, except Carol. She had been there longer but didn't seem to care if she got promoted or not. Much of her time was spent being angry at the government for a variety of reasons including JFK's assassination. But today, all of the usual irritants just didn't seem to trigger a response in Nathan.

After five, Nathan used his cell phone to reach this man called MacPherson. Following a brief conversation, he arranged to meet the millionaire at a local Starbucks. They started out with small talk about their individual interests, but the conversation quickly became dominated by MacPherson ruminating upon his own while Nathan just listened. Nathan listened as patiently as he could, reminding himself that this was the golden ticket out of his dead-end job and life.

"Wow, you haven't worked for anyone else since college? How did you manage to stay with one company for so long?" MacPherson asked once he finally took the time to review Nathan's resume. He certainly seemed to ask the most penetrating and toughest questions first.

"I am loyal to a fault. I keep my nose to the grindstone," Nathan replied in an effort to make himself sound better. MacPherson didn't let on that he knew that this would be a step up for Nathan. He had the wherewithal to know that he didn't need the absolute best architect in Denver to accomplish his work - but he did need someone who could do as he was told.

"I do need complete loyalty, as well as a desire for someone to keep at the job until it is done to my satisfaction. I would be leaving many of the day to day, details in Carmen's lap, but he will know exactly what I want. I also need someone who can keep his mouth shut. I don't want anyone to know where we are building or even to share that we are doing. If an employee uses a cell

93

phone to communicate any of this data with anyone other than myself or Carmen, I will have them terminated. If you work for me, I need a complete background check. Not just for criminal records, although I could care less about that, but more of a security clearance that you haven't spilled the beans in a coon's age," MacPherson dropped into a down-home drawl that came from his distant past. There had to be a story in the accent, but Nathan wasn't about to ask for those details. Nathan also realized that the warnings were more threats of retribution with powerful men such as MacPherson.

"I'll be happy to sign any confidentiality agreements. I have done those many times and on basically any deal I work on," Nathan stated somewhat defensively.

"I'm not talking about those!" MacPherson snapped emphatically. "I am talking about a top secret clearance I developed."

"A what?"

"Top secret clearance, man, don't you understand? My father had a top secret clearance when I was growing up. They not only made him take a polygraph over a billion questions, but then they asked all of his friends and family the uncomfortable questions to see whether he would be loyal and could be trusted with national security matters."

"Uh, ok. That won't bother me," a confused Nathan replied.

"Once you pass the security clearance then I will know I can trust you to help run the firm."

"Run the firm?" Nathan asked in astonishment. "I was looking for a job designing for you, not necessarily running the company. But, I am available to do whatever you need me to," Nathan concluded although apprehension had crept into his voice. He suddenly began to feel that he was stepping into something that was well over his head.

"I will get that set up then," MacPherson replied as he stood up to leave. The meeting seemed to be over with Nathan agreeing to be vetted for top secret clearance. Ending with a brief handshake, the encounter left Nathan's head spinning as he remained sitting with his half-finished Carmel Macchiato drink. He really had no concept of what his role would be in running the firm versus what Carmen would do, other than designing. After pondering the details of the meeting for about fifteen more minutes, he decided he wasn't getting any answers and left the Starbucks to head home.

ForeTold

CHAPTER 13

Groundbreaking news over the next few weeks consumed Nathan and Kathryn, making them almost forget about his meeting with the eccentric millionaire. The largest earthquake on record, registering a 9.9 off the coast of Peru, caused a tsunami similar to what had happened on December 26, 2006 in Malaysia. However the Indian Ocean tsunami looked like a small flood in comparison. The landscape of Peru was littered with the dead as nearly 400,000 people were killed within minutes of the quake. As the resulting tidal wave reached the Australian shores, seeming to gain momentum over the vast ocean expanse rather than diminish, many small towns in its path were wiped out without a trace and no one was found alive.

Kathryn would glance from time to time to the news reports that were constantly playing on the television stations, while researching a project for school. Her papers, spread across the round, glass-top coffee table, gave enough evidence that she should be busy for a long time. Nathan took the opportunity to retreat to the basement where he would secretly indulge his pornography addiction in between sessions of halfhearted research about the big designs that the *End of the World Preppers* loved to seek. He was recording every reality episode and documentary about prepping that he could find on the basement's DVR. However, as the weeks passed, his attention to preparing for the possible new job waned.

The ringing of Nathan's cell phone startled him out of a fantasy developing in his mind as he viewed a video on one of his favorite pornographic websites.

"Hello?" Nathan answered, as he quickly clicked off the screen in abject fear that the caller somehow could see the site on the monitor.

"Hello. My name is Ervin..."

"Oh, I don't need any magazines or whatever it is that you are trying to sell me. Wait, how did you get this phone number? I never get any telemarketing calls on my cell," Nathan interrupted.

"It is probably because this isn't a telemarketing call," the voice on the other end stated stiffly. "I was hired by a gentleman to look into your background to see about the suitability of hiring you."

"Who is it that you are calling for?" Nathan absentmindedly asked.

"I think you know our friend with whom you had a cup of coffee. I do all of his background and security clearance checks," Ervin replied.

"What, sir, do need to know?" an air of formality entered Nathan's tone.

"Tell me your five closest friends and give me their cell phone numbers. Then text each one informing them that I will be calling them. This will clear the way for me to ask them the questions I have about you," Ervin instructed, quickly getting to the point of his call.

"OK...hold on for a moment while I check my contact list, please," a reeling Nathan responded. His hands began to tremble as he brought up his contact list and began to zoom through the A's and B's, trying to come up with the requested names. As he continued through the alphabet, he started to worry that he would not be able to find enough names to report to Ervin. The thought caused his trembling to become uncontrollable, resulting in him dropping the phone to the carpet.

"What was that?" the disembodied voice spoke over the speaker that had turned on.

"Oh man, I'm sorry about that, sir. I am looking this stuff up, but I don't have that many close friends. Would my wife be a good one?" Nathan asked apprehensively.

"Not good. Needs to be someone not living with you. Do not call them or prompt them to answer the questions in a certain way, or it will invalidate you from candidacy. Just inform them that I need to ask them questions about you," Ervin retorted.

"You mean I won't be hired?"

"Maybe," Ervin sighed a little too loudly. "It means that you will have to find me someone else to talk to, because you would have tainted their answers, if you get my drift."

"OK, here they are," Nathan rattled off the names and numbers of five friends after a minute more of searching, only to notice he had barely completed the fifth before the line went dead.

"I hope I didn't give an ax murderer my friend's contact information," he sighed. The phone call had at least one unintended effect. It had refocused Nathan to the extent that he knew that he would not get back to his lustful internet surfing any time soon.

Nathan spent the next two hours searching many sites regarding the nature of the buildings he would potentially be designing. Each were underground with small halo stacks jutting out of their roofs and allowing for an entry hatch. The pictures didn't really show how the hatches would open, but the text indicated that they could be. Some of the sites showed dirty and rusted cars seemingly abandoned as junk behind old, tall metal fence lines that sported high voltage warning signs that seemed out of place. Each warned that when unauthorized intrusion took place, death could ensue. All the dwellings had various forms of camouflage to disguise the below ground entrances, making them undetectable to the casual glance.

He found that all had similarities, but the higher priced ones had luxuries that the cheaper models, built for survival only, did not. He also noted that some banked upon the need for only short-term use and lacked the storage for long-term supplies, while others offered enough space that life could be sustained for years.

Nathan sat back in his chair and pictured himself living within this type of bunker. He asked himself, *Could I handle the tight spaces or the pistol wars that might break out over three hundred square feet of living space?* He wasn't sure if he could, but he found it interesting that concrete and steel could provide the correct level of physical security against a nuclear holocaust, one of the end of the world scenarios imagined by many website writers.

For the next several hours, Nathan continued to Google apocalyptic shelters. The theories behind the necessity of these shelters were dreamed up by writers who could have written stories for the SyFy channel. Each was more detailed than the last, with predictions of everything from meteors, to earthquakes, to killer zombies roaming the plains, in addition to the classic nuclear disasters.

It then led Nathan to sit back and think of the multitude of horror movies which were related to this gruesome topic. It used to be around the time of Halloween that the horror genre would be rolled out in the public eye. He then remembered that he, along with his best friend Eric in high school, would watch these movies as well as the latest science fiction.

However, at this point in his life, though many movie titles had to do with zombies, aliens and ever-increasing catastrophes, he hardly paid attention. He would watch them on *Netflix* and occasionally saw them with Kathryn, but he didn't get the fascination anymore. He had come to believe that all would turn out as it always had in the past. There might be little changes in the world, but it would not greatly affect him and what he did. That thought drew him back to the task at hand and he worked until his eyes refused to focus on either the computer screen or the scratchings he had begun to pencil out. The clock read 2:38 in the morning.

ForeTold

CHAPTER 14

Night classes on campus were required for Kathryn's education. After classes concluded for the evening, she drove home in the old Honda Civic. Her backpack, which she had tossed onto the back seat, was bursting at the seams and almost kept her papers from falling out as she bounced over the speed bumps on the Aurora Campus. Kathryn wondered what new tragedy could be affecting Australia after the Tsunami, so she flipped on the radio to see what was happening in the world. She could barely understand what reporter was screaming into the mic.

She couldn't make heads or tails of what the reporter was saying. "Has to be in Australia where more looting and violence is occurring," she remarked to 850 KOA radio. Then she clicked it back off.

Without the noise from the radio, she quickly refocused on upcoming school projects. She verbally processed, while tapping her fingers against the steering wheel, all that she needed to accomplish. She still had to put together the teaching proposal on entomology for a seventh-grade class. It was a huge project that included a plan for four weeks of team teaching. She had started with an elementary teaching degree plan but soon realized that she needed to make herself more marketable to a school system that might move her from location to location until she achieved the stability of tenure and a regular classroom. So, she had taken on the daunting task of adding a middle school emphasis, creating a course load of a near double major. All this was done while holding down a day-job working for a lawyer who never had interesting cases.

She absentmindedly pulled into the driveway and was surprised to find that her garage door was open with

Nathan's car inside. She could not imagine what possessed him to not shut the garage door, especially when he constantly harangued her for pulling similar stunts. Carting her overweight backpack in the crook of one arm and her purse in the other, she found her keys weren't needed to open the door from the garage to the kitchen either. She began to yell for Nathan to ask why the garage was still fully open and the door to the house unlocked when she heard the same tell-tale sounds coming from the TV that she had heard earlier on the radio.

"What are you listening to?" she asked as she nodded to the TV.

"Ebola in Germany."

"Thought it was in Australia," she stated incredulously as the backpack banged against the couch and slipped off her arm falling to the carpet. Her gaze became transfixed on the screen where the news report indicated a gigantic scaled Ebola outbreak happening. Both Nathan and Kathryn remained glued to the TV as they watched the unfolding documentation, often switching from MSNBC to CNN and back to view different perspectives on what had become yet another catastrophic crisis. The couple stayed positioned in front of the television listening to news of the devastation until the early morning hours.

For the next week, nothing was discussed in offices around the world other than the massive devastation caused by the spreading virus. In addition, the ineffective use of resources other nations poured into Germany in an effort to help. People were dying as a result of the quickest moving sickness anyone had ever known. Normally, Ebola symptoms occurred in 8 to 10 days after contact, but a new strain had developed that spread and manifested within a day or two of exposure. Most people were debilitated once they contracted the virus and symptoms manifested and there was an 85% mortality rate.

"Mom, I know you've been seeing the events in Australia and Germany!" Samuel's voice pulled Kathryn out of another homework trance.

"Uh, yeah. How are you?"

"Great!" Samuel replied.

More puzzled than angry, Kathryn quizzed, "With all the chaos in the world, how can you say that?"

"In spite of all the tragedy that is surrounding us, I know that God is good. He said stuff like this will happen," Samuel replied, proud of being able to quote what the head pastor had spoken in the church service two nights before. "I was hired as the Worship Pastor last week in a new church only five miles from you. I would love to have you come hear me. God is moving in a unique way. Since this is my first job right out of CSU..."

"I am sure that He is, but what has that got to do with those countries?" Kathryn questioned her son.

"Listen mom, I know that you are not really into end-time events or anything, but here is the deal: these are just the tip of the iceberg. The book of Matthew talks about pestilences and earthquakes in diverse places. They are coming rapid fire. There is a time coming soon. It could be next month or years from now, but it absolutely is imminent that Christ is coming again. I want you to be ready," he said pleadingly.

"I believe in God...you know I do. I have been praying for those in Germany and other lands who are in harm's way. There is so much bad stuff happening that we need to focus on the here and now – not on those stories of future events that may or may not happen," Kathryn asserted.

"The here and now is totally important, mom, and that's why I want your heart completely tuned into what He is doing. He states in the beginning of Revelation that there is a special blessing to those who read and believe in the Book..."

"You think I don't believe in the Good Book? Come now!"

Samuel clarified, "I didn't mean that you don't believe in the Bible, but if you don't really take it seriously then you are missing out on what He is doing in the world and in your life."

Kathryn took on the teacher's voice that she pulled out for the classroom, "Samuel...I absolutely take the Bible as serious stuff. I just believe that you can't know what He is going to do. That one book you're talking about could be interpreted many ways. Those ways could be as you believe, but they could mean something different. It could be a hundred years from now or even a thousand. Also some believe to focus on the end makes us no earthly good, or however that saying goes," Kathryn replied, once again messing up the saying which was typical when she tried to use a quote.

"Mom, the Lord is coming back so soon! These outbreaks are another sign of that. I want you to be ready. I know I have said that before..." Samuel didn't know what else to say to convince her, so he trailed off.

"I know you do, son. We'll be there...your dad and I."

With that, the two talked guardedly about his new pastoral position. Samuel gave in reluctantly to the topic change since he was trying not to push his eschatological knowledge. He did not wish to upset his mother anymore. Kathryn, on the other hand, tried not to be irritated at the young man who assumed he knew more than she about the Bible, even though she had to admit to herself that he did.

Later that night, while her husband read, Kathryn's mind was plagued with the truth of the conversation, playing out what-if scenarios. She couldn't even quote the verses in Revelation to which Samuel had been referring, and that bothered her. She actually hated the many ways that the Church and popular literature ranted about the coming of the Lord. Her interpretation of Scripture on the timing of the second coming of the Lord was that it would not happen for thousands of years. In her opinion, future events could not be known for many reasons. She believed that God was in control but wasn't sure that He concerned Himself with things that would happen years from now.

As she got under the covers and reached for a book, her mind was still busy reflecting on the conversation with Samuel. Both Nathan and Kathryn seemed to be in their own worlds that evening, with very little talking. He was intensely engrossed in his NFL magazine which gave a brief overview of the Broncos' new free agents for the coming year. He usually bought two magazines seeking the latest information as well as one magazine on the fantasy football draft that occurred in the beginning of September. He would mutter the stats to her absent-mindedly knowing she knew little about football and cared even less about the game.

In her preoccupied state, she barely registered that he was speaking to her and could not even concentrate on the book she was pretending to read. She turned only two pages in the last hour. Kathryn felt in her gut a latent sense of foreboding with the events in the world that her son had seemed so excited about. All of the Middle Eastern drama, as well as other disasters around the world, seemed to make the newscasts craze for the latest photo of mayhem and death. Each channel was exclaiming their viewpoint, predicting the potential of more disasters to come. She wondered if they knew what they were talking about as she set her alarm for 6:30 the next day. At least it was going to be Friday.

ForeTold

CHAPTER 15

Kathryn had laid awake forty minutes before the alarm went off. She dreaded another busy day of work and school. She hoped the weekend would allow her to catch up...until she remembered that the yard and the flower beds were waiting for her and Nathan's attention. The weekend would take up more of her precious moments without any down time. She needed to write a lesson plan for ninth grade sociology, examining the after-effects of the Civil War upon slavery. At least she wouldn't have to dress up today since Friday's were casual day in the office. She really enjoyed the break from wearing skirts.

Normally, Nathan would have gotten up about fifteen minutes after she got in the shower, but this morning he already had the TV blaring as she stepped out and donned her purple robe. When she finished blow-drying her hair, she entered the bedroom and asked, "Why did you turn that on?"

"I wanted to see the beginning of free agency for the Denver Nuggets. They have 50 mill in cap space and are looking to splash this week. But then I saw all the channels filled with this," he inclined his head toward the television, his attention still totally fixed on whatever was being reported.

"All?" she trailed off as her own attention focused on the television. Upon the flat 42" screen was déjà vu all over. Nathan remembered how the events of the morning of 9/11 had played out. On that day, he had turned on ESPN to find out the latest Broncos' news. However, when he had turned on the television, all of the channels were showing live reports of a plane having hit the World Trade Center and only minutes later the second airplane hit the other tower. It was apparent that it was no accident; it was definitely a new world. Today's broadcast felt no different. Both wondered if this was the beginning of a new world in their lives.

"Reports are flooding in from about the globe of a...of a...I don't know what to make of it or even what to call it, David. People have left the building...I am sorry, but I don't mean to make light of it. Cut that..." the reporter was clearly making a fool of himself on the Denver local station, so they mercifully cut away to leave the serious coverage to others who would not waver in the face of whatever the latest disaster was.

Back in the studio, the camera changed the scene to show a popular desk reporter who seemed to have lost all the color in his face. "I frankly don't know what more I might say except for what we have been reporting all morning long. If you just now woke up and tuned in to our broadcast, something very unusual has happened: people have disappeared. Not just a few but tens of thousands, and it could be millions, all around the world. We don't know why, but we know that some were sitting in their chairs, as our producer was this morning in our briefing before our newscast, and then they were gone. There is currently no trace of these people."

Kathryn turned away afraid to hear more. She thought this sounded uncannily familiar. She was definitely not one to jump to conclusions, but she remembered the book called *Left Behind* portraying this same scenario and even though she had not finished the book, the similarities were remarkable. Could this be a joke? Kathryn also knew that Samuel had been mentioning more of this ever since he went to his new church. But, it could not be true, because she thought she was a Christian. Wasn't the Lord coming for her as well? But then she realized that she believed that Jesus wouldn't return for some time, so this disappearance had to have another explanation. She began to cognitively reorganize all of her weekend plans, ditching the studying and gardening for study of another kind...in her Bible, as soon as she found it. Then, she remembered something more important than the Bible in that moment: Samuel.

"What are you doing?" Nathan asked Kathryn.

"Shhh...Calling Samuel...he doesn't seem to be available at the moment. Maybe he went to work early to counsel distraught people," she replied. "And I'm one of them," she whispered to herself as she hurriedly threw on clothes, pulled her iPhone out of the charger, grabbed her purse along with her car keys, and ran from the house.

Kathryn drove in a panicked state. Her mind flashed back to a similar drive her father must have had when she was ten. Her mother had called her father at work and was only able to get out, "She's dead"...into the phone.

Her father worked forty-five minutes from home. When he finally arrived home after a very frantic drive, he found out that her mother had just run over the dog. His only daughter was not dead as he had believed. He lamented that it was the worst drive he had ever had. He had prayed and cried the whole way through traffic, in a time long before cell phones were ever used. This drive for Kathryn was no different, but she feared that there would be no comfort at the end of her journey of twenty minutes.

When she got to Samuel's apartment on the second floor, she rang the doorbell and then continued to knock incessantly. An older gentleman came out of the apartment next to Samuel's and scowled at her persistence, then thought better of saying anything, so he turned and closed the door. Tugging on her hair as she was prone to do when stressed, she started to leave, not knowing what would be the most effective means of contacting her son. As she got to the first landing of the staircase, she changed her mind and raced back up the stairs to knock on the door again, hoping for a different outcome. She did this several times as she debated with herself about what her next step should be. Finally, heading back down the flight of stairs and pausing on the landing, she was surprised to see the older gentleman had come back out of his apartment and was watching her.

With as much kindness in his gruff demeanor as he could muster he asked, "You lookin' for that Samuel kid?"

"Yes, why yes, I am...you haven't seen him have you?" she asked excitedly looking up.

"Nah, not seen no one. Sometimes I can hear his Jesus music kinda loud until I pound on the walls. He tends to be good about turning it down, though. Last night I kinda expected him to do so. You know he is dating a girl, don't ya? You gotta be his mama?"

"Yes, I am. Who's he dating?" Kathryn now changed her tactic.

"She's a little cutie from that Bible study he does up here on Thursdays. She's been comin' over for dinner most Friday nights but seems to leave by 11. Doesn't seem to be no hanky-panky going on over there," the old man exclaimed with an attempt at a smile. It was obvious to Kathryn that smiling was not something he did often.

"Well that's good...actually I am not worried about that. I have to find him!" She began to get frantic again.

"There's a bunch of people missin'. Wouldn't try to fill out no police report. Them cops ain't got the time for that," with the last comment he had turned and walked back to his apartment door, swinging it closed behind him.

"Uh, thanks," she uttered over her shoulder to an old man who was no longer there. She shook her head and after a few more moments of indecision quickly moved down the steps to the parking lot and back to her car. She headed home to catch Nathan and enlist his help with searching for Samuel. They divided up areas of the city where Samuel frequented and set a designated time to meet and report back to each other. Cell phones would be of no use since the panic following the disappearances had caused all communication circuits to be overloaded.

After hours of unsuccessful searching, they met back at the house and stared with unbelief and despair at one another, both having trouble grasping that this was actually happening to them. Samuel was now a statistic of what the media had dubbed MIW (Missing in the World). The numbers of reported MIW's was reaching staggering calculations of millions around the globe. In mutual confusion and fear, Nathan and Kathryn held each other for the first time in a very long time.

Finally, the emotional turmoil they had been through all that day seemed to catch up with them. They tried to rest on the couch in each other's comforting embrace with Kathryn's head cushioned on Nathan's right shoulder. As her exhausted mind drifted, Kathryn realized that while she found comfort in this position, the reason why they had finally turned to one another was devastating. Her son was gone.

She missed the news media conjectures expounding on why he was missing. With the TV's volume set on the lowest level and the screen split between CNN and MSNBC, she instead began to rail at the One who might have taken her son from her.

"Why did you do this?" she whispered into the night as she slipped away from Nathan and began to pace about the room. Inside she was screaming it. "Was I not good enough to take? How about Nathan?" she began pointing in his direction.

"I know..." she startled at the voice, at first believing that the Lord was responding to her distress, then realizing that it was only Nathan. Kathryn shook her head and mentally waved off the imagined response to her question that she hadn't really believed at all in the God of the Bible, but rather in a god of her own making. That god didn't exist and therefore had no power.

"What do you mean *you know*?" she asked Nathan.

"I know that you are upset over his leaving. But, there has to be a good scientific explanation for all of this," he said as reasonably as he could.

"Yeah, He did it," she stated vehemently and somewhat bitterly, pointing to the ceiling in the dark.

"Who did it? What are you talking about?" Nathan spouted with exasperation borne from exhaustion.

"I mean that Samuel was saying that God would take away the believers. But, why didn't He see fit to take us or the others on this earth? I don't get it. Were we not religious enough? Did we not believe enough?" she aimed her questions half toward Nathan and half toward the ceiling again.

"You were going to church two or three times a year. I believe in God. Not sure that He will answer you at this point, but I can't believe this crisis of worldly proportion has anything to do with Him," Nathan retorted.

"There has to be something more to all of this that I am missing. I have focused so hard on getting my degree that I...I...I don't know what I need to do now. Do I finish? Do I quit? What do *we* do now?" she again trailed off.

"You wanna quit school? With only two semesters left?" Nathan asked.

"No! I mean maybe. I don't know. Actually, I don't care about school right now. I have got to find Samuel!" She threw up her hands in exasperation and looked up towards the sky hoping an answer would miraculously come.

"We will look for him again in the morning. Let's go to bed to get a little sleep. Morning will be here soon," Nathan said as he dragged himself off to bed.

"Morning will be here soon," she repeated softly to herself. "Maybe then I can get some answers," but no matter how hard she tried, there was no rest for her that night. Racing images and jumbled thoughts disturbed any semblance of rest and she was destined to start the new day with red, swollen eyes from the tears that would not stop flowing.

ForeTold

CHAPTER 16

Kathryn was already putting on her makeup when Nathan awoke. He stretched and felt the tension of the previous night in his stiff, sore shoulders. As he got ready for the day, he shared with her the new locations that he intended to search, outlining his plans in detail. Kathryn seemed to be listening as he finished his morning grooming rituals. She had mumbled the obligatory *uh-mm's* periodically throughout his recitations. Once he realized that she hadn't added to the litany of destinations, he craned his neck around the bathroom corner to look at her.

"Aren't you listening to me?" he asked.

"Yep, but I'm thinking that I might check that church," she responded.

"Uh, that's a good idea. He might be going to church to prepare for those services. I will go to those other places. I also need to swing by the office to see how many of my co-workers are going to be there on Monday. My heart is not into going Monday. If it's anything like 9/11 was, my dad said no one went into work the next day," said Nathan. He squelched the guilt that started to rise since it was yet another lie, because he never wanted to go back to that office and really didn't think he would ever need to.

After getting dressed, he headed through the house only to find that Kathryn was already gone. He realized that she, as sleep-deprived as he, had lost all of the small courtesies that tend to be forgotten in crises, like telling someone when you were leaving and when you'd be back. Overnight, the world had reshaped the behaviors of its inhabitants who were all affected by the MIW's, and it would be sometime before it could pull its way out of its headlong spin. Reports were flooding in from around the

117

globe of death and destruction due to accidents that occurred when drivers, pilots, and other operators of moving vehicles had disappeared. Denver was no different in this capacity and had no answers for the numbers of accidents along the highways and side roads.

With cell service still being down due to an overload of communication circuits, Nathan pulled out a pad of paper and a pen and began plotting his route with a list of the different directions in which his son might have gone, beginning from his apartment. He started his morning with a cursory view of the apartment building as he climbed the stairwell, as Kathryn had done the previous day. The neighbor that Kathryn had encountered sat upon his stoop drinking coffee, kicking his chair back on two legs and rocking it toward the wall.

"You must be the papa. Your wife was already here. He ain't in there. He ain't nowhere. It's been quiet as a mouse across the complex," he chuckled at his joke and waved his hand like it was a magic wand, as if he had the ability to still the ill winds that were blowing through the North Creek Apartments. Nathan visually swept the buildings following the motion of that moving hand. Either people had disappeared here as well or were glued to their TVs. *Probably both types*, Nathan thought.

"So you still haven't seen anyone?" Nathan asked as his mind scrambled, trying to make sense of what was going on.

"Nah. It's all over the world. They call them MIW...Missin' in the World. Thinkin' that's a pretty clever title. Musta' taken all night for them yokels to come up with that one. You should be headin' for the hills. If I'd had the cash, I woulda plunked it into land. Dumber than rocks those media pukes," the old man said in between slurps of coffee.

"Uh, yeah, you're right," Nathan muttered. "Gotta be goin' now," he spoke over his shoulder as he threw his right hand in the air as a cursory wave goodbye, eager to leave the conversation.

Nathan returned to his search, noting possible routes his son might have taken. Samuel's car wasn't in the covered parking area designated for apartment residents. His was missing but many seemed to be parked at home. After exhaustively scouring a five-mile range, Nathan happened upon a Pizza Hut and suddenly saw his son's car out in the parking lot. Nathan swerved hard into the lot cutting off vehicles whose drivers responded with honking and a few classic one finger salutes outstretched in his direction. Nathan pulled in beside his son's old, blue Hyundai Sonata. Peering into the window, Nathan noted a jacket on the backseat, but the keys weren't in the car. The doors were locked and he didn't want to set off the alarm so he turned toward the restaurant itself.

Nathan hurriedly opened up the doors to the Pizza Hut and began to scan the people within. He allowed 30 seconds for his eyes to change from the bright sunlight to the darker wood paneled interior that older locations like this tended to have. Once his eyes had adjusted, he realized that only two other people occupied the locale while several workers were behind the counter. He noted that the salad bar was disheveled, and the lettuce looked stale. Several of the servers had multiple stains on their uniform shirts and the shirt tails were hanging out. The overall picture was one of dejection.

He searched in almost every booth appearing as if he were playing a complex game of hide-and-seek with a five-year old in the dirty restaurant. After wandering throughout the joint for some time, an annoyed server asked him if he needed to be seated.

"No, I am looking for my son," Nathan frantically replied.

"How old is he? We haven't had any children in here all day. Maybe check at the Denny's?" the server retorted with no emotion.

"He's not a little boy! His car is out front. He's disappeared!" Nathan's voice raised as he finally turned to the server only to see her walk away without another word.

The employees allowed him to check the bathrooms and the hallways until Nathan was thoroughly exhausted by the efforts. The patrons and workers had seen this sight played out several times...a scene that was being played out over the entire world. His son was in fact MIW.

Nathan retreated to his son's car. As he leaned against the hood of the car, tears flooded his eyes. It had been years since he had cried and he had almost forgotten what it felt like. Despair felt like a physical blow to his gut. No longer worried about setting off the alarm, he clutched the blue sedan until the frustration boiled out of him, drying up the tears and replacing the physical pain with a need to strike something. Using his knee, he hit the side of the car. The dent to the door was significant but didn't match the pain to his knee. He didn't care about the resulting throb radiating down his calf. He only cared that the madness caused by the missing people might end. He hoped the police would come to his distress, but they seemed to have bigger problems of their own. No doubt the wheels of justice were slowing as many of its workforce were permanently retired by disappearing from this earth.

Needing something to focus on, Nathan began to search around the car for Samuel's keys. As the moments passed and he failed to locate them, his anger began to build. Taking several deep breaths, Nathan reined in his tumultuous emotions and tried to think of a plan of action to follow.

He decided to go back to the apartment manager for the keys to Samuel's apartment. Nathan figured if he could find the extra set of car keys Samuel was sure to have, he could move the car back to Samuel's place.

It was painful getting into his car with his throbbing left knee but focusing on driving and the task at hand allowed him to gain control over his emotions and focus on the road. At the apartment complex, his reddened eyes told the assistant manager that this was a distressed father, and that he should not ask too many questions. The assistant at last walked him to the apartment to show him inside. There he noted a couple of – what appeared to be - family pictures on the wall. Once he recognized Nathan in those pictures, the man left him in peace.

Nathan seemed to move in slow motion around the apartment. In the kitchen, he picked up a dirty knife that lie beside the butter dish and set it in the sink replacing it with a clean one from the kitchen drawer. In the living room, he placed all of the remote controls in order on the coffee table and moved the bills beside the computer screen in Samuel's second bedroom into a neat pile so that he could find them later. As he set the bills down, Nathan realized that he would need to pay these bills or they would go into collection. The momentary worry that Samuel's credit would be ruined was replaced with the staggering truth of his loss. Nathan began to truly realize that his son was gone.

After spending almost an hour aimlessly rifling through Samuel's belongings, he finally found a second set of keys to the car. This brought another round of tears from his swollen eyes. As Nathan's eyes swept through the tiny apartment from his vantage point at the front door, he noticed a spare key to the apartment had been laid on the edge of the kitchen countertop by the assistant manager. He realized that the kid knew that this was the occupant's father. Nathan carefully secured the lock on the apartment door and headed out to retrieve Samuel's car.

As Nathan started away from the apartment, he recognized that he could not take more memories flooding his mind, so he headed toward his own house instead. Then he remembered that he hadn't tried to call his wife in the last five hours while he had been searching. He attempted to call her and was surprised it actually seemed to go through. When she didn't answer her phone, he left a message about finding Samuel's empty car. He was used to speaking to her voicemail, as Kathryn tended to leave her phone in her purse and commonly would not hear it ring. At this point he had no idea when he would retrieve Samuel's car and was not sure that it was important.

CHAPTER 17

Kathryn chose another route. She didn't believe she would find her son, so she began the quest for what her son might have believed. She shoved her iPhone in her purse even though she knew communication systems were overloaded and probably wouldn't be working for a while. She would have to attempt to connect with her friends and family as systems became available, but this wasn't the time. In this instance, her son made all of this very personal. She had already shot off an email to her boss letting him know that she wasn't coming in Monday or Tuesday because of her son. She was mildly surprised that he had responded back quickly, telling her that she was welcome to take all the time she needed. He had lost his mother who was in a memory care unit in Arvada, who he hadn't visited much over the past years because she had forgotten who he was long ago. With that bit of communication out of the way, Kathryn felt relieved that she could focus on her son and finding out more about what he had known about these disappearances.

She drove towards Samuel's church around ten in the morning hoping for some answers. At each stop light, even though she knew she wouldn't see her son, she couldn't help but scan the faces of those walking the streets or study the cars parked along the side of the road. As she neared her destination, she yawned widely and realized she might need something to help her focus and carry on for the next few hours. Spotting a Starbucks, she signaled and turned off the road and into the drive-thru.

With her Grande Café Mocha in hand, she pulled back into traffic and continued on her way to the church. The drive had taken somewhat longer than usual, much like Kathryn, other drivers slowed down to better visualize the wrecked cars off on the side of the road due to the many MIW's.

Since it was Saturday Kathryn assumed there would not be very much activity at the church. However, as she pulled into the parking lot, she noticed that there were groups of cars interspersed throughout the lot.

As Kathryn gazed out at the scene, she remembered past conversations with Samuel of an impending event like this, a small measure of hope was building inside her that she may be able to see Samuel again. With a desperate sense of hope, she could almost picture him up above with his Maker, singing and praising before the God he had known intimately.

Her mind began to wander, she realized she had loved to hear her son sing and play but really wasn't into all of the outward emotional displays that he tended to express with his music. When her early dreams of a great marriage didn't pan out the way that she hoped, music had become an annoyance, especially when she heard love songs. She just hadn't been able to stand them. Even coming from a band she liked, the music and lyrics still reminded her of things in her life that had not turned out the way she had hoped. Talk radio or nothing at all was preferred in her car.

After a few moments, she shook her head and purposefully reined in her thoughts, trying to focus on the reason she had come here. She opened the car door and got out and walked toward the church. As she opened the doors to the church and entered the dimly lit foyer, she noticed groups of people huddled about. Any movement of the doors opening and closing caused each person in the foyer to look up in expectation of perhaps seeing a loved one.

Like sheep without a shepherd the flock congregated together. No leaders in the church were there to give them comfort, direction or answers. All their pastors were among the MIW's. Everyone in the foyer had stunned looks on their faces. Half the people knew they missed what they thought was a sure thing, the other half had no idea what was going on. The half that realized they had missed it simply wanted to know two things: Why were they still here and who else was in the same predicament?

If a stranger came in, everyone immediately turned their heads back toward their huddle. As recognized members of their church came in, they said nothing. The look in their eyes said it all, *You too*. The shock and awe that filled their hearts would in no way be squelched by any church belonging connection they may have had. They knew what happened but they did not understand why it did not happen to them. Without any pastors left to explain why, they staggered at the thought of what's next. They knew just enough to know horrible events were still to come. How could they survive? They thought *How could have God abandoned us.*

Kathryn's initial response as she was greeted with this scene of heads turning away in coldness was to turn around and head back to the car. But then she realized the question she must be able to answer was *Why am I here?* Somehow, she realized that if she had known a little less than she did then she wouldn't be here. And it wasn't as if she knew much of these people's situations. She couldn't afford to be judgmental at this point.

Instead she made as little eye contact as possible as she maneuvered her way through the main sanctuary doors that were open. She sat down on one of the chairs in the main sanctuary hoping that there would be one person who would walk down the aisle to explain where their loved ones had gone, and why they themselves were not included with them. She suspected this phenomenon was related to the strange event that Samuel had called the Rapture, but then she realized that she hadn't bought into the idea, even when he had tried to explain it to her.

Something Kathryn had never seen before was a group of people in the front of the sanctuary on their knees at the altar. They were sobbing with tears flowing down their faces, crying out to God asking for forgiveness. The cry's for a second chance were unashamedly articulated without care to who was listing or what they thought about them. Some were saying, "Jesus I know you love me and I am ashamed that I was found unworthy, please forgive me, search me and clean my heart of all impurity."

Anytime anyone came into the sanctuary, Kathryn found herself turning from her trance in hopes of a reunion with Samuel or at least a few answers from one who might know something concrete about the event. One woman with hair disheveled began to hand out copies of a scribbled page starting in the back of the auditorium. The pages rustled as they were handed from the giver to the receiver and murmured questions started to hum throughout the rows.

"I am sorry. I don't know more than what is stated on this page. I know it doesn't look professional, but this is what I was asked to do. I have worked for this man's father at Lockheed Martin for years now as his front office staff. The father was very religious, but his son was not before the disappearances occurred. The son, the speaker for the event outlined on this page, wrote this up, and I was asked to pass it out in this church. I will learn what he is talking about at the same time that you do. Please don't ask me more," the stressed red-headed woman in her forties begged.

"What's this?" Kathryn asked when she received her copy. The only response she received was a finger plunking on the page and a shoulder shrug indicating that the page had all the information that was to be gleaned at the time. Once the woman had passed out fliers to all those present, the mourners rose as one to follow her out of the sanctuary, arriving in the foyer where a whole new commotion was being created by the words on the flyer. Each time questions were thrown her way, the woman begged them to come to the event that was planned at the Arapahoe High School gym on University and Centennial at six the next evening.

Kathryn stood a moment watching the commotion and then quickly read through the flyer she held in her hand. The top contained an address and tomorrow's date. The note read:

All who see this page are seeking a truth that cannot be known without the Spirit who reveals it. I messed it up until this point and was given a visitation by the Lord Himself who told me of this truth. You might not believe what I have to say, but I will say it from every rooftop or doorstep until the Lord tells me to stop. I know what is happening. The world will come up with their own agenda to explain it, but for those who seek His face upon this issue, the words will bring answers of life. If your spirit rejects the world's explanation, then I say you are ready for the truth that will lead you in a new direction and you should come to learn more. If this flyer bothers you, then you should also come. The choice is yours...
Armin Paley.

Then his prediction was eerily fulfilled in Kathryn's midst, "What a quack!" one stated and threw the flyer into the air.

Another said, "I gotta verify this with CNN or maybe MSNBC News. One of them will know more than some local guy, wouldn't they?" the man asked those around him hoping that his theory of truth might be verified by his weak conviction of the sources of evidence.

A tearful woman pleaded, "I am going, and I need to hear what this guy's gonna say. What have we got to lose?" as she stood beside Kathryn. Kathryn squeezed the woman's shoulder in comfort and confirmation that she agreed with her comment.

Uncharacteristically for her, Kathryn took up the banner raised by the tear-stained woman, "People, people, I agree we should seek answers. I don't know for certain where my son is. I have been here for an hour waiting for a sign or a word that would give some explanation of truth. No one has offered anything until this flyer. I have a good feeling about what we might learn!"

Some were swayed by Kathryn's words, but others took up the opposite banner. "Nah, he can't know anything. How could he? He's trying to get you to pay into his coffers just like this church did to my wife. I was sick of the money she gave these shysters here. I was hoping that she was huddled in a corner like I heard those people back in California in the 1990's...what were they called...*Heaven's Gate*? The ones who killed themselves? It's more likely that they ran off to drink the Kool-Aid than whatever his supposed truth is."

"I know what to believe," another man interjected.

"What's that?" Kathryn boldly asked.

"That science has the answers. My wife was wrong. I did love her, but she was becoming kooky in the last few years. It was Jesus this and Jesus that, I was getting sick of it. I had even thought about...well, never mind. I was hoping that she wasn't dead, but this convinces me that she probably is. When the scientists get a hold of the evidence, they will let us know through the News on TV. Don't be morons; listen to science," the man concluded as he tried to lead a group out the door. After a few seconds some were persuaded by his words.

Kathryn and several of the others felt that the excuses were weak and lame. They made little sense and those left in the foyer of the church returned to studying the hand written page in hopes of gleaning more information about what the meeting was really about.

A grey-haired gentleman name Drake broke the silence, "I know what happened. The truth is Jesus came back for those who were ready. The answer I seek is why He did not take me. I don't understand I was a member of this church for 20 years, even an elder. Well...until last year I left the church when that stingy pastor would not take my advice on the church budget. I was right to be offended; after all I have done for this church!"

"Perhaps if you are right, the answers await at this meeting. After all there are no pastors here with answers," Kathryn stated firmly, trying to portray a hope that she didn't know if she really felt, but knew was somewhere deep inside of her. It was the kind of hope that sprouted from a seed of faith that knew that answers were forthcoming.

It was getting late, Kathryn walked to her car preparing to return home. As she did so, she found her eyes drifting to the Colorado skyline that was most beautiful tonight. The sun sinking over the mountains transfigured the sky into what those who lived here called an alpine glow sunset. It's when the red setting sun's rays bounce off the bottom of the clouds back toward the ground giving everything a rosy glow. She stared into it for some time believing that a revelation was about to unfold that would change the course of her life. She wondered if she could get Nathan to come along with her to the meeting at the gym tomorrow and began to hope that she was up to the task of convincing him to tag along.

That night the couple sat about the dinner table, which was uncommon for the two of them to do. Each discussed what he or she had found. Both had their opinion and endeavored to entreat the other to his or her camp.

"We have got to find a rational explanation for all of this! I cannot believe that aliens have taken him. You can't either that...that..." a whispered curse escaped Nathan's lips as he tried to evade the emotion his voice betrayed.

"I don't believe in aliens!" Kathryn bristled.

"Isn't that what you are saying with this meeting tomorrow night? What about work? You have school and I have a project..." he cut off his own words that attempted to restore normalcy in a changed world.

"I told them I might not be in this week," she lied.

"What about school? Are you quitting again?"

"Hey, wait a minute! I quit for you last time. I got you through college, so that we could have a family like you had wanted. Well, we both wanted that last thing, but I gave all of my credits up for you. I lost so many of them when I started the process again last year. Now, I don't know about any of it!" she realized that as she made each comment her priorities changed. She now understood that nothing would be as important as what she would learn tomorrow night at Arapahoe High.

"What do you mean you quit for me? I took that cruddy job for us. I hate it! I was and always have been treated like a lackey instead of an architect. I would quit..." he caught himself because he didn't want to expand this fight with more inflammatory comments.

"You're not hearing me, Nathan! I have to find the truth," she silently begged him to learn it with her. She needed the support that he really hadn't given over the last few years. He had been excited that she might have a job that could pay better than she was currently making, and mentioned that having a teacher's health care plan would be superior over the small company benefits he paid for dearly.

"One of us has to keep this house afloat!" he boomed. As soon as the words escaped his mouth he understood he had truly inflamed her passionate response.

"Keeping us afloat? You have to be kidding me. What do you...?" instead of questioning him, she stormed off knowing that she was about to lose it and if she did she would never get him to come with her. She headed straight for the garage door to take a walk to clear her head.

Her only revenge was the satisfaction gained from slamming the door on the way out, knowing it would resonate throughout the house. Both of them were spinning out of control in word and thought, and she understood that it easily could end in a climax of a destroyed marriage. But who was she kidding? Their marriage had a few good nights of passion a year but more empty stares during meals than anything. Meal times usually denigrated into iPad playing while watching the recent DVR event recorded each night. Then while he would continue to watch the SyFy channel's recording or football, she would leave to clean or plan something else.

By the time Samuel had left for college and then moved out on his own, they had forgotten who the other one was. Even the stilted, infrequent conversations between them when Samuel was in high school had digressed into silence. They didn't have a marriage anymore. She had even begun to notice that he would suddenly click off of the iPad screen, and cover it with the case as she walked back in the room. Kathryn knew that the images stored upon the device were salacious. They denigrated her, knowing that she had gained ten pounds over the years. She knew that his mind raced with thoughts of what once was. Nathan seemed to stop looking at her like he used to.

As she walked her mind returned to the expectation of learning the truth which tomorrow may bring. Relenting due to the spat, she believed she would have to go to the gym alone. As this understanding settled, her anger quelled and a strong longing to know truth began. She was resolved to go wherever it took her, she thought as she rounded the corner to home.

Kathryn spent the rest of the night lamenting the life that Samuel would never have: marriage, children - her grandchildren, career advancement...the list was endless as well as the challenges. She had pondered if Samuel would be a better husband and father than Nathan. She shoved aside the thoughts of Nathan's perceived failings, and the accompanying resentment at what it all had done to them. As the anger subsided, sadness washed over her countenance as her heart despaired of ever seeing her son again. The tears began to flow once more, making a mess of her face she knew, but she didn't care. He was gone and was not coming back. She walked back into the house with less bluster than when she left.

As Nathan walked into the room, he searched for a reason for her crying. "What have you learned?" he asked.

"That you don't even care about our son. You act as if he didn't exist. How can you work at a time like this?" she confronted in tears, the resentment and anger returning with a vengeance.

"You think I don't care? You..." he stopped his words before they blew up in both of their faces. He stalked away to disappear.

"Yah, there you go, hiding from this family again!" she cried all the louder.

Back in his home office in the basement, Nathan could barely contain his anger. He pounded the keyboard that he had returned to. He spoke as if she were there in a play of the mind: *I do all of this for us!* As he jabbed at the computer screen with another backyard design.

"You'll never know," he whispered, knowing that she could not understand him in more ways than one.

CHAPTER 18

Kathryn awoke the next morning to take a quick shower and prepare for the day. She headed out the door around six, making it her earliest Sunday morning in memory. Due to the tension that was emanating through the house, she didn't feel the need to say goodbye, but sent one over her shoulder anyway in a hushed tone that a snoring Nathan would never have heard.

She drove up Broadway toward Englewood looking for a coffee shop that might be similar to an old one she remembered in Kansas, where you could load up on coffee and the prevailing winds of gossip. Only north of Englewood did she find such a place that was leaning toward being more of a dive than the usual places she frequented.

She asked for a table for one and brought out her iPhone, notepad, and Bible. She actually had no idea what to do with the Bible, but it made her feel close to her missing son. She had not done anything like this since she was in high school in Olathe where she might write poetry or make entries in her diary about a boy who had done her wrong. On this fateful Sunday, she just wanted to sit nearest to the loudest group and listen to what they had to say. She was hoping that maybe she could glean some new information.

As the theories being touted of the MIW's were discussed by the variety of patrons at the coffee shop, Kathryn could hear the half-baked logic behind each position. Some voiced support for one theory or another, while others insistently controverted each view. The leading concepts ranged from alien abductions; a field of energy against those who offended Buddha or Allah; and then finally the Rapture. She tuned her ear to that last reference. It didn't appear that anyone present knew enough about it to elaborate on the how or why. It seemed as if most people had more to say about the other half dozen far-fetched theories that had been voiced.

"What about that Rapture thing?" Kathryn asked as she turned to the jean-jacketed figure whose large belly pressed against the edge of the counter.

"I don't know. There was a series of books back in the 1990's that talked about this thing called the Rapture," he explained.

"Yeah! I wanna see Bruce Willis go up in the space ship and knock those commies outta the sky!" Another bemoaned.

"It's a comet that he knocked out, you moron!" his closest companion slugged the bemoaner.

"I bet the Rapture is the end of the world," another table offered. No one really had anything to say about it since no one knew what it meant so the comment went unacknowledged.

The conversation turned into a litany of movies in which the themes were about the end of the world attached to the worst critique of each Kathryn had ever heard. Since no one seemed to have anything to say that would give her the information she was looking for, she began to tune out the conversation around her and process her own thoughts. She started with writing down the word *Rapture*, and then typed it into her phone for a definition. Since the day before, some cell service had been restored and she hoped she would be able to find what she was looking for.

The sketchy service allowed Siri to spit out likely definitions or references to it such as Wikipedia's guide to the word, and then there were more strange references from a variety of sites. She read information about the church getting taken away, sometimes without their clothing - maybe a naked heaven - Kathryn considered, her eyebrows raised in speculation, and other times about people disappearing before one's eyes. It seemed to make some sense; but if the Church was taken away, then why were the buildings and many church members still there? She didn't realize the definition of *church* was more than old buildings of antiquity which was all her search was bringing up. Kathryn nevertheless underlined the word *Rapture* to investigate it further, as well as the word *Church*. The other comments she heard swirling in this place had little other than science fiction to back their claims of whodunits, so she finally decided to leave.

She drove to different locales across Englewood and Littleton, sometimes crossing into Denver territory. She didn't know why or where she was driving but realized that her location wasn't important at this point, so she just kept going. After three in the afternoon, she remembered that she hadn't had lunch but didn't even care about it. She doubted that she would eat before the meeting that night. She hadn't really felt like eating since the day of the disappearances. *"Why would I start now?"* she mused.

Around 5:30 PM, Kathryn found herself only a mile away from the parking lot of the school. She was always one who arrived early for a party in high school. She had half-heartedly tried to fight her habit on this Sunday, but knew that this meeting was important enough to get there early and to get a good seat.

"No one will even be there this early," she muttered to herself as she approached the parking lot. "I bet I am one of only five or so to show up and we will spend our time wandering through the building searching for the correct room," she continued. But, as she pulled into the lot, she was amazed to see that it was full. People were walking up with the flyer she had seen at her son's church telling her that she was in the right place at least. She parked and got out of the car and followed a group as they entered the school building. They flowed down a hallway until they stepped into Arapahoe's gym. As she gazed around the room she noted that the stands were filling up quickly. This wasn't a joyous meeting, but there was an air of expectancy that spoke volumes of the desperation of the attendees, who were busily scanning the gym for who was in charge.

"Please take any seat available, and we will try to find more chairs along the walls. Wow, I didn't know this many of you would be here. We will start at six though," announced the same red-haired woman from the day before. She sounded nervous as she spoke through a mic that stood at half court. All waited anxiously, attempting to browse through apps on their smart phones to ease their tension.

The slightest movements toward the mic caused heads to snap up towards half court until it was realized that the person walking that way wasn't the speaker. Finally, a gentle and wispy man of about 27 stepped purposefully toward the microphone. Kathryn noted that he did not have a single note card or an iPad to reference for speaking. He looked down at the hardwood floor and closed his eyes while muttering to himself briefly before raising his head and addressing the waiting audience.

"Thank you for coming tonight. I know you are all anxious to know what occurred days ago. When I tell you what has happened to our world, I imagine that the first thing that will ensue is that many of you will get up and immediately head for the doors. But, if you will listen to my evidence, I will lay out the events that have led us all here.

"I am Armin Paley. I grew up in New Jersey. I am a stock trader *by trade,* if you will pardon the pun and a Jew by race. For years, my mother would preach to me about being a good Jew and following the faith as their parents and grandparents had done. Grandma actually went to Israel to live out her life in the Holy Land. I didn't have any desire to enter the family plans for my life as a rabbi. I went to all of the right schools for a religious Jew and heard the stories, but I didn't believe them. I thought that they were tales to entertain children, such as David swinging a rock toward a big man's head. They were fanciful enough for me to ignore the details of each story." As Armin warmed to his topic and appeared to relax, he began to gesture with his hands, adding emphasis to what he was saying.

"But, what if I told you that the disappearances, the MIW's as the media calls them, is a message to us sitting in this room and also to the rest of the world? Would you think I was crazy? I too, have lost my mom and dad in these disappearances. Now what is important is how we, and how others respond to the disappearances. It was the Rapture of the Church!" he stated confidently and then paused to let what he had said sink in.

As he expected, more than thirty people began to grumble about crack pots and religious fanatics. Rudely jostling those they were seated next to as they passed, they stormed out of the gym. The anger that emanated from those leaving was palpable, but finally the last one left after trying to get his wife to come with him, but she would not budge from her seat on the bleacher. The rest of those present, including Kathryn, were not swayed by the commotion and anxiously waited for things to settle down so Armin could continue. No one wished to hear about objections but real possibilities regarding their loved ones.

"OK, now with that out of the way, I can move on. Since most of you have never even looked at a Bible before...well let me ask: How many have read your Bibles before?" Only about five people in the crowd raised their hands. "Of those of you who raised your hands, keep them up now...how many of you have read it more than a few times outside of church?" Almost all of the five people dropped their hands. Only two people were left with their hands up signifying that they had read more than slight bits in the Bible. Kathryn was honest to admit that she really hadn't looked much at a Bible in years even though she had professed to be a Christian to a few individuals.

Armin consoled the crowd, "It's ok! Neither had I. Well, you have to know that I studied it a lot in college, because I wanted to put my dad in his place as a Messiah-believing Jew in my teen years. I went to Jewish middle schools and was indoctrinated in all of the Old Testament traditions for my Bar Mitzvah. But, I didn't get along with God. I saw what I had mistakenly perceived as lies that my dad portrayed in his life and didn't intend to live with a God who tolerated them. What I didn't understand is that my dad, in his later years, had accepted Yeshua - who is Jesus. He wrote me a letter that outlined much of what I am going to give you tonight. I am not going to quote the Bible for you. Afterword, I will give all those who wish the verses from the Old and New Testaments, which are both parts of the Bible, so that you can study the details for yourselves.

"The Lord visited me shortly after the Rapture. He commissioned with a seal on my forehead as one of the 144,000 Israelites listed the Book of Revelation. This is a far cry from my vocation working at a firm as a day trader from New Jersey.

"When the first firm I worked for asked me to pad the books, because I also have an accounting degree, I was more than happy to do so. It would promote the firm's growth and my stock options. Once the stock market leveled off in the company's last year of existence with poor gains, my company took it hard and was listed as one of the least reputable firms to work for. I was then laid off. As time went on, I ran out of cash and savings.

"My parents had moved to Denver to be near the Jewish Hospital since they are renowned for their lung cancer treatments, for my mom had been diagnosed with lung cancer. I had nowhere else to turn but to my dad. He graciously took me in, and I hid out in my room in the basement of their home," he stopped to cough and catch his breath. Kathryn then noticed that it was a ruse to allow his emotional state to calm after having mentioned his parents.

"So I had the humiliation of living with my parents again at 26 years old after having been out on my own for four years establishing my career. In this last year, I thought about women more and got on some of those dating sites, but I did not get one date. My dad then started to bother me about his Christian beliefs. I have to admit I argued with him some. In spite of my being somewhat negative in my responses, my dad came back each night to talk me through it.

"I started playing computer games in the basement, but only a few weeks after our discussions had begun, I turned the games off and began to read his Bible. My motive was to try to discredit him on any point. I would hit him up with perceived contradictions that I found, but he eradicated everyone them. As I saw the supposed missteps through a rational thought process that my dad walked me through, I finally realized I had found none at all. Now, I know what you are going say: NONE...come on! There are none, Armin?

"Christ came to pay a transactional fee for you. Have you ever heard of it that way? There is a price on your head, the same as a contract killer makes a contract to remove his enemies. Satan has a contract to kill every one of you. He is searching every part of you to gain legal access to do so. He won't give up. His kingdom is comprised of cronies who carry out the killing.

"Your ransom is more than you could pay in three lifetimes. The real Jesus came and paid the ransom fee to cancel the killer's contract on you. The ransom was his life. He died on the cross to pay a ransom for each one of us.

"Satan doesn't want you to know that the ransom has been paid. His cronies are made up of the demons who inhabit this world. Even if you find out that the ransom was paid, they keep feeding you their lies that it wasn't. The lie is you need to fork over more dough until it is paid. Please stay with me on this extended metaphor that I think will make sense to you in the long run," Armin paused as he wiped the sweat that had begun to bead on his forehead. Kathryn was paying close attention making sure she kept up with what he was saying.

"But you want to hear the real scoop? Armin asked, a smile lighting his face. "It is that you owe nothing, the process begins by believing in your heart that Jesus died for you and then was raised from the dead, and confessing with your mouth that 'Jesus is Lord.' His lordship means your life belongs to the One who paid the ransom. The catch is that you still have to tell those cronies that your ransom has been paid. Once they hear it from your lips, then they are required to leave you alone. They love to keep trying to remind you, but you have to smack them down by repeating that the contract is paid in full by Jesus. The benefit of repeating that to them over and over is that you are really reminding yourself of this transaction. Does that make sense?" he asked and paused once again to allow his listeners time to process what he had said.

Kathryn had never heard the Bible spoken of in this way before. It was a hope-filled message and the legal jurisdiction analogy Armin used made so much sense. But there was a problem; something was happening in her heart and she couldn't even see Armin anymore for the tears that were filling her eyes. She could not wipe them away fast enough to focus on the man's face. She took a few deep breaths trying to get her emotions under control. If she let herself go, she knew she would become a blubbering mess. She could not allow that. To her utter amazement, she found the people sitting around her were fighting the tears just as much as she was. All around her people were reaching for tissues or using a hand or shirt sleeve to dry their tears.

Armin continued, "Do you know that your missing family and friends knew of this transaction? My dad and mom sure did. And, because they did, they escaped, which is known by them and now me as the Rapture of the Church. It was the final release in which the contract killer has no more legal claim upon our loved ones.

"But I must tell you more. My dad didn't really know this. Over the last few months I started to realize that there was another revelation in the Scriptures that wasn't completely evident before," Armin amended thoughtfully. The people were now leaning forward. It was a good thing that Kathryn decided to record the whole message on her iPhone, because she would have to re-listen to it.

"Scripture is God-breathed - which means that it is true. Everything about God is truth, so any time He interacts with us it is in truth. God's character does not change one tiny bit, but mine has in the past few days. God's Holy Spirit has come into me to dwell, and this is my first time to say all this...please forgive me..." he said as he once again began to choke up.

"Dude! You're doin' awesome...we love it," one person shouted bringing about a much needed release of laughter from the crowd but also causing more tears to flow. Spontaneous applause arose from all over the gym with shouts of encouragement for him to continue.

"OK...thanks for that! It's God, you know. I couldn't do it without Him. His visitation authorized me with the power of the Holy Spirit. He has given us a living relationship that is confirmed in His written word. I just was stupid enough not to believe it before. I know that is harsh, but I didn't want to believe it. But now I am here and I am going to take full advantage of this knowledge I have found.

"So where were we? Oh yeah, all of the stuff about the end of the world is true that some have bantered about for decades. Soon we will see the beginning of the period called the Tribulation. It is all over Scripture in many fashions but clearly stated in Daniel 9:27. It is a seven-year period in which the worst kind of stuff will happen. I really don't want to get into it now, because that isn't my message. But so you can understand, the Tribulation will begin with the rise to authority of the one Scripture calls *Anti-Christ*. He's one bad boy. He will be confirmed when he ratifies a seven-year treaty with many nations for peace, especially focused on the Middle East, that includes Israel. But this thing called the Rapture that our loved one's just experienced has been conjectured about vehemently for approximately 150 years; however the reality is that it was there in the Bible all the time. My dad and I argued about it somewhat over the past year.

"There are three primary views of the timing of the Rapture: Pre-Tribulation, Mid-Tribulation and Post-Tribulation. What that means is that there were groups of people who believed in each one and felt that the others had to be wrong. In my discussions with my dad, he would have me read about each view. Our debates could get really heated between especially the Post and Pre-Tribulation positions. Post-Tribulation meant that only one Rapture would occur at the end of the seven-year period, the Pre-Tribulation meant that only one Rapture would occur before the seven-year period. And of course you guessed it, and the Mid-Tribulation meant only one Rapture in the middle of this seven-year period.

I debated each of these positions frequently with my dad who was sure about the Pre-Tribulation Rapture, but he admitted that the others could be possible. Now we know that the Pre-Tribulation Rapture position was certainly correct, but I'm here to tell you that it is not the only one. There is a reason all three positions have been held since the early forefathers of the Church. That reason is there is Scriptural evidence for all three.

"At the time, I would debate from my observation that if they were not all true, then the Bible wasn't true, because it was contradicting itself. I made my mom crazy to the point she would leave the two of us to contentiously defend our stated positions. My dad gave me every book on it he could find and even made a point of telling me that I didn't need a job, because he felt it was more important for me to learn.

"What I didn't see at the time was that all of these positions were Biblical and the explanation was that all of them would transpire. That is the biggest revelation that I have had. You heard that right, people! There is more than one Rapture. You can get on the next train outta here. It's coming!" he lifted his hands in triumph and all clapped loudly even though they may not have completely understood what they were applauding for.

"I want to tell you more about it all tomorrow night and for many more nights to come. I also wish to share with you corroborating evidence I found by this guy, Jeff Swanson, who revealed it in this thing called *The Plan Bible*. I recommend that you buy this eBook or better yet, get the app and study it. It was designed for us living during this perilous time. You can find it at www.PlanBible.com.

"But more importantly, I want to give you an opportunity to come forward and accept the payment for your life, so that we can put the contract killer out of business. He has to cease and I believe firmly that in these last seven years, while it is going to get bad...I don't know how to say this, but there will be special God-given graces that will advance your understanding in a very short timeframe. It does not have to take you years to

143

figure it all out. Come forward tonight to receive the reward that was spoken upon the cross with Jesus Christ stating: 'It is finished!'"

Kathryn rushed forward finding that almost all in the gym were also doing so. She didn't know if Armin would have time for each one, but she just asked God to void the contract upon her life. She knew that there was legal jurisdiction for the contract, as Armin stated in the mic, her sin opened the door for it. As an unexplainable peace flooded her whole being, she knew inside her very core that that *killer* at the doorstep would now have no more room in her life. She also had a sense that the devil would be worried and she purposed in her heart that she was going to keep him frazzled for the rest of her days on the earth. Jesus had made a new way for her. Her sins had supernaturally been disposed through Christ's body on the cross and left in the heart of the earth. The tears continued to flow down her cheeks as she silently praised and thanked God for what He had done long ago for her through Jesus at the cross. All around her others did the same. It felt amazing to know that the transaction, while being paid two thousand years ago, was as good in this gym tonight as it had been then.

CHAPTER 19

Kathryn stood in the parking lot at Arapahoe High until after midnight listening to other's testimonies of how the King of eternity had dispensed His grace upon them. People wandered between the cars in the parking lot, moving from one group to another, hugging complete strangers until weariness finally overtook them, and they began reluctantly to leave.

Kathryn was thrilled that she had prayed with Armin, if even for a short few moments. She then lingered in reverence and listened to the other's prayers. She did not really know how to pray herself, but hearing the heartfelt words spoken aloud made her cry more each time one of her new brothers and sisters entered the Kingdom with her. It was as if heaven's gates were opened so wide that anyone could step in if they would only ask and receive what Jesus had done for them. Out of the few hundred in the crowd, only a precious few didn't enter through those gates that night. Kathryn now knew where her place was in eternity, and she made it a new goal to find an opening in that place for her husband as well.

She started home with a new sense of joy that she had never experienced before. It was an immeasurable peace that seemed to eclipse the chaos of all the emergency vehicles that continued to weave between the slowly moving traffic and empty cars that had yet to be moved off of the roads. The craziness of the city seemed to be increasing with each passing moment, but in spite of that, her mind was focused on the things above.

She pulled into the garage after a longer than usual drive home.

"Lord, thanks for getting me home through that!" she called out and then felt a little silly for saying a prayer that didn't end in Amen. But she shook her head and smiled to herself as her newfound peace and assurance once again washed over her causing her to suddenly feel great knowing that she now had a personal relationship with the King and she did not need to always stand on formalities with the One who knew her better than any other. She sighed a little as the thought crossed her mind that this was what Samuel had been trying to tell her about in the days before the Rapture.

Kathryn climbed out of the car, grabbed her bag and walked carefully through the garage and into the house wondering if Nathan was awake, but when she heard the loud snoring in the bedroom, her unspoken question was answered. She was so disappointed that she could not tell him all that had transpired since she had left the house that morning. She now wanted to share every aspect of her life, especially her new revelation, with Nathan so that he could also walk through that gate and be with her.

She sat in the dark living room with the only light coming from the flickering blue circle of her internet DVR that was locked into the on position so it never turned off. Kathryn reached for the remote to shut it down, but instead found herself reaching for the Bible she had found just a few days ago. She allowed her fingers to flip the pages to the middle of the Bible, and she noted a book with the heading of *John*. But her burning eyes and burry vision could not be ignored any longer. She had to sleep. It had been too many sleepless nights and stressful days for her to continue on. She quietly set the Bible aside and made her way to the bedroom where she prepared herself for bed. She then slipped into the bed beside her husband and uncharacteristically snuggled up toward his back and wrapped her arms around him.

The next morning she was still in bed and in her half-awake state once again reached for Nathan, but his side of the bed was already cold. She groggily realized he was already up and shaving, and so continued to doze off and on until she heard him grabbing his phone and car keys as he prepared to leave for work. She quickly sat up and looked at him, seeing him in a whole new way.

"Love you hon...I'll be praying for you," she sheepishly called, feeling a little awkward saying the words and nervous about how he may respond, but really wanting to start sharing her new faith with him.

Her words stopped Nathan in his tracks and he turned back toward her with a puzzled grin on his face. "Uh...thanks. I'll see ya later," he called briefly searching her face but then turning and walking out.

As she prepared to start her own day, she felt a burning desire to begin the day with prayer. She realized, however, that she hadn't the slightest clue how to do it. She had prayed in church when she was younger and had, on occasion, desperately prayed toward heaven when bad things occurred in her life. She wanted to be able to say that she had conversed with God before, but she now realized that was a lie. Knowing she needed to start somewhere, she reverently got down on her knees next to the bed and began to thank God for what she had experienced last night. While it wasn't eloquent or formal, she knew she spoke from her heart.

After several minutes of her expressing her feelings of gratitude, she rose and thoughtfully started the day. She showered and dressed, intending to stay around the house while she caught up on neglected housework from the last three desperate days they had had. She cleaned the kitchen and bathroom all the while reflecting on what had happened. A contentment enveloped her while she worked as she intermittently sent up little tidbits of requests and comments for her husband and for her own future to a God she now knew would listen and answer.

As she vacuumed the carpet she continued saying, "God, I really don't know what to say. I feel stupid for not knowing what my son knew. It was all in front of me. I know that I should have heard Your voice before. I should have listened...I am babbling now...listen to me. Oh yeah God, I know You are listening to me, but I need to know what I should say to You. It can't be the thees and thous, because I don't know them enough to say them correctly. Can't I just talk to You?" She then shut off the vacuum and felt a strange tingle run up her spine.

"Thank you, Lord, I am gonna take that as a *Yes*. I am sorry for being so slow, because I heard we have so little time. I think I need to quit school and work as well. I don't know...maybe I can keep the job just to talk to people," again she experienced the same tingle that felt like a peace flowing from the Father above into her spirit.

"Well now, I will keep the job to talk to people, but I think that I will quit school since *You* seem to like that idea. If we were going to be here for forty years, then I would keep going to school but it doesn't make any sense now. I know that Nathan is going to...uh what's a more Christian way to say this?...have a conniption! I need to make sure that what I replace school with is something that You want me to do. Please, tell me more of what You want."

Kathryn found herself in an on-going conversation with her new Father throughout the entire day. She felt her faith and confidence in Him growing by the hour.

Later that evening, Kathryn heard the garage door opening as Nathan returned home. In her excitement and anticipation she almost leapt toward the door, opening it in time to see Nathan clambering out of the car holding a large tube of drawings as well as his briefcase. She noted that he looked especially haggard.

"How was your day?" She asked in concern as she reached for his briefcase to help him as he came into the house.

"Uh, well long and tiring," he replied obviously confused by her greeting. "You feeling OK?" he queried his forehead creasing into more of a frown.

"What do you mean?" She asked, acting as if she didn't understand, but she knew that she hadn't really put forth the effort to greet him when he got home for a very long time. She leaned toward him and kissed him on the cheek, something else she hadn't done for over a decade.

Not quite knowing how to respond to her overtures Nathan muttered, "Well, never mind. I gotta do a whole bunch of work tonight."

"Why don't you tell me about it?" She offered as she followed him downstairs. She set his briefcase upon the desk where he could easily reach it.

"Well, outta the eight designers in the office and the five salesmen, three designers and two salesmen went MIW, and two more quit because they are waiting for the end of the world. That leaves us very shorthanded, and the owner, Doug, doesn't believe that people are going to rebuild decks as they once were. He wants us to finish out the projects that are paid for, then he has the rest of the sales staff going door to door to the ones who had started their deals to find out if they are still there. The news has reported that many unfilled large business orders made prior to the disappearances have been cancelled.

"You know those friends I meet with on Wednesdays for lunch? Steve, who works at Hearing Rehab Centers here in Aurora, said that they did the same thing. They found that lots of people who had ordered hearing devices are not even at their homes. They have just disappeared and the company is left holding the merchandise.

"I even met a guy at Home Depot named Joshua. He mentioned that the store is totally empty of customers, well, not totally, but has been super slow all weekend.

149

They haven't felt this type of business slowdown since 9/11," Nathan wound down looking at her with a scowl on his face.

Kathryn took a deep breath and silently prayed for courage. Solemnly shaking her head she replied, "I have seen that type of chaos everywhere I have been the last few days as well. I also don't think it's going to get better anytime soon. I'd like to ask, would you come to a meeting with me tonight? I think it might help answer a lot of questions," she concluded looking at him hopefully.

"What?" Nathan asked incredulously.

"I wanted to tell you all about it last night. Oh, Nathan, that meeting at Arapahoe High was amazing. I have learned why the disappearances occurred. Are you interested in knowing what's really going on?" she asked hoping that he would take the bait.

"I guess..."

"Well, here is what I..." Kathryn began but was interrupted by Nathan before she could get any further.

"...As long as you don't mention the religious theory. The radio's been playing that idea along with the others all day," he stated as he put his hand out to stop her.

"The religious theory, as you put it, is actually the truth. This guy Armin is one of the 144,000 from the Bible and he gave me so much insight into what is happening. The disappearances were the Rapture and there is another Rapture coming soon, or at least I think so. I accepted Jesus last night. Oh Nathan, I really want you to hear him," she pleaded knowing that her speech made little sense to him.

"Armin, isn't he a character from the Bible? Did he show off his long white beard in the high school?" Nathan joked, laughing as he moved papers around on his desk. But as he looked up to see if she was sharing his humor, he saw a lone tear drop from her cheek. She was looking away, and he knew that he had hurt her.

Rolling his eyes, Nathan spoke in exasperation, "It's been a long day, and there is so much going on. I don't even know if I am gonna have a job after these projects are done. I want to stick around, and be the last one standing to show that I am better than any of the other designers, because you know I am. I am the only one left with the degree and the experience, and I am frankly scared that they might fire me. It's a tenuous time and then with the MIW's like Samuel...I just can't wrap my head around it. I don't know that I ever will, and I certainly have no time to go to a meeting," he trailed off turning back to the work on his desk.

In a bold move, Kathryn reached for his hand, the tears flowing down her face, unable to express any further thoughts in the face of his rejection, but still wishing to connect with him. Nathan, thinking the tears were due to him having mentioned Samuel's name, softened a little and drew her close for a moment, his sadness deepening as he once again considered his missing son.

ForeTold

CHAPTER 20

Armin addressed the returning crowd, "I have been studying for quite some time about this next phase of God's plan. I have consulted with a few different sources as well as the main One from on high," he said with a grin as he pointed toward heaven. "Here is how I believe it's going play out," to the crowd that had grown by another fifty people.

"As I stated in my first message there is more than one Rapture, or as the Bible refers to them as a harvest of souls. There are actually three harvests of believers. A picture of this is seen in Israel, where there is a Wheat Harvest, a Barley Harvest, and a Grape Harvest. I believe the Wheat harvest is the Pre-Tribulation harvest of the Faithful Church. John the Baptist announced Jesus at His first coming that He would separate the Wheat from that chaff found in Matthew 3:12. In ancient times the Wheat was thrown up into the air, the chaff blew away in the wind. A perfect picture of the mature Wheat kernels, or Faithful believers, being taken into heaven in a Rapture. Then the chaff represents those who did not believe are blown away by the wind into the Tribulation period, were we find ourselves now.

Another way to look at it is the Faithful Church were those which believed, by doing God's will, without seeing. Jesus hinted at this after He arose from the grave in John 20:27-29. It states: 'Then He (Jesus) said to Thomas (one of his disciples also called 'Doubting Thomas'), "Put your fingers here and observe My hands. Reach out your hand and put it into My side. Don't be an unbeliever, but a believer." Thomas responded to Him, "My Lord and My God!" Jesus said, "Because you have seen Me, you have believed. Blessed are those who believe without seeing.'"

"Now, what does that mean?" Kathryn was surprised to see Drake from the Church asking the question.

Armin went on without hesitation, "Well, on the surface it means what it says it does. Doubting Thomas could only believe what he saw. But the New Testament states that a blessing comes for those who believe without seeing. You see, the Faithful Church has had a promise, unfulfilled up until three days ago, of His second coming - which was His Rapture spoken of in I Thessalonians 4:13-18. This passage talks about the coming of the Lord for those believers. I would also submit that these are the Faithful who believed the promises of His coming without ever seeing any physical evidence. They probably have already received their special crowns mentioned in I Thessalonians 2:19. His reward to them is better than the reward that we can obtain because they believed His Word without visual evidence. Actually, Scripture mentions a definition of faith as being the evidence of things hoped for and the promise of things unseen. The Faithful walked out this Biblical definition of the Word by doing the Father's will in everything they did. This group of MIW's as the news calls them, are what we now know as the Pre-Tribulation Raptured," he stated pausing only slightly to move his notes around. All in the gym were hastily scribbling notes of the revelations presented.

"Once the peace treaty is signed by the *Anti-Christ* with many nations, this starts a seven-year countdown to the end of this Tribulation Period. Some believe that this covenant is only with Israel, but Scripture indicates it is with many nations. It will be the beginning of a very turbulent period. However, after seven years Jesus will return to this earth to set up His kingdom.

"I think that we could see that treaty very soon or even tomorrow, but we cannot know the exact moment of it until after it happens. We don't exactly know why other than it brings in what the Bible indicates as a time of false peace and safety. That period of time is only three and a half years long, because the *Anti-Christ* defies the treaty and will enter the Temple in Jerusalem to proclaim himself to be god.

"We could get sidetracked regarding who is the *Anti-Christ* or what will happen next, but let me just tell you that Scripture foresaw you today. Did you know that? It refers to you as the next harvest, the Barley Harvest, found in Revelation 7:9-14. It speaks of you as a great multitude that will be taken out of the Tribulation period. In God's mercy, He has given you time to come to Him, because it is His will that all would come to repentance and know Him as found in 2 Peter 3:9. This Tribulation period could have happened in a blink of an eye with an instant conclusion by the One who already has seen all things. Don't kid yourself about these seven-years. He doesn't need it to show the world that He is the only God. He only requires one second to accomplish that, so making a choice to serve Him is required on our part. He has given this world seven-years to make sure that no one is left undecided on the fence.

"Think about this: while our friends and family who are now gone in the Pre-Tribulation Rapture were being identified as the Faithful Church, we were messing around by not really believing. In the Hebrew culture, we know what you believe by your actions. We were not living in the truth of seeking the Master's will. Because we did not truly believe, we did not truly seek His will. We were playing with God, because we didn't really want to accept Him. Some of us were maybe even active in the Church but not really submitting to the Master's will. But you know His will now, don't you?" Armin asked, pausing for a response.

"Yes we do!" the audience intoned as if they were prepared to state it. Kathryn screamed out with all her might. She knew it was the truth but had yet to learn how

155

walk out the truth. It was similar to her watching a football game with Nathan, but not really understanding how they figured out the plays. She knew a few of the rules, enough to watch it, but could not get into the nuances of the game without the full knowledge of how it was played. She knew football without understanding it. Using this analogy to process what she was hearing helped her understand her limitations regarding what she was learning.

"But who are you to teach this? Aren't you one that didn't know the 'Master's will' just a week or two ago?" Drake rose and asked skeptically as he made quotation marks in the air with his fingers.

"You are completely right. I was so dumb in this. I actually had more education than most people, but I didn't know what in the world I was studying. I had heard that when you studied the Bible and didn't believe it, that you might still glean some understanding from the reading. The reality is that I had no idea what I was studying. It was as if I had taken Calculus 2, but really had never taken Trigonometry to prepare myself for the course, not to mention Calc 1. You can't really hope to stay up with a higher level college course without having a good foundation. Now, God is impacting me moment by moment and bringing to my remembrance what I have studied before. I must re-read all that I read over the past year at my dad's house. Now that I have accepted Jesus as my Savior, God's Holy Spirit is with me, helping me to understand what God really meant, Armin refuted Drake's skepticism who sat down again feeling chastened and satisfied all at the same time.

"The Hebrew people are God's Chosen nation. We were chosen to be a light for the entire world to come to know the one true God, the Creator of heaven and earth. He made hundreds of promises to my people thousands of years ago that are about to come to pass. However, we were blinded to the Messiah's first coming. It is now close to His return, and a group of us have come to see the truth. Now as servants of God we are fulfilling the mandate to be the light to the entire world.

"My firm belief is that Scripture calls me one of the 144,000. What does that mean? We, *the 144,000*, come onto the scene right after the Rapture of the Faithful Church and are discussed in Revelation chapters 7 and 14. We are Israelites but have never been with a woman before in that way...I mean...well, you know," he sheepishly grinned. Laughter from the crowd drowned out his embarrassment.

"We are supposed to teach the truth. My assignment is here in Colorado and possibly other states around me. I don't know the exact limit of my jurisdiction yet. I have been in communication with many others, but since we are a small number throughout the entire world, I am the only one I know of in Colorado. I guess there could be others here but I don't think so. I am supposed to help prepare the way for new converts to come into the Kingdom of God.

"I weep for my people the Chosen nation. The Tribulation period purpose for them is to bring them back into right relationship with God the Father. This can only be done by experiencing the removal of sins accomplished by Jesus, or as I call Him, Yeshua. They are the Chosen people and are losing their blindness day by day, but they don't see it entirely yet. They will though," he said excitedly and began to pace around the lectern.

"God states that His will is that no one should perish. He is patient and faithful - there is that word again - to forgive you. Your wakeup call was the Rapture. You must understand that your sin had made you dead and kept you separated from God. When you accept Jesus as your Savior, you are now alive and can understand why He came to this earth 2000 years ago. You know it or you would not be here!"

"Should we worship you since you are God's servant?" another well-meaning question came out.

"What?! Have you not heard me? No way! I am just a Jewish messenger sent from God along with my 143,999 brothers. We are to only worship the God who created us and sent His son to die for us and gives us His Holy Spirit to help us live for Him.

"But getting back to you...here is what Scripture states about you: it says that you will be ones who will go in the next Rapture. Did you know that? Some of you might already know because you were here before. But you new folks..." he paused making eye contact with a few he recognized as not having been at the previous meeting.

"I have started reading some books on this time period after I got saved last week," another woman held up a book. "They never mention another Rapture. They only argue for either a Pre, Mid and Post Rapture, not multiples. You made a comment that it was all of them, but how? I don't get it."

"It is all in Scripture so let's lay that out for you," Armin began and then went on for almost two hours showing how each Harvest was pictured in the Old Testament in Zechariah chapter 6:1-8. He demonstrated that the next Harvest, also known as the Mid-Tribulation Rapture, is found in the New Testament book of Revelation chapter 7 where it describes a great multitude coming out of the Tribulation and being caught up to heaven. Along with that group, chapter 14 states the 144,000 are also redeemed from the earth before the second half of the seven-years. There were other references to the Sheep and the Goats in Matthew 25, but Armin promised to talk about them later. He told the people gathered that they would come to know and understand deeply as they studied Scripture. Armin also encouraged any who had not already done so to settle their belief about the mercy of God given through His Son that would bring them redemption and save them from the wrath to come. He warned that they would have to endure a few blows, meaning that there would be some persecution for believers during the first three and a half years of the Tribulation, but that God would Rapture them up to meet Him in heaven.

He then hinted that those who waited until after the Mid-Tribulation Rapture to convert to Jesus would find God's mercy, discovered in a third Harvest. However, the persecution of many blows would come to these people known as the Great Tribulation Converts in Revelation 14:16.

Kathryn was eternally grateful to know Jesus as her Lord and Savior. She was so hungry for truth that she continued to attend the meetings that Armin held, so she could learn even more. She prayed that Nathan would be taken in the next Harvest with her, but she had serious doubts that he would come into the saving knowledge of Jesus at this time. Nathan continually dismissed her when she tried to reach out to him as she studied and grew in her faith. The on-going separation of their beliefs seemed to widen the gulf between them. Kathryn also knew that explaining to Nathan that she was not going back to school again would put an even greater fracture in their relationship. Thankfully, she knew that she could lay all of the burden of her relationship with Nathan at the feet of the One who could do something about it. She continued to pray for him at every opportunity.

ForeTold

CHAPTER 21

Over the next six weeks, Kathryn buried her nose in a book or iPad app studying Scripture. She hadn't bought a new dress or blouse since before the Rapture. But she did thrill a little at the thought that God had a completely new wardrobe set out in the biggest closet she could imagine in her house in heaven that He was preparing for her. She suspected, though, that the closet would hold little delight to one who was quickly finding that her first love was Jesus Christ.

It was liberating to Kathryn to use the money she had to help bring others to a saving knowledge of Jesus. She would take someone to lunch so that she would have the opportunity to share her story.

Nathan noticed that her attitude around him was much sweeter. He, at first, was puzzled and wondered if it was fake or not, but the behavioral change day by day was noticeable and consistent enough that it seemed genuine.

He was furious that she had quit school but would not even discuss with her why he felt as strongly as he did, believing that she already knew why. He didn't want her to hear fear in his voice due to inability to provide the income and health insurance benefits as he had in the past. In his mind he had counted on her teaching job to pick up the slack.

The unrest at his current job was increasing daily and he was feeling the pressure at the office to go out and find more sales leads, even though he was a designer and not a salesman. There were precious few new jobs coming in to create backyard gardens and living spaces since the disappearances that his wife was convinced were caused by the Rapture. The company was rapidly running out of money, and the comments from the owner, Doug, indicated that layoffs or a complete shutdown of the company was around the corner if they could not jumpstart something quickly. The challenges the company was facing after the MIW's was progressing into a situation of staff-wide depression. Doug would be shut up in his office with the doors closed having heated phone conversations. Then he would storm out of the office, his hair disheveled, stress written all over his face and frustration in every move he made, adding to the unrest and low morale.

Kathryn knew that the decision for her to not return to school was adding to the stress in their relationship. She struggled with feeling guilty about the situation but was learning that was not the way she should think or live. She had read in I John 1:9 "If we confess our sins, He is faithful and righteous to forgive us our sins and to cleanse us from all unrighteousness." She was starting to understand that she didn't have to carry the weight of things that were wrong in her life as she did before she was a believer. Through her study, the Holy Spirit was revealing to her each day how Jesus had paid the penalty long ago. This weight was actually a low grade anxiety that the Bible states is sin, for it says to be anxious for nothing in Philippians 4:6. Her part was to cast her care onto Jesus, which is to place this sin on His body on the cross because He disposed of it nearly 2,000 years ago. Her job was to release it by faith. For now, she had to be reminded daily and sometimes several times a day, but she was growing in awareness that part of the walk of faith was to overcome that sense of guilt by trusting in the knowledge of His redemption plan for her.

So, she gave effort to listen more to Nathan's increasing concern over his work and to be less judgmental. Nathan's mounting concerns helped her realize that the company was dying even though Nathan professed his belief in its solvency. Although she never let on, she felt that unemployment would be his future soon enough.

The news related to inflation and economic disruption with the mass of humans who disappeared from the earth grew bleaker as the days progressed. The U.S. could not compensate for the lack of shipping and trucking that had occurred since the disappearances. Normal shipping routes, through the middle of the country, were at a standstill without goods being delivered and the lack of supply for the demands that existed caused the dollar to slip further down in value.

The quick rise of a new world leader in Europe who touted a global monetary system was making the headlines. Many saw him as a savior to America's problems with his solution of smart biochip technology. The smart biochip could be placed in the hand or the forehead. It contained all pertinent information of an individual's financial and medical records, and was very secure. The biochip not only authenticated the ID of a person, it gave them the ability to perform transactions instantly. It was an advanced version of the same technology that had been commonly found on every credit card already in use.

People across the world clamored for the media to provide some type of entertainment as an escape from the constant coverage of the downward spiraling conditions. In response, the networks added more graphically intense reality shows in the place of more news telecasts. It wasn't just the lewd nature of the shows that were glorified on the channels, but the unabashed brutality and criminal activity including real rape and murder scenes as networks fought for higher ratings. Kathryn would have hated these shows before she had given her life to Jesus. Now her reaction was heart-breaking compassion for lost people being deceived by Satan's kingdom.

About three months after Kathryn had accepted the Lord, she was home slightly early from a slow day at the law firm. As she walked into the house she found Nathan already there. Without even looking at her he announced in shock, "I was let go today. Things were a lot worse than I thought. They even started selling the furniture and computers. The office secretary wiped the data from the hard drives, and they sold them for pennies on the dollar, as if the dollar meant anything anymore. We were given two weeks' severance pay, and Doug was tearful as he shook each person's hand as they left." Nathan finally looked Kathryn in the eye and asked, "Kathryn, what am I going to do?" Not knowing how to respond, Kathryn just put her arms around him and held him tight as tears began to run down his cheeks.

"Hey," she began as she pulled away with a bright smile of hope. "Who was that guy that wanted you to build those shelters a few months ago? Maybe with the way that things are going that is the wave of the future. As short as that may be."

Ignoring her last statement, Nathan latched on to what she had first said. "You're right! I gotta find that guy's name and call him! I bet the panic is setting in, and those with the means will be looking for ways to protect themselves and their families. If this does turn out to be the wave of the future I could make a killing and then retire on the earnings from this! Great idea, Kathryn!" As he hugged her briefly, a new excitement replaced the shock from moments before. Nathan ran to his office to search through his briefcase for the card he needed as he reached for his iPhone to make the call.

"Carmen Luongo, please?" Nathan asked when the call was answered while his hands began to sweat. "Uh, Mr. Luongo? It's Nathan Covington. I don't know if you remember me, but I am that architect that you met several months ago who helped design your landscape project. You had recommended that I call a Mr. MacPherson. We interviewed and I was cleared, I think, by his background investigator."

"Ah, yes, Nathan, how are you?" Carmen asked.

"Well, not too well. The landscape company I was working for went out of business today. I guess there is no one who needs new backyard living spaces in light of current circumstances," Nathan responded.

"I know, but can I tell you something Nathan? Business for me has never been better. MacPherson is letting me basically run the company. He really has dozens of other activities to keep up with on his billion dollar projects, so he leaves the day to day operations to me. I'm the one you needed to call. I can bring you on now. I have more work for people like you to help design our underground fortresses than I have been able to cover.

"We would want you to work from home. Our customers will not allow the designers to travel to the sites, at this point, because they value their confidentiality for security purposes. Also, the government would love to get their hands on our places. We can accomplish all we need using some high tech, hands-on computer equipment that we can deliver to you. Meetings will go through video conferences from your work area. You had mentioned that you had a sliding glass door from your basement to your backyard. As part of our required security measures we would need to put mirrored glass on that. Additional measures will include having drawn shades installed on all basement windows which will need to be kept pulled down at all times so that prying eyes are not allowed to see the plans. We would also put a security system in your house that would also serve the purpose of allowing us to scan for listening devices.

"You would start at $250K per year plus all the equipment. I will also have you get a car from a friend of mine who has a Lexus dealership. The ELS 980's that we use in this company come equipped with glass impenetrable to radar detection. Also cell phones cannot be traced while inside of the car and the GPS systems don't interfere with the Bluetooth capability of the phones so any conversations will not be interrupted. You can pick out the color if you like. How about it?" Carmen asked as his flurry of words came to an end, while Nathan wondered how this man could know so many details about Nathan's basement and about how much he was working in it.

Nathan, stunned by the generous salary amount and unexpected benefits, stammered as he tried to get the words out, "Uh I...I...guess I have to say yes! Yes! When do you want me to start? It's Thursday now, I can start anytime!" Nathan finally got it out. He felt like shouting in his delight but maintained control and sobered his facial expression as if Carmen could see him over the phone.

"Great, I will be by there on Monday. Expect our security teams to arrive at your house on Saturday bright and early to set up the new window treatments in the basement as well as all the scanning and security equipment. Once that is done, I will have my computer people install all that is needed on Monday morning while you and I go for coffee. But for the rest of the time, just chill a little. Be ready to hit the ground running on Monday though, because we will be swamped with projects for years to come. It will be 80-100 hour work weeks. I hope you can handle it. Oh, I almost forgot. Spend the weekend going to get the car at the Lexus dealer. That'll be fun for you to do. And one more thing: I don't want you talking to anyone about the job at any time. Got it?"

"Absolutely! I am up for the challenge and totally understand! This is turning out to be a great day! I can't wait to see you on Monday. Thank you, sir." But the last sentences were spoken to a dead receiver. "He probably has no time to chit chat," Nathan spoke aloud as he saw that the screen on his iPhone had gone blank. He sat in his basement planning out the changes, but then caught himself because he knew that Carmen's people would be doing it for him. He would have to tell Kathryn to stay out of their way.

After a few hours of putting all of his landscaping drawing and drafting tools away in preparation for the new equipment to arrive, he went upstairs to tell Kathryn the fantastic news. While there were parts of his story, such as the security this job would afford them that she loved, she had a curious look on her face when he told her of the house modifications that would be necessary.

"Why would they have to do all that unless they are doing something illegal?" she asked.

"Whaddaya mean, illegal? You are blowing this out of proportion! It is absolutely legal!" Nathan shouted, unsure of whether he was trying to convince her or himself of the legitimacy of the new job. Her point about the extensive monitoring and security was valid and something to which he really had no answer, but his abrupt way of cutting off her next set of questions left little room for her to argue. Then she tried another tactic.

"If there could be legal entanglements involved, I could have my boss at the law firm look over any contract he might give you," she offered. And after a pause, "Are you really sure about this?"

"These people expect complete anonymity for their projects. I think the cameras are for our protection from competitors, stuff like that. I am sorry, I really don't know some of those details, but what I don't get is why you aren't happy for me? With you not getting a teaching position because of being out of school now and staying in your dead...well...job, we needed a break like this. Now you can either stay in your position as long as you want or quit. You can even go back to school full-time if you

167

would like to." Nathan was playing every card available to deflect the incoming questions and redirect her, especially since he didn't have all the answers. He also did not want to jeopardize an opportunity that would save him from having to face the bleak future he thought would be his just that morning. He felt their world would be fine after it was reconciled to the new changes that had to occur to make this new job a success.

Kathryn, in response to Nathan's outburst and unwillingness to take her concerns seriously, really shut down after that. She had been hurt and insulted by his words. He had essentially told her that she was being selfish to not keep up with her schooling to get a better job. He had also intimated that her instincts didn't matter when it came to a perceived invasion of her household. As she turned to move to another part of the house to get away from the charged atmosphere of Nathan's presence, Nathan called her. However she didn't want to hear an apology or anything else from him, so she kept walking. Instead she sighed deeply while praying silently for wisdom in how to deal with the situation.

Still feeling hurt and frustrated, she finally hurried out the back door and picked up her work gloves and a hand-trowel from the wicker table in the backyard so she could do some gardening. The corner of the back yard had a spot where she had envisioned a small flower garden. She admitted to herself that she really wasn't interested in gardening right now, but digging in the dirt seemed like a therapeutic thing to do at the moment. So she began to prepare the ground for its new purpose.

After several hours of tilling through grass, weeds and rocky dirt, she was reminded of what she had read the day before in Matthew when Jesus had talked about casting seed upon the rocky soil. She began to think that Nathan was either the thorny growth or rocky soil, she just could not figure out which one. She was also tormented that her response to him had not been as good of a witness as it could have been.

She was gripping the handle of her trowel so hard that her hand and arm began to cramp. Her gloves were caked and stained with dirt as were her knees. In the mist of her emotional and physical pain she began to question what she had learned. Was this how sin was in the life of the unbeliever? And if one did believe and Jesus completely washed the caked dirt and stains away, was it really gone? If the price for cleanliness had really been accomplished upon the cross around 2000 years ago, and He was returning soon, how could sin still be active within a person? These were questions she wrestled with devoid of the aid of mature believers, for they were taken in the first Rapture.

Kathryn sighed and stood to her feet. In the midst of pulling off her gloves, she froze, as she felt a familiar tingling sensation as the Lord started to essentially download into her Spirit what He wanted her to understand. Occurrences like this had become commonplace. She had no idea how she was hearing from God, but she hoped she wasn't the only believer receiving daily messages in this time of trial.

The Father was telling her that He had removed the stain of condemnation from the earth through the sacrifice of His Son, who came not to condemn the world but to save it. The Father patiently waited for each one to come to Him, accepting of His great sacrifice. All it took was a choice to believe. The choice would remove sin and condemnation from her heart as easily as a shower cleared the grime and dirt from her body.

She also believed that she and all who had made the choice to follow Jesus doing His will, would arrive in heaven in next Harvest before the three and half years of the Great Tribulation. That realization revealed to her one other point - she could endure all things through Christ who strengthened her. With that truth emanating

169

through her Spirit, she asked herself, *What is the rest of my life in comparison to eternal life with Jesus?*

As she prepared to take a shower and get cleaned up her thoughts continued. The world as a whole was spiraling toward an existence without God, while growing remnants of people were seeking Him with all of their might. Battle lines were being drawn and people's souls hung in the balance. "My husband is so far behind the wrong line," she said to herself as she showered.

But then the Lord chided her for that thought. He reminded her that if one were against Him, then eternal separation was the only outcome. Something God does not desire for anyone. He wanted Nathan to come to know Him.

She felt the Holy Spirit enlightening her understanding of what eternal separation really meant. The unbeliever's Spirit is already dead; because once there is sin in the spirit it is dead. Only acceptance of Jesus' sacrifice can return it to life. Eventually when the body of the unbeliever dies, the soul will be separated from God forever with its dead spirit. The choice to believe or not is the decision of this time period known as the Tribulation.

As Kathryn finished her shower and got dressed she reflected about how she didn't even go clothes shopping anymore but only went for the basics, not because of a lack of funds, but simply because material goods didn't have the slightest value to her anymore.

Her thoughts were interrupted by a Television News break:

"The prevailing world leader Cartiff has just done the impossible. Peace in the Middle East! The signing of a monumental seven-year treaty with the whole world for peace with Israel has marked a new age in world political evolution. All nations are joining in the chorus of adulation for the only man who has been able to accomplish this feat in all of history. The nations are shouting, *'We now have peace and safety!'*

Cartiff's vision goes beyond this treaty as he is working toward the unification of all religions so they can coexist. Meanwhile the United Nations is calling for a vote to elect Cartiff as the first *Supreme Chancellor* of the world."

Kathryn stood with her jaw opened as she experienced Biblical prophecy fulfilled just as Armin had stated it would. The reality of the Scriptures was sinking into her heart that all was true. The remaining time on Israel's time clock was now ticking backwards. There would be seven-years to the end of Satan's kingdom. She had a new sense of urgency that time was very short. The other realization was the one the Bible refers to as *Anti-Christ* has now been revealed, Cartiff!

She had no spiritual fear of him. She had to be fearful, that is to be reverent, of the Father in heaven, but not afraid of any man. She felt determined that over the next several months she would learn as much as possible about God's ways and His Kingdom.

ForeTold

CHAPTER 22

That Saturday was tumultuous for Kathryn as she watched work crews setting up security cameras and other high tech equipment all throughout her basement, changing out the glass in the slider door to mirrored glass and hanging new window treatments on all the basement windows that would provide maximum privacy. She could feel her blood pressure rising as they installed surveillance and scanning equipment about the kitchen as well. Although she quelled the anger and frustration instantly, she refused to have it throughout the rest of the house. She would not be spied upon.

Later that afternoon as the security installation crew prepared to leave; she overheard Nathan comment to one of the workers that he was going to the Lexus dealership to pick out the car the company was providing for him. He also mentioned that he was selling his old car for cash. Although Kathryn harbored concerns about the extravagant perks of the new job as well as the heightened security now in their house, she didn't try to protest knowing that it would be pointless with him in his current state. He was on such a high from all the changes that he supposed were to the good that he could not see the world being pulled apart by the seams.

Some of the more commonplace occurrences in this new world were that street lights would malfunction at night leaving streets in total darkness. Small stores were devoid of inventory for many days and even weeks until shipments arrived. Marshall Law had been in effect since the disappearances. The dwindling members of law enforcement barely could carry out their various tasks. However, the Marshal Law grip was beginning to loosen somewhat.

At this point, even though it had been several months since the disappearances, what was usually a forty-five minute commute could take ninety minutes, not because of increased traffic, but because of obstacles on the roadways still had not been effectively cleared. Each time more normalcies were achieved in the balance of city services, another weather disturbance or riot would throw Denver off kilter once again. Some people tried to do something as simple as mowing their lawns to bring a little order to the chaos and get back to what felt like normal, but few had the resources to afford the price of extra fuel for lawn care. Others struggled with the ability to pay utility bills as costs increased upwards of a thousand dollars a month for anyone trying to maintain their homes.

Amidst this backdrop of deterioration, Nathan went about his plans for the afternoon, proudly stopping at a KFC and paying for overpriced chicken on a nearly maxed out credit card knowing that the company credit card would be supplied for his needs at $2500 a month on top of his salary. He was excited about his new salary since it would be more than he had ever made before, but he couldn't stop a nagging feeling that there would be little available to purchase due to all the instability in supply. He figured he would be able to save lots for a rainy-day fund. Nathan dreamed services would snap back on like power does with a replaced blown fuse.

After his quick lunch, he pulled into the Lexus dealership on south Quebec in Greenwood Village. He was so excited that the day he had been dreaming of for so long was finally here, but his excitement waned as he noted that the place was so rundown compared to what it had been just a few months ago. He could see two salespersons standing outside. Both were smoking cigarettes as a third man picked up trash around the lot in front of the showroom preparing for a Saturday afternoon of potential sales. The lot, though, was almost empty of customers except for one person sitting in his car in front of the service door waiting for assistance.

In previous attempts to browse for a car, he had always felt that the salesmen were somewhat brazen and trying to take advantage of him. So this time he would not exit the vehicle until he built his courage to handle the onslaught of questions regarding his personal financial state. Feeling confident, he popped out of the vehicle with excitement and slammed the door a little harder than necessary, startling the poor salesman whose name tag identified him as Horace.

"What can I help you with today, Mr.?" Horace asked as he reached out to shake Nathan's hand.

"Just call me Nathan. My boss, Carmen Luongo has sent me down here to pick out a new car. I also want you to buy my old car. I want to walk out of here with cash in my hand and that new 980," Nathan stated forcefully, delighted at being able to best this man at his own game by dictating the terms of the deal.

"Ah, OK then." Horace stammered as he blinked with surprise at the directness of the communication. "I will have my manager look at your car to check the mileage and other pertinent details and to see what we can give you. We really don't have much use for older vehicles here anymore with all that's happening," Horace stated unconvincingly as he gestured at the landscape around them.

"Well, that's funny, because I know Mr. Luongo, your long time, very good customer who would say differently," Nathan retorted, startling himself with his overt candor.

"No...no...no problem, Mr. Nathan," Horace stammered again placing his hands in front of him with surrender written in his eyes. "The 980's are around the side if you want to look at them. I have to get the keys for the three we have that Mr. Luongo requires us to keep in stock for him. They are the ones furthest under the awning in our secured yard. We try to keep them separate from our regular inventory and less accessible to those who might steal them. I will bring out all three sets of keys but the only real differences between the three are the interior and exterior colors. They are all equipped according to Mr. Luongo's specifications. Can I get you something to drink while I get my manager to look at your car?" Horace asked as he held his hand out for the keys of Nathan's car.

"Sure," Nathan replied as he tossed the keys to his old car to Horace and headed around the side of the building. He hoped to never see those keys or the car they went to again. He was slightly disappointed that the salesman didn't catch them, but seeing Horace digging in the dirt to retrieve them brought a small smile to Nathan's face. "I'll take a Bud Light, or a Coke, if you don't have a beer," Nathan called over his shoulder.

He made his way around the side of the building to the small fenced in area under the awning. A service technician hurriedly keyed in a code to unlock the gate, and then opened it so Nathan could gain access to the area where the cars were being kept. It was not a cramped area for three cars, but it would take some maneuvering to extract them from the secured lot. He figured once he made his decision he would allow the salesman to maneuver the car he wanted out of the area, so he would not be responsible for accidentally scratching his new pride and joy.

Nathan slowed his pace and arrested his rambling thoughts as he ran his hands along the smooth lines of the vehicles. The sedans were of significant luxury, of course, and pinstriped lines added a jetted sleekness to the design. All had heavily tinted windows. There was a black with midnight wheels along with a white car, both of which were fine. But, it was the third car that caught his eye. It was maroon with cream interior and maroon had always been his color of choice. His hand touched almost every inch of the surface of the outside of the car. He even caught himself swiping some grime away that had accumulated as a result of dirt and water mixing and dripping through an occasional hole in the roof of the car-lot awning. Nathan was beginning to grow impatient as he waited to get inside of the car when he was finally greeted by the new car manager and Horace.

"Mr. Nathan? I am so glad that you came down today," the slick manager intoned as he offered Nathan the Coke he had brought for him.

"Just Nathan, if you please. Do you have the keys for this one?" he asked pointing to the maroon one.

"Sure, Horace has them. The key is actually a wristband in the form of this watch," the man said, holding the watch-like key for Nathan to see. "Once it is in the vicinity of the vehicle, the car will unlock. As soon as we code the circuit to your matrix of skin and wrist measurement, no one else can use that car other than you. Anyone else who attempts to open or start the car without this device would receive a shock if you are not around. So even if someone takes the wristband, without your matrix to interface with, the key is useless. We can also make a designated key coded to your wife's matrix, and we could even do one for your mistress if you so choose," the manager offered with a sly wink. Even though Nathan was annoyed with the connotation of unfaithfulness, he ignored the comment and allowed the ruse to continue and let them believe he was a player, not wanting them to be disappointed with his supposed image.

"Ah yeah, that's cool," Nathan responded. "So do I use the key to drive it?"

"Let's get in," Horace said and then stepped up and indicated that Nathan should get in the driver's seat.

177

For the next hour, Horace familiarized Nathan with the many features of the car, while he also allowed Nathan to ask him questions as they drove about Littleton Boulevard and Broadway, then back to the dealership on Quebec. There were no ends to the luxuries the car afforded. Nathan allowed Horace to hook his iPhone up to the car and once the Bluetooth connection was established, more functionality was gained as the phone synced to the open-sourced console. The luxurious seat seemed to enfold him once it was adjusted to his body position. The car had a 4.5 liter engine with 400 horse power but achieved a hybrid rating of 40 MPG in the city. It had power to burn but luxury enough to exceed anyone's standards. His dreams were finally coming true.

After the four dealership employees spent two more hours taking care of the details, Nathan had the coolest watch he had ever tried on and an ancillary extra watch in a beautiful presentation box sitting in the passenger seat beside a check for $3500 for his old car. They had cleaned up the exterior for him and sent him on his way with a full tank of gas. He texted Kathryn that he wanted to take her out to dinner with the new ride he had picked up.

Before he drove it home, he took it on the highways around C-470 in hopes that he might have fewer obstacles in his way and could open it up just a little. Unfortunately, he was disappointed that he could not achieve much more than 70 MPH due to unrepaired potholes and many more abandoned vehicles than expected, so he made his way home just as the darkness of the night set in accompanied by a cool autumn breeze.

As he pulled into the garage, he wasn't prepared for how wide the car was. It took a slow-go to ease it into the short part of the three-car garage in which he always parked. After he slipped into place, he started pushing the navigation buttons and checking out all the gadgets once more as he customized it to his liking. After about thirty minutes he was ready to go in to show his wife.

"Come on out to see it!" Nathan called to Kathryn as he walked in the garage entry, his face beaming with excitement.

Plastering as genuine a smile as she could on her face, she reluctantly walked through the door Nathan held open for her only to find more luxury than she had ever thought she would see sitting in their garage. In her experience, cars like this were reserved for high-powered lawyers and people who wanted others to think that they were more than they really were. She hated the idea of the attention the car might garner with it being such an ostentatious presentation during the most desperate time in human history. "Honey, it is very pretty," Kathryn stated honestly.

"You gotta sit in it...actually, let's go somewhere," he implored of her.

"I guess we could go for a short ride, but it is almost too late for anything to eat - you were gone so long, most places are closed," she responded as she buckled into the passenger seat.

They drove for more than forty-five minutes, stopping at a fast food chain that was a little less run down than most and open surprisingly late. He didn't want the smell of the food in his car so they ate inside and discussed the necessary things that went with the new job starting up. He told her that he was getting a credit card with a $2500 a month limit for all the items he might need as well as food when he would be out on the road.

His new salary and car were overwhelming to her. She sensed that he was in far over his head. It wasn't as if he could not accomplish a huge design, but he was moving from small time designs to a gigantic one overnight. She knew that his mind would be incredibly focused once he told her that he would be putting in 80-100 hour work weeks. Her hopes that he would have a spiritual renewal began to sink. She also sensed that she would be essentially abandoned by him even though he would be in the house all the time.

"You haven't said much. Aren't you excited for me, for us?" he accusingly asked.

"No, no, I am excited for you," Kathryn replied earnestly. "I just don't understand where all this money is coming from. How can Carmen afford it? I know you told me, but it doesn't seem to explain how so much is coming all at once. When you first met him, he didn't hire you at that time, because there wasn't enough work. Now, there is a ton of work, and all the luxuries one can imagine in the midst of a world turned upside down with grief and heartache. It is like seeing the separation between the ultra-rich who don't care about anyone else and all others. I feel like the earth is mad and spinning out of control with a need for a Savior. We are on such a short spiritual leash!" she concluded.

"You are right about one thing," Nathan replied. "We may only have a short time. Once these eccentric rich people get in their new digs, then I might be out of a job. I am hoping that I am one of a select few doing this so that I am on the inside and can have work for five or ten years even if it means long hours. Then, we could start to look at retirement with enough of a nest-egg to settle where we want without need for debt. But I need you on board with this," Nathan stated firmly.

"I am trying to be. We don't have ten years left on this earth though," Kathryn answered.

"Let's go home, you are probably getting tired. I know that I am after working on this car deal most of the afternoon and having all the installations done at the house. Tomorrow, I've gotta get the systems up and running in the basement that they installed today. I would also really like to go to one of those car accessory stores to see what I can find to put in this new one!"

Nathan's response about the accessories told her that he hadn't even heard what she had said about the limited amount of time they had left. She resigned herself to the fact that he was just ignoring everything she knew in her heart to be true. Her vision of a loving marriage with Jesus at the head of it was fading. If she didn't believe that she was going to be leaving this earth soon with the next Harvest, she surmised that a divorce would be inevitable. But she also knew that the Scriptures were clear. She would not initiate any divorce - that would be up to him. But she knew she had to fight for his soul every day even if it meant that she would lose her marriage because he would leave. It seemed strange to her to view it in that light, but his soul was far more important than her marital needs or his feelings for her.

ForeTold

CHAPTER 23

The next several months passed with Nathan working hours that burned his candle at both ends to the point in which he felt he might snap. He didn't take the time to worry about caring for the lawn, because water was too expensive to use for such trivial things anyway. He also took for granted that Kathryn was caring for the rest of the household chores since he was so consumed with his work. The computers and video monitors in his basement ran constantly and his engrossment in what he did left him oblivious to the world around him which was seeking order in the midst of chaos, but failing to find it.

Around midnight each night, Nathan would allow himself a forty-five minute break to do what he pleased. During most of these timeouts, he tried to keep up with what MSNBC or CNN had to say about the world. Regional affairs were constantly dismissed or downplayed and replaced by worldwide news that highlighted stories about globalization projects going on in other parts of the world. What most people didn't realize was that such projects, along with the media attention, was an attempt to unify everyone into a global community.

Things on the home front, however, were not very good. It was extremely difficult to drive through the city, especially at night, as there were fewer workmen available to replace transformers causing all of Denver to look dark and disheveled. Stores had limited stock and supplies even though some trucks could be seen delivering goods, but not all of the items needed were coming in. Stealing of cars was not a major issue, but the stealing of groceries was and food had to be carried in duffle bags so that they weren't recognized as such. Skirmishes throughout the world indicated the unrest of citizens trying to get their own needs met, as governments were too overburdened to meet the demand.

It was during this time that Kathryn started a Bible study group at her house with Armin as the primary teacher. The group meetings averaged an attendance of twenty to forty people twice a week. Kathryn was becoming proficient in assisting Armin in leading people to Christ. She longed for the day that would bring Nathan from his dark basement into the light of the Gospel, but he hid in the recesses of video chats with work crews. For the most part he could not be seen or heard from upstairs. However, on a rare occasion she could hear him cussing at a subcontractor regarding misplaced plans or materials.

One particular night in the middle of the Bible study, the volume of the voices reached a fevered pitch. Kathryn stormed downstairs, "What is going on down here? I can hear you dropping the F-bomb every other word!" she hissed at him in frustration closing the door behind her.

He only looked up in disgust as if she were one of the moronic workers about whom he complained. He held his hand up to stop her question as he continued his tirade, "You have to know that if the outlet of air isn't sufficient, then they will suffocate down below. I designed plenty of room for those intakes and outflows to have an almost continuous sweet smelling air. Get it done!" he then broke the connection with a stabbing thumb to the remote, and the screen went blank.

"Is there any possibility that you could not scream every invective you can think of? Or are you trying to remind us believers that the *lost* will be left behind?" she chided sarcastically, immediately regretting her words and hating that the term *lost* referred to her husband.

"I am *lost*. These people have no clue. When the disappearances occurred, why did they take all of the good ones?" he snorted a forced laugh only to swallow it back, because it reminded them both about Samuel. "I gotta get out of here!" he picked up his phone from the charger and bolted by a dazed Kathryn who was fully realizing that she didn't know this man anymore.

As he headed out to his beloved Lexus 980 in the garage, he was sure that the ugly scene of two weeks ago would not be played out with another person parked behind his car. As he suspected, there was a perfect yet small zone for him to back out of the driveway and into the street. The last time someone had parked behind him, they had received a tongue lashing from Nathan for their impertinence. Since that time, Kathryn always directed the traffic to her house for Bible study on where to park in order to protect those who entered her home from her husband's rude comments.

He tore out of the housing development not really knowing what his direction might be. Two miles down the road, he pulled into a convenience gas station, and then noted that the sign stated that they had no gas. It was curious, because he had never seen a sign like that before. He had heard his parent's talk of long lines during the seventies when fuel was rationed so badly for America. He also knew that his grandparents, during World War II, had had to survive on small amounts of gasoline per week. Those days were circling back again, he guessed. He pulled out almost as quickly as he had entered. He suddenly began to notice the decay occurring to his familiar streets. He wondered with some concern if this was an indication of things to come.

"How long has it been since I have really paid attention to the condition of these streets?" Nathan asked himself aloud. "Way too long, I see!" he answered himself. Unlike typical Friday nights from a year ago, there were very few cars out and about on the roads. Denver was normally bustling with activities from malls to professional games to wine tasting events. Now, however, there were no Bronco games, no Nuggets, no Avalanche, and no fun. He remembered how he used to peruse the sports channels, but since the lack of funding for anything other than basic needs, football seasons for colleges and the pros had been cancelled. There were promises of seasons re-opening next fall, but he was beginning to wonder if that was overly optimistic on the parts of those in charge. Even the new leader of America, who would not call himself anything but the Governor of America, stated that he was a huge football fan and lamented with sporting Americans about the changes that had occurred in the past year and a half. He had tried to make commitments that once the shipping flowed again from the East to West coasts then all would return to normal. The problem was that conditions really hadn't improved. The same impassable streets remained so, and diners and restaurants continued to have precious few customers.

Nathan had hundreds of dollars in his wallet at any given time due to his new position, but it could not buy him many of the things that had comforted him before or that he had always thought could. There were commodities of all types that could be purchased if one new the right person. Trafficking sites and the black market were booming and it was well known that police and other officials looked the other way in exchange for some of those commodities that would make their lives easier.

As he drove south past C-470 on Broadway, he saw a motorcycle cop without his siren or lights on, negotiating with what seemed to be a motorcycle gang. In this particular location this would normally be a site of meting out arrests. But, arrests for most crimes were occurring less often these days. People from all walks of life now packed concealed weapons. Trading tables replaced store purchases with sometimes violent bartering. Best Buy had long since closed its doors while Wal-Mart only had meager supplies of food and clothing at incredibly inflated prices.

As he continued to drive around, he started to pass by a Wal-Mart that was still open, so he pulled in to see what he could find for purchase. Grabbing a cart and starting at one side of the store he slowly made his way around, perusing the nearly empty shelves. He found some somewhat fresh produce in that section of the store and chose several perishable items along with a few long-term food stuffs he had found toward the middle of the store. As he pushed his cart toward the checkout, he spotted a rack of candy that included a few bags of something that he hadn't purchased in a long time – in fact since Samuel had been quite small: gummy bears. They were $25 per bag so most didn't want to waste their money upon that frivolity. But since he had the money, he thought he might as well spend it and he could then eat the gummy bears slowly on the drive home. It should have made him feel wealthy to be able to spend so much money for so few items, but instead it overwhelmed him with a feeling of despair. What was this world coming to?

When he arrived home from his drive about the city, the Bible study had long since concluded. He drove into his garage and closed his car after gathering his purchases. The light from inside the house suddenly flooded out of the door into the garage as his wife stood holding it open for him.

"I am sorry for being angry with you," Nathan said quietly as he stopped at the door. "I just had to get away from everything."

"I know you did," Kathryn responded in understanding. "Is there a way that we could drive up into the mountains to see the beauty of the leaves changing? I know it would cost some money, but I think you could use a weekend away even if it is on really short notice," she offered.

"Hey, that's not a bad idea. I could check in with the crew if I get clearance for the Silverton worksite. I will call Carmen and ask about that in a little bit. I'm sure he won't mind since I believe he owns a house over there. You wanna pack, and I will get my work gear together?" he asked.

"Sure," Kathryn said, a smile lighting her face and joy filling her heart as she turned to go do as he asked.

CHAPTER 24

The trip was relatively slow going over roads that were sometimes barricaded and had only a little of the snow cleared. They occasionally had to drive illegally on the shoulder of the road in order to get through. Finally, they arrived in Silverton around seven o'clock Saturday evening. It was late September, and the snows were already coming to the High Country. Both Nathan and Kathryn had been in Silverton two times for excursions over the years of living in Colorado but really didn't remember much about the area. The town of about 500 people had been laid out originally with one main road that was paved with curio shops and restaurants dotting the 25-mph throughway. Two other parallel streets were dirt roads in the style of an old west gold mining town. Many of the shops had closed up or had broken windows without signs. Several die-hard stores remained for the residents and the end of the world Preppers who had migrated into the area. Since few goods were coming into town, the prices of what was available were astronomical. It appeared though, that the people that remained in Silverton were wealthy beyond the couple's understanding, because they were somehow able to buy what they needed.

After their long drive where they had found only a few snacks for purchase along the way, they decided to check into one of the few rooms available. It was located over a restaurant and was furnished with an all-wood bedroom suite. The overall look was reminiscent of an old styled log cabin.

After dropping off their backpacks and essentials, they wandered down in search of a good Mexican meal. They only found one restaurant that served Tex-Mex cuisine. Since it was between the main meal hours, they were the only two in the restaurant and were waited upon by the bartender who had stains upon her apron.

"You want some water? Or a beer?" she asked.

"Do you have a Coke?" Nathan asked.

"I gotta few of those. It's twenty per bottle. I get them from time to time, but not often enough to keep a good stock so it is more than the beer and wine. Some of the residents make their own alcohol, which I carry, so that tends to be cheaper and is actually tasty as well," she added.

"I'll just stick to the water and two chicken tacos," Kathryn decided.

"Yeah, I will do the same, except a Coke and water on the side," Nathan chimed in.

As they waited for their food, they both attempted to use the internet on their phones but quickly realized it was downgraded in this town to a 5G signal so it was very slow going. Kathryn was receiving occasional text messages from Armin and other Bible study attendees of the miracles of faith occurring as more and more people accepted Jesus as their Savior. Each text she read like that, she reveled anew in the glory of Christ.

She kept up with all the changes happening with members of the group through group messages that contained codes that they all had decided upon during one of the Bible study sessions. They knew the world was getting to the place where there might be prying eyes from government organizations trying to identify the Christians popping up each day. The *World Neighborhood*, as they called themselves, was extensive with new levels of invasion of privacy. After a fairly good dinner with very little intimate talk, they agreed it was time to get a good night's sleep.

The next morning was a beautiful crisp day with Colorado's famous deep blue skies stretching over the snowcapped peaks splashed with brilliant yellow aspen trees. They were ready to walk the streets to see the lay of the land. Both had separate sets of motives in their wanderings.

"Do you see how many open-carry handguns are on the streets?" Kathryn remarked to Nathan in a soft voice.

"Yeah, I noticed that. It is almost as if they have chosen to go back in time 150 years to when one's rights were protected by the use of a gun," he responded.

Nathan's car fit right into the landscape of Escalades and other higher end SUV's the residents of the town drove to traverse the roads in the winter. Backpacks were also a common site as seemingly everyone used one to carry their results of trading with the shop owners who, instead of touristy-type paraphernalia, carried essential heirloom seeds, guns and supplies that only these people would wish for. Haggling was normally reserved for Americans when they vacationed in Mexican towns or overseas, but this was the new norm of economic exchange of Silverton. It made the tenor of the town change to one of pent-up energy with a hint of suspicion. Somehow, the edge of emotions was relieved by the energetic commerce and need for interdependence upon one another.

Later that night, Carmen Luongo called Nathan to invite them to a private dinner being held at his second house located at the base of the hill near the cemetery. At six, they drove up the hill from where their room was located in the center of town to Carmen's mansion. There was a security guard posted at an iron gate – the only break that could be seen in a six foot wall that encompassed the estate grounds. Trees within the walls concealed what went on within them from anyone trying to see. Carmen spent almost the first hour of their visit showing the two around. They were a little stunned to realize that this estate was one of two that he owned other than his Denver residence. He showed the couple his high security vault utilized exclusively for his own

191

prepping needs. He also told them of MacPherson's ranch that was in a hidden location and even bigger than what they were seeing now. He explained that MacPherson was also utilizing the underground facility and owned the biggest bungalow yet built underground.

"I thought you had mentioned when I first talked to you that you didn't believe in the prepping thing," Nathan said incredulously.

"Good memory," Carmen replied with a smile. "I did feel that way. But, the world's changing conditions day by day has convinced me that the money I was saving for my retirement will not be needed. Besides I have to tell you: two months ago, my team of anti-hackers, as I call them, found that someone was trying to hack into my IRA accounts. I also had some offshore monies that were being accessed illicitly and stolen. Once I found that out, I started to move the money around so it was harder for anyone to trace. This has been happening to our customers as well. Their funds are being raided by the government who goes in and changes their passwords and then drains the funds out of the accounts. So we set up a daily monitoring system to watch for this. As we notice that passwords have been changed, we hack the accounts and change the passwords again. That last change is encrypted making it harder for the government to access that account again and buy us some time to move the funds into a completely new account with all of the access codes missing from governmental files. The owner of the account can then access the money. Once I realized the extent of the robbery that was happening within my own accounts, I moved all my funds into cash and gold as quickly as I could. It cost me a lot to do so, but I recommend that you do the same," Carmen said as he pointed to the bewildered couple.

"Government? What are you talking about?" Nathan asked shaking his head as he tried to wrap his mind around all they were hearing. It sounded like something that should only happen in a movie. "Anyway," he continued, "all we have is about a hundred and twenty thousand in our accounts. We haven't had the money over the years to save more than that, and the stock market crash wiped out a bunch of what had accumulated. We moved some into T-bills because..."

"Get your money out of that investment!" Carmen interrupted. "That's the easiest way for the feds to take it. They have banks working with them when it comes to monetary acquisition, and they love to target anything that we once thought was secure. It's like a new game to them. They have been spying on us so long that they can anticipate what we will do before we even consider it...and the digital age has only made it easier for them."

"I believe it," Kathryn agreed.

"Hey," Carmen tapped Nathan on the shoulder with the back of his hand. "Why don't you use my secure server to change your accounts now? Send them anywhere you want. Then cash them in. I can help you with all this if you need me to. We can work something out where you transfer the money to me and I will give you the cash if you want to do something immediately."

"Honey, I have been saying that for a while now!" Kathryn interjected. "Armin predicted it over a year ago. The Bible mentions a *Mark of the Beast* that will be required and no one will be able to buy or sell without this mark," Kathryn said and then went on to explain more of the Biblical details to the both of them.

"Please, honey, don't include Carmen in your crazy end of the world themes," Nathan began looking over at Carmen with hands upraised in protest, "I am sorry for my wife. She is taking the Bible literally nowadays."

"Wait...did you say *mark*?" Carmen asked Kathryn.

"Yes! I could show you," she excitedly suggested to Carmen who now forgot all about where they had been going and led her to his dining room table that was being set for a steak dinner.

Nathan was left on his own in front of the computer screen. He watched as a screensaver image of the dig site swirled into form and then disintegrated only to repeat the process over and over with other pictures and diagrams. Mesmerized, Nathan leaned over the desk to see the progress over the months as he realized the images contained both older and newer designs. Some of these pictures of the prepping site were familiar being pictures he had worked, but a few were not. One picture caught his eye, but when he tried to use the backspace button to get back to it, he held it down too long and activated the windows desktop. Shrugging his shoulders, he decided to take Carmen up on the offer to move his money.

He pulled his passwords out of his wallet to access the secure site. He began to suspect something wasn't right with the accounts when he logged in and it asked him to renew his password today of all days, even though he monitored the money monthly at the very least. The fear sparked by the request in light of the information that Carmen had just shared with them told him that he had to move his money out now. Once he got into the account he noted that instead of the $85,000 or so he expected to see in there, only $47,842 was showing up. He searched to see if the markets were down again, what he found instead was a notation of amounts two days ago when his password was accessed to pull almost five thousand dollars out. He knew for a fact that Kathryn didn't have these codes, because she didn't want to worry about them. A fierce panic set in causing sweat to break out on his forehead. He could not determine in any way, no matter how thoroughly he tried to trace it, where the money had gone. Normally, he received updates by email stating that a change had occurred or funds had been deposited, but this had triggered none of those notifications. He also found records that his notifications were recently changed.

"Carmen, can I take you up on your offer of cashing in my account? If I transfer the money to you, would you cash it in for me today?" Nathan asked rushing in to where Carmen and Kathryn were in deep conversation, somewhat out of breath from the fright of what was happening.

"Sure, I told you I would," Carmen responded, nodding his head.

"What's wrong, honey?" Kathryn asked with concern in her voice.

"They took money out of our accounts!" Nathan said, still having a hard time believing this was happening to him as he led them back across the hall to the study where the computer was located.

Carmen and Kathryn crowded behind Nathan at the computer as he pointed out the amount, explaining that it was significantly less than what was in there a week ago. Carmen shared that he had lost forty thousand dollars before he realized what was happening. There was a panicked look on Nathan's face as Carmen helped him transfer the money from his account to one of Carmen's local ones. As they finished the transaction, Carmen promising to have the cash for the couple before they left to return home, Nathan glanced at Kathryn and was irritated to see that she looked somewhat peaceful and serene rather than upset.

"How can you not be ticked off?" Nathan asked Kathryn somewhat accusingly.

"I am bothered about this but not surprised," Kathryn explained calmly.

' "How did you know that this was going to occur?" Carmen asked, interested to hear what Kathryn would reply. It seemed that their earlier conversation of a one world economic system run with microchip technology had whetted his appetite for new information and perspective.

"I didn't. I just know that the government isn't the same one that the founding fathers set up," Kathryn answered.

"Well that much is obvious to the casual observer," Carmen remarked.

"I know it hasn't been for many decades, but that isn't what I am saying. Once the *faithful* believers were taken away in the Rapture, key governmental office positions that were vacated were filled by people susceptible to evil influences. When I say evil, I really mean the devil – Satan himself, as I was telling you earlier in our discussion about the *Mark of the Beast*. You see, I believe that everything we are experiencing today is a result of the battle of good and evil that has been fought over mankind since the beginning. Of course I also believe that God is over Satan and his cronies. Satan is about to be reduced in territory when loses the privilege he has had through the centuries to visit heaven and will be restrained to this earth. That, of course, will mean he is angrier than ever and will wreak more havoc on this earth than has ever been seen," Kathryn said earnestly.

"I am sorry, Carmen, for my wife," Nathan interjected, a note of derision in his voice. "She can sometimes preach her view. I respect her right to do so, but I heartily disagree," he countered, not realizing or caring that he had just put her down in front of his boss.

A stern look of resolution came over Kathryn and she spoke with a boldness that she would not have had in the past. "What has occurred recently was predicted thousands of years ago in the Bible. There are too many examples in Scripture of prophecies that have been proven reliable for me to get into. But can I tell you about a section such as 2 Thessalonians 4:17 where it talks about the Rapture of the Faithful Church into heaven?"

She asked Carmen. Her earnest words and gentle manner in the face of Nathan trying to shut her down had successfully eliminated any possible rebuttals. Nathan tried to open his mouth to refute her but could not figure out a good enough argument.

Carmen was more intrigued than ever with what Kathryn was saying and their discussion continued. All through dinner he peppered her with questions about concepts with which he was struggling. Kathryn smoothly answered each question, occasionally astonished she knew the answers. She had come to realize over time that when she operated in such a way giving effective responses, it was a sign that the Holy Spirit was speaking through her. Her only regret was that Nathan seemed not to be listening to the conversation that night and remained preoccupied with his financial losses.

The evening went long; the conversation going back to the building project after Carmen realized that Nathan was not inclined to participate in the discourse going on between him and Kathryn. After coffee was served and the dialogue wound down somewhat, Kathryn and Nathan excused themselves to return to their small hotel room downtown.

ForeTold

CHAPTER 25

For the next few days, Carmen and Nathan were busy with the Silverton building project known to the residence as *The Ground*. Since that kept all of the two's attention occupied, Kathryn took this time to walk the town and listen to the random conversations looking for opportunities. She would occasionally interject a word seed of truth. Avoiding pointless debates, she did not push her views and beliefs to pressure anyone. A few people joined her in her stroll through a store or two to ask her more questions about her views. She happily answered their questions. One woman, Susan, was so touched by what she heard that she asked Kathryn to lunch.

Susan Stanton shared with Kathryn the story of her thriving money laundering business in Vegas. With the corruption of the current government and laws that enabled that corruption, Susan spoke openly and without fear of recrimination about her former occupation. She recounted a story of a life consisting of a series of increasingly wealthy men used as way-stations. These men gave her physical comfort until moving on to the next more lucrative prospect. She spoke with some regret of how her childhood gentleness and kindness for animals and strangers had been replaced by hardness. Through challenging business decisions, she turned a small operation into a phenomenal big business making her super rich. She was aided, at one point, by her money laundering partner and lover. Her business had grown to where the profits would have run into the multi-billions of dollars, but she found out just in time that her partner was enacting a coup. She had been able to make off with about a hundred million dollars before her empire came crashing down and she ended up literally on the street.

Susan went on to explain that she actually didn't mind the turn of events or miss the man who had caused her ruin. It afforded her the ability to walk away and retire from the budding racket she could no longer emotionally afford. So, she had moved to Silverton to build the in-ground retirement home that she had deemed necessary when considering the precarious nature of the world's financial mess. She, like the other investors, moved close to the project site and lived in the last place they would ever see above ground, or so they reported to one another. It was an ultra-wealthy but eccentric bunch of preppers who populated this once touristy town.

"How do you know the future? Are you hooked up with an on-line psychic?" Susan asked, only half-jokingly.

"Me? No! I hear the still small voice of peace," Kathryn replied solemnly.

"What was that?" Susan asked, her eyebrows raised.

"The still small voice of peace found in Jesus. I am just learning to live by it," Kathryn mused as she stared out the window of the hamburger joint.

"Uh, OK, but seriously, how do you know that stuff? How do you sound so sure about what has happened? Preppers like me will act as if they know what's going on because of our power connections and we are classic liars. We sense changes coming in the wind and tell people what we think. People believe what we say to be true....just because we have money and power," Susan admitted what Kathryn had suspected about this demographic of ultra-wealthy preppers.

"My son is one of the MIW's," Kathryn began. "Since his disappearance, I have learned that what the Bible says is true. I have come to believe like my son did. Jesus is the Son of God and came to this earth 2000 years ago, lived and taught about the Kingdom of God and then was crucified on the cross for each one of us. He was the sacrifice that would make a way for us to get back into a right relationship with God the Father. God raised Jesus from the dead and He has promised to come again for all who believe in Him. Since the disappearances, I have sat under the teachings of a man, a Jew, named Armin. He is one of the 144,000 that is listed in Revelation...sorry; it's the last book in the Bible."

"Yeah, I know what revelations are," Susan replied, fascinated by the manner in which Kathryn related what she truly believed.

"No, it is the Book of Revelation in the Bible of which I am speaking," Kathryn corrected. "It is the written account of a vision that the Lord gave to one He knew and loved named John. Revelation is all about the time in which we are living. It's an uncanny view into our predicament, and it gives us a timeline to show what comes next," Kathryn explained with her customary waving hands when she became excited.

"So, you set your clock by this book?"

"Yes...but that's..."

"If it's that good, then we should all study it to know what is going to happen next. That way we can be proactive instead of reactive. Is it really like an insider trader sorta deal?" Susan asked, grasping a little of what Kathryn was saying, but missing the bigger picture.

"Yeah, you could look at it that way," Kathryn began and then felt the Holy Spirit stirring her toward a different track. She continued, "I have come to think of this book as an indicator to the lost, and I am sorry to be blunt, but you are one of the lost. I personally don't worry about what will happen for me as a believer and really neither does the rest of my cadre, but those who are lost will face much worse to come."

"Whaddaya mean? Don't you live and die by what the predictions bring?" Susan asked incredulously.

"Have I studied it since I first believed? Kathryn asked and then answered, "Yes. Do I continue to memorize it? Yes, but not for the reasons you might think. The fate of the world is certain. As for mine, I put my trust in Jesus Christ. There will be more disappearances to come as those who believe like me are taken to heaven to be with Jesus. I believe I will be taken in the next group. My son believed and was ready and went in the first disappearance, what we call the Pre-Tribulation Rapture. You see, Susan, I am not scared by the disaster events predicted to come next. Is it possible that I will die before the next Rapture? I hope not, but if I do die, I believe I will be immediately with Jesus in heaven.

"There is no way I can lose. The Bible indicates that to live is Christ, to die is gain. I would be honored to go the way of a martyr, even though I am uneasy of the thought of the pain of death like everyone else. When I understand the truth about my relationship with Jesus and the eternal future He has for me, why do I really care what happens next? I only care about it because I know I need to witness to people like you who still need Christ," she explained.

"So, you think that you are better than me?" a sullenness came over Susan.

"Absolutely not! I was a sinner – I did so many things wrong in my life. What changed me was my faith that I was washed in the blood of the One who made me. The only difference between you and me is that I have received Him and you have not. I am now perfect in my Spirit in Christ because He is perfect. Not that I do perfect things here in the body, but God's grace is sufficient to cover all my mistakes and help me to do better. My focus now is upon the relationship that I have with the Father and Son for eternity. Once you believe in this way, then your fate is as secure as mine. I spend more of my personal time searching the Scriptures for an understanding of my departure from this earth - whether it be by Rapture or martyrdom. I will go to either gladly. I am looking forward to my next step, like my son already took, into heaven."

"The government states that the MIW's are...an evolutional change perpetrated by aliens to remove the weak. It is somewhat plausible as a concept," Susan retorted.

"But let me ask you something: if you believe that hogwash, then why don't you buy the rest of the silliness that they shovel?" Kathryn dished right back at Susan with the same type of wording she had used.

"Because they are lying about the other stuff. Things are getting worse, and we have to take cover. They have stolen money and resources from all of us. They want to control what we think and feel about them!" Susan responded, her voice raised slightly in agitation.

"Exactly! So, if you believe that about the governments of the world who are now specifically under the control of Satan, the father of all lies..." she gestured all around her, "then how can you accept their alien lie about the disappearances? You don't have to answer that, because I see on your face that you don't really believe it."

"Girl, you sound like my lawyer," Susan laughed relaxing again.

"Well, I used to work for a law firm before they had no more work for me a few months back. Some of it had to rub off on me," Kathryn joked back.

"I promise you this: I am gonna think about this very seriously," Susan said, almost to herself.

"I think you're missing one thing," Kathryn responded just as seriously.

"What's that?" Susan asked.

"There's not much time," Kathryn said solemnly.

"I know you say that. But I'm not ready to give up my place in *The Ground* yet. But, I'll be looking into the claims you are making, because they are tremendously compelling," Susan said thoughtfully. She took the Bible that Kathryn handed her, then slipped a card back to Kathryn. "Just in case you need it. I know you believe that you won't, but I have no one else. I extend this to you if you need...I mean, want to. It is a spot on the last potential lifeboat in my underground apartment, if you wish to use it."

Holding the card as a precious gift and token Kathryn asked with tears in her eyes, "Are you really sure about this?"

"Yeah, I am!" Susan replied.

"I appreciate it," Kathryn responded with genuine thankfulness and then continued earnestly, "but I want you to know that the Lord is coming for me soon enough. As I said before, living is all about Jesus Christ and dying gains me everything. There is nothing I am scared of. I know my place as it relates to the world, but I spend my time trying to grasp the understanding of what my new home in heaven will be like. I figure I will be there a year or two from now. If I die early, then I get that mansion in the sky a little sooner than I thought."

"Well, this is a get-out-of-jail-free for you or your husband, but it can't be for both," Susan explained as she pointed at the card.

"I will give it to him," Kathryn stated, "because I don't know if he has his ticket..." she trailed off as the joke fell flat and tears once again formed in her eyes as she realized this wasn't funny.

"Honey, don't worry about him. I will tell you that if you go in your Rapture, then all you have said is true and I will be completely on board. Then, I will invite your husband to use that card." Susan tried to reassure Kathryn, impressed with the genuine and fierce conviction with which Kathryn had spoken.

They hugged. Susan dropped a hundred dollar bill on the table to cover the two hamburger meal costing forty dollars with a nice tip. They went their separate ways with Kathryn feeling such loss for a dying soul. She found a wooden bench along the street and sat in the warm sun praying fervently for her new friend to realize the truth and come to believe in Jesus as her Savior.

She was reminded again of Jesus' parable about the sower and the seed, just as she was when she was working in the garden spot at her house months ago. She wondered if Susan was fertile ground or choked seed. Choked, maybe, because she would allow the cares of the millions of dollars she had to draw her away from the Lord's calling. Kathryn looked down at the card she still held in her hand. She knew that she had secured Nathan's passage on a ride of refuge, but she wondered just how safe it would actually be.

That night, Kathryn and Nathan ate in relative silence, each lost in their own thoughts about things that did not need to be voiced.

The next day the extended Silverton weekend came to an end. Kathryn and Nathan packed their belonging and headed out for the slow drive back to Aurora.

ForeTold

CHAPTER 26

Another year and a half passed as the distance between the couple increased as much as the Aurora temperatures outside which soared past 110 degrees. Those in the southern states had learned the concept of air conditioning with high summer temps long ago, but many Coloradans did not know how to combat the heat. The weather patterns throughout the world were too unpredictable for most weather forecasters to report with any accuracy. Tempers rose as dramatically as the temperatures outside. Police all over the Denver area only responded to the most violent crimes.

Kathryn broke the silence at the breakfast table by asking, "Have you heard the news?"

"What news?" Nathan still waking after a short sleep the night before.

"Cartiff has made a worldwide edict. It was broadcast across all the channels early this morning. You know that identification smart biochip they have been pushing for the past couple of years as the solution to all our economic problems?"

"Yea, I guess," Nathan responded nonchalantly.

"They are going to mandate everyone on the planet get one!"

"Oh..."

"The *World Neighborhood* will be injecting everyone at police stations, court houses, and hospitals around the globe. They are claiming this will reduce the crime and remove the need for citizens to carry large amounts of cash. They are throwing in an incentive as well - significant debt forgiveness. The *World Neighborhood* is mandating all commercial transactions will require this implanted biochip!"

Nathan responded, "Calm down, Carmen Luongo sounded as if he would be willing to pay us cash instead of traceable electronic transactions. We shouldn't worry about such things."

She went on, "Homeland Security is now our regional arm of the global government. They will still be in charge of dispensing the biochips to everyone in the US. They are saying the benefit for receiving an injection immediately is there will be no charge and with less wait time.

"However, if a person chooses to wait until after the New Year, then a 35% sales tax will be enacted on top of a $3000 charge for the injection!"

Nathan attempted to reassure her, "Let's wait and see. Political things have a way of coming and going. Remember Probation in the 20th century?"

What the couple did not know was anyone found after an imposed June 1st deadline without the new ID could be arrested by any bio *chipped* citizen around the world. Along with serving prison time and being charged with fines for noncompliance, a hefty bounty would be paid to those who turned them in. Any assailant would be forgiven on the spot if the injured party did not have the ID chip injected in their head or hand. This system would increase the prevalence of citizen arrests throughout the world.

The edict caused a flurry of activity by unethical people. Criminal networks were already being set up through internet sites that would pillage a person economically, while roving gangs accosted them physically. They would turn in the *non-chipped* to the identification stations hoping for an early reward.

It seemed to those who recognized what was occurring that the governments of the world had aligned themselves with both the criminal elements and police forces. They had found that they could use and manipulate both parties to bring society into line with their bigger agenda. They, of course, couched it as being for the betterment of society when explaining their reasons to the general public.

Meanwhile, the Bible study continued to meet at Kathryn's house, but with no cars evident in the driveway so as to not arouse suspicion of an unauthorized meeting. The attendees parked in retail parking lots and walked for many blocks to hear the *Good News* for all of humanity. Kathryn had moved all the couches and other furniture out many months ago allowing for more chairs to fill the space. Armin spent one night a week teaching at Kathryn's Bible study. The rest of his week was engaged in driving all over the region to teach wherever the Spirit led. Great multitudes of people had converted to Christ. Armin found strength inside his spirit where the joy of the Lord resides. However, at times his energy was being stretched as the need of these new disciples was great in order to combat the prevailing deception.

On this night the meeting began in Kathryn's living room with forty people packing the small space and waiting expectantly.

"Life is different now, I know. We have seen our share of discrimination, but nothing will prepare you for what is to come next if you haven't made a choice for Christ," Armin began.

"Whaddaya mean? I lost my job because someone thought that I was reading a Bible. I have suffered innumerable persecutions!" exclaimed one man with short-cropped hair.

"We, new converts, will have light blows in this timeframe," Armin responded.

"Light blows? What does that mean in relation to what that man just said?" an irritated woman who came for the first time, blurted out.

"It means we new converts to Christ, in comparison to what is to come next, will have a few blows of persecution. After we are gone the persecution will be unto death. We live in a time in which the rules of the game have changed. We lived in a time, only three short years ago, that allowed us to think whatever we wished and act upon what we thought. In Revelation chapter three, Jesus judges the Laodicean church harshly, stating that He wishes that they would be hot or cold, but because they were neither, He was about to spit them out of His mouth. That church, as some are today, was lukewarm, not really having chosen to follow good or evil. What the world will go through over the next four years will be what it takes to get everyone off the fence and either choose God or choose Satan."

"So, are we being spit out of His mouth?" Kathryn asked knowing the answer to the question she posed but aware that some in the group were wondering. She had perceived correctly that her role was to guide the group into new understanding.

"In one sense, we are spit out of His mouth, because we chose not to be faithful to what we all knew in our hearts. We all had an inkling that something ominous would befall us if we sat on that fence we were on before the Rapture," Armin said and paused to allow the people to reflect on the state of their souls now and before that fateful time.

"God states that He desires for all to come to a knowledge of the Creator and begin a deep relationship with Him. He wants us to know Jesus. Many of you in this room have done that, and most of you are paying a price for your new faith. You, Conrad, are feeling the nature of the few blows as we speak," Armin rested a hand on the shoulder of the man who had asked the first question.

"How did you know my name?" Conrad asked in surprise.

"I didn't, but the Master told me as you walked into this house. He wants you to be with Him, Conrad, for eternity. Some people feel that heaven will be just about comfort, and that certainly is a part of what we will be feeling. The more interesting thing that I have realized about our being in heaven is that we will be learning for eons about the creation and the Creator. There are near death testimonies of those who have been to heaven and returned. They state those in heaven now will aid to instruct us about how the Master works out His perfection.

"The blows of persecution feel harsh now, and I know they are for those of us who have tasted this country's previous freedoms. God mentions though, that those who wait past this next Harvest will have many more blows coming their way, as Scripture states in Luke 12:47. A large portion of the martyrdom spoken of for these times will occur in the final three and a half years. The Gospel of Matthew indicates that the next timeframe will start in a matter of months and is called the Great Tribulation. The Gospels term the blows as severe, indicating that death and other unspeakable atrocities will come to those in the last part of history. The Devil described in the Book of Job, currently has access to God's heavenly throne room. He will bring great wrath after being thrown out of heaven and will be restricted to the earth. This war in heaven will bring the ultimate persecution to God's people," Armin paused at this moment allowing that information to sink in deeply for those around the room who hadn't considered Satan's tactics.

"I also want to talk to those believers who have made the decision for Christ about a question that has been posed to me," Armin continued as he pulled a wadded piece of paper from his back pocket. "What the Lord has revealed to me, confirmed time and time again, is that we are to study eschatology to convince the *Lost* of

211

what is to come. The sufferings will come from the *Anti-Christ*, who is *Supreme Chancellor* Cartiff, aren't really the biggest issues that we should study. Those who give their lives to Christ now and obey Him will be taken in the Barley Harvest. I am so glad that you who have joined here together tonight are so interested in the discipleship that Christ instructed us to do. Now more than ever, it is important that we disciple the *Lost* to bring them into a saving knowledge of Jesus Christ.

"There are people throughout the centuries who have spent a lifetime getting to know the Father intimately. Many of you are experiencing God's abundant understanding illuminating your heart in order to bring you up to speed as quickly as possible. In the past this understanding would have taken decades of study to accomplish. You are also sensing the importance of maintaining your physical body as God's temple. Your understanding heart and strong body will help lead others to Christ. The seeds you sow into new converts will reap eternal benefits for both them and you. Is that not exciting?" He asked. He could sense the excitement all around him coming from those who had made their mind up to go in the next Harvest of God. They were sitting on the edge of their seats. They realized that they had a mere few months left before that next Harvest that would give them a resurrected body and to be with their Creator!

"Consider this as we close for the night: many pastors have talked about how the earth was created in six literal days, which I heartily believe for many reasons. I believe that the Bible is true and science is only limited knowledge. God was the only witness actually present at Creation. He told us what occurred in His Word. He said it only took Him six days and on the seventh day He rested. The Gospels speak of Jesus preparing a place in heaven for us. Can you imagine the place that He has spent more than 2000 years to create for you and me? A personal mansion for each of us? If it only took six days for Him to create the wonders of the world around us, just think of what that mansion is going to look like after 2000 years of that!! Now, consider that He has not only prepared a place for you, and it's not a retirement home as we think of it on this earth, but He's also ordained a profession in which we will engage forever. That is why you need to be studying the Gospels and the Epistles as well as the Prophets in the Old Testament who speak of the wisdom of the Lord. You are preparing yourself for that eternal eventuality more than you are for what the earth will see over the next few months." With that, he closed with a prayer and found a few more coming forward to seek entrance into the Kingdom. Those new converts shed tears of joy knowing a party was occurring in heaven for the new residents.

ForeTold

CHAPTER 27

Two nights later, Kathryn received a disturbing call from Conrad, "Kat, you there?" Conrad asked in a whisper.

"Yeah, Conrad? What's the matter?" She replied somewhat confused as it was three in the morning.

"I just heard something outside of my house. Now that I accepted Jesus, I had my Bible out again at work..." Conrad explained, still whispering, but was cut off by Kathryn.

"What? You know that is dangerous. I love it that you are reading the Scriptures since you accepted Him but..."

"I know, I know. Someone is looking in and around my house. They'll call it search and seizure I'm sure. It is the police with one of my co-workers. I can't believe that with all of the rape and murdering going on they have the resources for this...and to a good citizen!" he murmured into the phone. Kathryn heard wind blowing in Conrad's receiver giving evidence that he had gone outside into the blistering heat of the night that was becoming more unusual for Denver.

"Hate to tell you this, but we aren't good citizens anymore," Kathryn said, not trying to be funny, but it brought an ironic chuckle from the other end of the line.

"I know we aren't. I just can't get over it that I am going to jail for as a subversive," Conrad said with an odd tone of serenity in his voice.

"No, don't let that happen!" she exclaimed into the phone. "If you can make it out to the back-fence line, I can meet you about a mile up in that old housing development north of your house. That should throw them off your trail. You can stay here," Kathryn offered as she pulled on her shoes holding the iPhone in the crook of her shoulder.

"Hey, I'm gonna see the pearly gates before you do..." he trailed off causing Kathryn to abruptly cease her preparations. She could hear shouts through the phone and the sound of Conrad's labored breathing, then a shot rang out and she could tell that the phone had fallen to the ground. She listened for a moment more and then disconnected the call as she realized what had happened.

"No, no, no...no, this can't be!" she screamed at the now silent phone in her hand as her tears began to fall.

The yelling upstairs didn't even bring Nathan up from the basement as she sat for what seemed hours crying for the death of a brother. She was nearly furious at God for taking him and in her anguish she began to yell toward heaven. "I thought that You were our protector? Why did this happen?"

"Who are you talkin' to?" the voice of her husband made her drop the phone in fright.

"God..." she responded shortly bowing her head as more tears started to flow.

"He's not listening, you know," Nathan sardonically stated placing a hand on her right shoulder as he noted her tears.

Her flesh desperately wanted to just tell Nathan to *Shut Up!!*, but she kept her mouth closed instead. However, she indicated her annoyance by moving away from his touch. He got the message and retreated back to the basement, which wasn't her intended response. She thought to herself, *Would he ever try to reach out to her again?*

Kathryn's surprising response from God was, "No." Feeling a strong anointing, she proceeded to inquire the Lord about her first question about God being the protector. The impression she got inside her heart was, "I am your protector. However, faith is the shield that is required for My protection. Conrad was just a baby in his faith. He had not learned how to appropriate faith to manifest My protection. He is with Me now and I am his protector for all eternity." Kathryn's tears turned to joy as the comforter of the Holy Spirit had reached a new level inside her.

On the outside the unfortunate truth was that martyrs were increasing throughout the planet as the culmination of the sins of the world was coming to a climax. Conrad would not be the first one to die. In many nations, as vast multitudes were converting to faith in Jesus Christ, it gave more license for those yielding to the devil's will to kill off what they perceived to be the problem.

Kathryn's short lived joy of comfort was stagnated by the thought of people being so deceived to do Satan's will. It seemed that life was being discounted at an ever increasing rate. But, she felt the Holy Spirit continue to comfort her with His presence and with the gentle reminder that the Lord weeps for those who were unfairly persecuted for His name. Then the still small voice returned, "They will be vindicated! When I return, My justice will be served. Those who murder will be murdered; those martyrs who are Mine, will be resurrected to rule and reign with Me for a 1,000 years." As she dried her tears, an even greater peace washed over her as the Holy Spirit confirmed the Word she had heard inside her heart. Then joy started to rise up as she become grateful that she would meet Conrad again, when she finally enters heaven herself.

As she removed her shoes, she mentally calculated the date from the beginning of the Tribulation and realized that her time on earth was fast coming to a close. She resolved to continue in her spiritual preparation, knowing that in the short time she had left, she wanted to *Share the Word* with all she could. She believed she would one day soon be seated at a feast in heaven with Jesus and all the other new converts and she wanted as many as possible to be there with her. That meant diligent study of the meat of God's word. Her new found intimacy with God inspired her to pursue His presence every waking moment with every breath and every thought. Her relationship with God was now an all-consuming fire.

CHAPTER 28

Kathryn repeated the proclamation to herself, "I will not be offended today by anything that Nathan does." This became her common morning exercise. She knew that Cartiff's seven-year treaty was now almost halfway completed. The world had morphed into a place of horror. In response, Kathryn found herself more and more contemplating the glory of heaven. She had found when she did this it turned her feelings toward Nathan to sympathy and love instead of her negatively reacting to his anger that seemed to be mounting each day. He ranted about the smallest things every time he emerged from the basement. Apparently, nothing was getting done effectively enough for him.

"Lord, What does he need to see You? Bring people along his path that will help him find You." Her continual prayer was offered as she lightly applied her eye shadow. "Also, bring Susan from Silverton to a knowledge of You. She has heard the gospel. Let the seed of truth grow within her heart, even though now she is too preoccupied with things that don't matter. I pray that she does not experience the many blows foretold in Scripture of the Great Tribulation to come. However, far better for her to convert at that time than never at all. Neither Nathan nor Susan deserve..." Kathryn cut off her prayer right there, because she knew that all deserved worse than they receive. Even the wicked were procuring grace from on high.

It was February, and as unusually high as the temperatures had reached in August, they were dipping to new lows this winter. Traditionally, there were heavy snowfalls and cold temps during a Colorado winter, but this year the cold was especially biting and the thermometer was dipping lower for longer periods of time.

Tuesday, it had begun to warm up into the thirty-degree range with only a light wind. But already too many work stoppages due to material shortages and freezing, snowed-in roadways plagued Nathan's every virtual step regarding the worksite in Silverton.

The fences were up around *The Ground* as they called it. Many of the residences were finished with the owners working on the final furnishings. Others, however, still had problems with basic plumbing and electrical issues that affected completion of the walls. It wasn't as easy as above ground projects to rip out dry wall and tear into concrete to repair a mistake. Additionally, each wall was reinforced with steel and Plexiglas. The electrical work and plumbing had to co-exist with these materials so the bunker would be protected from most nuclear blasts other than a direct fifteen-kiloton strike. Of course, no one really knew the correct ratings on the reinforcements, because the effects were mathematical in nature and not born out in actual experience. The billionaires and the few millionaires in the cliquish group requested only the best and most efficient storage units for them and their wares. They were banking on being able to survive for at least five years underground in spite of the tragic circumstances they believed would annihilate the rest of humanity. Most doubted that they would have to be under for that long, but they were trying to become as completely self-sufficient as they could.

The news from around the world was mind-numbing to even the casual observer. The acceleration to the implanted biochip was starting to give Nathan the shivers. Not for the rash reasons his estranged wife gave him for the end of the world scenarios, but for his own understanding of governmental tracking of which he didn't want to be a part. His generous salary and benefits from his new job afforded him a newfound independence and he was able to store cash at an alarming rate from anything that he had previously known. He was also very thankful that he had been able to eliminate all their household debt before the biochip became mandatory. Global officials issued veiled warnings to those who were in debt that over spending could be curbed. In the next breath they then promoted the biochip and essentially promised an earthly do-over when it came to credit scores – in other words, get the chip, get out of debt. The draw to the *chip* itself had become an international phenomenon. Recipients created a social network viral buzz showing off what one could do once received. Hairstyles and tattooed designs that framed the areas of the implanted chip on the forehead were most popular with the younger generations who had college debt enough to choke a horse. All those debts were forgiven for this new society of global believers, or at least that was what the media was purporting. The only few holdouts were seemingly the religious right in the extreme minority and the high upper class that balked at this level of governmental control.

Because Nathan had paid off everything with his salary, he really didn't care about the draw of a lack of indebtedness to the system. He felt outside of the system for the first time in his life. He was experiencing an aspect of life only the rich knew. In the back of his mind, he realized that they may never accept him as an equal even though he had built their castles in the ground for them.

At first when this project started, Carmen and Nathan would privately joke about the nature of the paranoia displayed by these affluent eccentrics, knowing that MacPherson was right in *The Ground* with the group. Although most would associate such paranoia with those who were severely without means and had little grasp upon the realities of the world, this time it was the super-rich, who had a heap of hard-to-come-by data, to support why they had reacted in this way.

One day though, Carmen called to tell Nathan that MacPherson had died in a construction accident in their

221

bunker. He had been directing some of the work but placed himself haphazardly in the way of a steel wall that was not secured in place yet and it had come down upon him. Two days after the incident, as the community solemnly buried him on a hillside just outside his creation, it was learned that Carmen had been given complete control of the company. He was left with enough provision so that he could finish the project. Since the rest of the bunker community had at least known of Carmen, if they didn't know him personally, his ascension was comfortably welcomed and the transition from one leader to the next went virtually unnoticed. It seemed that the future inhabitants of *The Ground* were just happy to know they would not be inconvenienced by a delay in construction due to MacPherson's untimely death.

The media, in its downward spiral of evil, began to broadcast shows displaying effects on people the conditions around the world were causing. It was not uncommon to watch video of the most current fashionable people stepping over the dying on street corners without stopping to give assistance. The homeless and destitute population seemed to grow at disquieting rates in each city. Bio *chipping* became the focus of a new reality series in which those who were against it were pitted against those who had already been *chipped*. Not surprisingly, those with the biochip always seemed to win, somehow having had access to homemade weaponry to which the other side never did. Death came to the screen in all its carnage replacing the mock gore of decades before where special effects were used to portray the dying. Somewhere along the way TV executives had thought it was easier to have actual people play roles where, unbeknownst to them, they were scripted to actually die.

As Nathan's work cycled its way toward a close, the thought that he was nearing the end of all things troubled the back of his mind. The project winding down was caused by a lack of parts available to complete portions of the underground bunker right away or with the actual completion of other portions. He was thankful that the majority of the underground complex had been completed. He found his work time dwindling from the 90-100 hour weeks to less than 45 hours, but at odd intervals he also found himself with more menial tasks such as babysitting delinquent shipments.

The really disturbing part to Nathan was that he began to wonder if Kathryn might be right about her Bible info. Was it possible that the world was pulling itself apart at the seams? Were there sides to be taken in a cosmic war? If one had to take sides then which one was he on? His heart pounded inside of his chest as he asked himself these questions that he had never concretely considered. "I can't take sides now though. And do I really want to believe in Kathryn's God anyway?" Nathan asked the TV hoping it would somehow give him a solid answer. But, all it spat out was more despairing news of chaos. It did seem, to some extent, that the end of life as he had known it was near.

He chose to turn off the TV for once and sauntered upstairs thinking he might be interested in pancakes or an omelet to eat.

The smell from the kitchen wafted through the bedroom and into the bathroom startling Kathryn out of a reverie. She had been sitting with her coffee and makeup brushes not attending to either one for more than fifteen minutes, so wondering about the enticing odors she was smelling gave her an excuse to get up and investigate the source. To her amazement, she spotted Nathan cooking eggs with cheese, tomatoes and chicken on the stove.

"Can I help you with anything?" she asked incredulously.

"Nah, I'm good...well, actually, you can make the toast," he responded not looking at her.

"No problem," Kathryn replied, deciding to play along and see what was really up with him. In ten minutes, he surprised her again by setting two plates at the table and dishing up their eggs. They talked about their early marriage for the first time in years, and then turned to a few laughs together about memories of their son which brought tears to both their eyes.

"You know, he is in heaven...you could go there too!" Kathryn said quietly.

"I hear ya," Nathan replied, causing Kathryn to hold her breath in hopes that he really had heard. "I know you believe this stuff, and I felt this morning that there might be more to it than I have thought. I admit that many of the things you had told me about have happened. That *Mark of the Beast* thing is eerily similar to the bio *chipping* that they are advocating right now. And don't worry about it," he placed his hand out as if to stop a potential barrage he felt might come from her, "I won't get *chipped*. I don't think that either of us needs it. It is made for the poor and the middle class who have massive debt. We aren't there anymore. We can always buy things until this passes. Maybe, in time, the *World Neighborhood* will repeal the law requiring it. They might find that the only ones getting it are the poor, but that it hasn't gained enough traction with the rich. I want you to know that I am thinking of our future and trying to prepare for any eventuality," he finished, hoping his words had comforted her.

"Well, I so appreciate this breakfast. It's been a long time since I have had this kind of meal. I am sorry that I haven't made anything like this for you in so long," Kathryn replied as she thoughtfully wiped her mouth and then stood to clean up both plates. She sighed deeply as she rinsed the dishes, knowing that the conversation about *the Mark* wasn't going to go anywhere at this point. She sent up a silent prayer and left it in the Lord's hands, because she had already spoken her peace about the subject many times. What else could she say without getting irritable with one who didn't want to listen? She knew she had said enough and that the Holy Spirit would have to continue working on Nathan to open his heart to receive the truth. She silently expressed her gratitude that there finally seemed to be a crack in the hard shell surrounding Nathan's heart. At least he had finally admitted that there might be something to all she had said.

Surprised that she hadn't pushed her point home more thoroughly as she had done in times past, Nathan somewhat gratefully changed the subject. "I don't really have much to do today because the shipments are delayed for the next several days. Work isn't gonna happen. You wanna watch a movie?" he asked.

"I wouldn't mind if there were any good ones. Most of them portray actual violence, meaning I would have my eyes closed through 75% of it. Is there one that would meet the lack of violence criteria?"

"I don't think so. There aren't the cool movies anymore that are just fun. They tend to push an agenda of death. Do you want to take a drive to the mountains instead?" he asked.

"You know, I would love that," Kathryn said in relief, her face lighting up. "Do we have the cash on hand to do so? It could cost a lot with gas being $7.58 a gallon. We can save some money by packing a meal or two, though, if you want me to do that?" she asked, hopeful that they might spend a little time together as husband and wife before she left this earth.

"Yeah, we can do that. Go ahead and pack some stuff. We'll go see the mountain scenery."

ForeTold

CHAPTER 29

The couple drove off through the Aurora streets and to C-470 to head toward the mountains. It took more than ninety minutes, even on a Saturday, to reach I-70 in the Golden area to start toward the foothills. So much of the drive out of Denver was congested with areas of poor road repair - some so bad that the rough roads would scrape the bottom of the vehicle as they slowly drove over them. There were also many traffic lights that didn't work. People were no longer very polite in waiting their turn to go through intersections, everyone seemed to think they had the right of way. Wreckages still dotted the landscape, some from new accidents piled close to those that were significantly older. But, once they hit the foothills, the congestion loosened up enough to allow 65 miles per hour speeds. Kathryn was almost tempted to roll down the window to smell the mountain air, but thought better of it as she remembered the freezing temperatures.

As they continued to drive, they began to see military vehicles which blocked their view of the mountains. There were trucks of all types and even a few tanks. They didn't have the American flag displayed prominently on them like normal military vehicles. Careful perusal did show a smaller version of the American flag on the sides of the vehicles, but it was dwarfed by the prominent black and blue colors of the *World Neighborhood* flag. It was a poor joke among citizens that if you didn't comply with the *World Neighborhood* orders, their flag would make you black and blue.

"It's a good thing that I packed your car with winter gear, survival gear and enough clothes for several weeks, not to mention a nine millimeter with two clips of ammo,"

Kathryn remarked as she looked over her shoulder to see the tanks roll by.

"What? I knew you were packing a few things in case of an emergency, but I never realized that you had put clothing and a gun in here. I hope we don't get caught with an unregistered gun," Nathan said earnestly, beginning to sweat at the thought of what the *World Neighborhood* members would do if they were caught.

"Well, I hope you are praying," Kathryn stated, "and while you are at it don't do anything to draw attention to us," to which, Nathan rolled his eyes.

As it got closer to lunch time, they finally turned off onto a side road that actually didn't have any signs, because they didn't want to be in the way of the military and accused of something as simple as loitering. For that matter, they didn't really want to encounter anyone else either. The snow crunched under the tires as they drove slowly to find a place where they could sit in peace and eat a sandwich without being bothered by anything. It took them about three miles, on a mostly abandoned road, but they finally saw a downed tree in a small meadow off the side of the road. With only a few inches of snow on the ground in this area, they pulled on their heavy coats and boots and trudged out to the small clearing. Even though it was 32 in the Denver area, it was only 25 degrees in the foothills, and for the moment their newly chosen picnic spot was directly in the sun. They found an elongated relatively smooth area on the tree trunk to sit upon and then took a few moments to just breathe in the fresh scents of the thick pine trees around them. They listened to the wind breaking through the tree tops above. Fortunately for them, the wind was not hitting their position, tucked into a small valley as the area was. But the sound it made in the highest branches was soothing and relaxing.

They ate mostly in silence, enjoying the ability to just be still and enjoy nature. After about thirty minutes, they began picking up their trash and returned to the car. They then decided to follow the small road a little farther up into the hills just to feel like they were on a new adventure. In reality, they really had nowhere to go and nowhere had they to be – at least for a time.

After going a short distance, the road began to narrow. Moments later, they spotted a mid-sized cabin with overgrown, dead vines covering it so thoroughly that the color of the cabin was indiscernible. Even the windows were covered so thickly that there were only tiny peepholes through the branches that could be seen. The couple decided to drive up slowly so that they might not startle the residents of the place, if there were any. "What is this place?" asked Nathan.

"I think I might know. It has the tell-tale signs of one of two issues: either it is truly abandoned like houses we have seen in the Denver area, or it is a safe house for believers," Kathryn said as she peered intently out of the front windshield.

"You've been reading too many spy novels," Nathan tried to chuckle to show his sarcasm.

"What? No, I haven't," Kathryn replied, stung that he wasn't taking her seriously after having had such a pleasant day together. "You haven't noticed them over the last few years? People can isolate themselves like this to be off the grid. They don't have any power brought in, and they have no city water, using either a well they have dug or a fresh water source like a stream. They rarely use cell phones, preferring instead to use short band radio to communicate to different areas. They look like the houses those Raptured left behind – totally abandoned, but they are really safe houses. There will be more coming soon," Kathryn reported.

"I don't want to be a believer if that is how I have to live. I am not sure that they do either," Nathan's reply was surly, the pleasantness of the morning seeming to have definitely worn off. Curious though, he parked the car and stepped outside.

"No, Nathan. They live like this because they have chosen to do so. People will still accept Christ in the time to come, called the Great Tribulation. That period starts once the *Anti-Christ* abolishes the Israelite sacrifices in Jerusalem's Temple. He defiles it and puts up some image of himself to worship. As soon as that happens, the Bible clearly states that those in Jerusalem should run to the hills. The Lord will protect them in an unknown wilderness place. I believe that safe houses like this will become even more important in the next few years. I am still hoping that you will come with me in the next harvest, but I will accept it if you at least become a believer during the Great Tribulation. That's my prayer for you, Nathan. Not that you will suffer, but to become a resurrected believer for eternity is greater than this natural life. I've talked with you about all of this for some time, and I hope that the Holy Spirit brings it into your remembrance when I am gone," Kathryn said, tears filling her eyes as she talked to him inside his prized Lexus.

"Let's just check this out. It could be cool," as Nathan climbed out of the vehicle deflecting the conversation in a new direction.

They walked without any stealth to the front door, because they wanted anyone who might be there to see them as they came. They didn't want to be the victims of a double-barrel shotgun. Nathan knocked firmly on the creaky screen door. After waiting about thirty seconds with no response, he reached up to pound on the heavy wood door inside of the screen door when it opened to a scraggly bearded man.

"Whatchu want?" the man asked gruffly.

"We're not lost if that's what you mean. Shalom Aleichem," Kathryn spoke up, surprising Nathan into silence. He was surprised even more when the door was swung open wide upon Kathryn's last greeting, which Nathan didn't understand at all.

"Welcome!" the man beamed through his hairy visage and ushered them into the cabin.

"Please come in and join us by the fire. What are you two doing up this way?" the man's wife asked, and they looked up to see her come quickly around the corner. She had no makeup on and a tangled single braid of dirty blonde hair tinged with silver was pulled over her left shoulder. The woman was kindly in nature and had a hospitable spirit about her. Kathryn suspected that her hospitality had been exercised very little since they shut themselves up.

"I am Sandra Farrell and that is Sonny Farrell you met at the front door. The kids behind the banister over there are Sarah and Shoshanna," Sandra introduced everyone, pointing her finger in the direction of two girls no more than twelve and fourteen years old who were the spitting image of their mother.

"That's a lot of S names to keep up with. Doesn't make you cuss now and again when you stumble over everyone's name, does it?" Nathan asked with a snicker but subsided when the others didn't join in his humor.

"Would you like some cocoa?" Sandra asked, but scurried off before they could give their affirmative remarks, believing no one could refuse something hot to drink during the present cold snap.

Sonny used his foot to nudge a log out of the way that had rolled down the huge woodpile stacked next to the massive stone fireplace. He then picked up a smaller log and tossed it on the fire, causing the fire to crackle so loudly the couple jumped in surprise. "So, what are you doing up here?" Sonny asked again.

"We were just trying to get away from the city. Nathan's work has finally slowed down with the freezing temperatures. We wanted to spend some time together

231

and smell the mountains once more before Graduation,"
Kathryn smiled as she spoke the last word.

"Never heard it called that but I like it. Graduation's
gotta be soon," Sonny replied with a gentle smile as their
kindred spirits confirmed their common faith.

Nathan stayed quiet as he only half listened to the
inside conversations between Christian converts that
were going on around him. He didn't have an inkling of
what they were talking about most of the time. They
prattled on about various topics that ranged from seeing
the face of their Savior, or the beards of the long-dead
prophets, a conversation which made Sonny stroke his
own.

The fire and the cocoa, combined with the fresh air
of the afternoon, began to do their work on Nathan. He
remembered that hadn't brought any of his electronics
with him and since there was no way to reach civilization
at the moment, he settled into the couch, which had a
somewhat smoky smell to it, but was otherwise
comfortable. The heavy crocheted afghans that were
thrown over the back and arms of the couch - easily
accessible to provide further comfort. They reminded him
of his grandmother when, as a child, his family visited his
grandparents in the middle of the Oregon hills. Heat was
a luxury in Oregon that his grandfather didn't have when
he grew up and would not turn on later in life until it was
below freezing. Nathan's mind continued to wander as his
eyes remained focused on the blue flames of the fire,
licking the blackened bark of the logs. But as the
conversation droned on around him, he could only hear
the crackle of the burning logs and smell the mesmerizing
scent of the fire. It wasn't long before his eyes became
more and more blurred and he finally just had to close
them.

Seeing that Nathan had fallen asleep, the others
reduced the volume of their voices to a spirited whisper.

When his heavy and steady breathing betrayed his condition, Kathryn admitted to them that Nathan was not a believer, and that admission allowed her to tell much of her story. The couple listened intently, asking pertinent questions from time to time to better follow the events as they had unfolded. For their part, Sonny and Sandra admitted that their isolated living conditions made them hungry to hear all that Kathryn cared to share. Her story more than kept their attention as the afternoon waned.

Over the next two hours, as Nathan slept soundly, Kathryn commiserated with them about her missing son, struggling marriage, and the work for God's kingdom she felt compelled to do. They could easily tell how much Nathan's refusal to believe, along with the on-going stress of the strained marital relationship, weighed on Kathryn's heart.

"That's too big a burden for you to carry. You need to cast your care onto the Father," Sandra said as she reached out for about the tenth time to place a comforting hand on Kathryn's shoulder.

"I know it is, but I think that Nathan is getting closer to the thought of God," she explained. "At least I am hopeful that he is."

As the darkness deepened outside the windows, the only light in the room emanated from the fireplace. Sonny got up and assisted Sandra to draw heavy curtains over the windows to keep the firelight from shining out. Avoiding drawing attention, nothing was left to chance.

Nathan finally awoke to find the fire burning a little lower and that that everyone else had retired to the kitchen and were softly singing as they prepared a meal. He rose from the couch and stretched, pinching the bridge of his nose and rubbing the sleep from his eyes as he strode quietly to the doorway of the kitchen. The whole family, along with Kathryn, was busy either pulling out food or getting out dishes to set the table.

Nathan drew their attention, "Oh, and I am so sorry for napping on the couch. I haven't done that in years. Frankly, I can't remember the last time."

After a brief awkward pause, Nathan broke the silence, "Don't you think it's time to let these good people get back to their life? We gotta get to ours as well," looking at Kathryn.

"Not to worry, Nathan. It's all good," Sonny said, still looking at the dishes in his hands. "Anyway, you aren't getting outta here. You missed seeing the amount of snow falling. Without plows, these roads fill in, and the snow will bury that Lexus. Your wife brought it around to the back and got some clothes out of there. There's no going anywhere tonight, maybe not for a few days. Sorry bud."

Almost panicky, Nathan thought of the things that he was going to miss. His iPad and laptop were back at the house along with the desktop with its two huge monitors. His phone could be charged, but that was about all he had brought with him on this supposed short trip.

"Do you have a land line?" Nathan asked.

"Sorry no. We got rid of it last year when the world went really nuts. I guess you could say things were crazy before that too, but it just got to the point where we did not want to be tracked up here. Now, we have a little internet, but only at certain times to keep the feds off the track. We don't use it continually for more than 20-40 minutes, and then we turn it off for several hours," Sonny explained to Nathan briefly.

"Sorry to say this, but you guys sound a little paranoid," Nathan said, more worried about his work than anything. He jumped in surprise when Kathryn slugged his shoulder from behind, scaring him.

"Apologize!" she demanded uncharacteristically.

"I am sorry," Nathan said sheepishly. "I'm just worried about my work schedule."

"Don't worry about it," Sonny replied. "We don't have enough time to be angry with one another."

They finished the preparation for the meal and Sonny invited Kathryn and Nathan to join the family at the table. Once everyone was seated he bowed his head and said a simple blessing over the food, remembering to thank God for bringing the guests into his home.

Nathan ate quickly and then excused himself to search the cabin for a place where his iPhone might see one bar of signal. He didn't even notice a smidgen of bar movement from the network in this shell of a house. He then sought a Wi-Fi signal and found one that was password locked. "Sonny could you give me the code to the Wi-Fi?" Nathan asked, offering his phone to Sonny so he could enter the code for him. Sonny dried his hands and, taking the phone, entered the code. He then made sure Nathan knew he could only use the Wi-Fi for 40 minutes and no more.

Nathan sat on the couch and settled in for a search of any roads that might be passable. The National Weather Service was warning of a Clear Creek County blizzard. It was predicted that the snow would top 24 inches in the mountains and foothills, and then pile up slightly more in Denver over the next several hours. At times, storms would push against the Rocky Mountains, and then move slightly back toward the east again where they would stall and dump significant amounts of snow upon the Front Range. These conditions often accounted for more snow fall than the higher mountains received. The warnings about this storm coming across the forecasts were one of those predictions, and Nathan became concerned about his job and contacts.

All of his shipments were really in trouble if there could be no FedEx deliveries. He messaged his boss about his predicament as he came to understand the conditions would shut them all down for a time. Carmen responded back that since the shipments hadn't come in for the past two days and the storm was breaking over them, the people had decided to hunker down in their bunkers. Carmen reported that another storm system threatened southern Colorado for the next day as well.

Nathan was off the hook for the time being, but he still didn't want to stay in this cabin for many days. It reminded him of a commune. If he could just find a passable road nearby, he might consider braving the roads sooner than the Weather Service recommended.

That evening, they were graciously given the guest bedroom which Sandra had straightened up to allow for their stay. With nothing else to do but go to bed, although it was still early, everyone began to prepare the cabin and themselves for a long evening.

Strange and enticing fragrances wafted down the hallway, beckoning Kathryn to find the source and she disappeared from their bedroom for twenty minutes, while Nathan heard Sonny bringing in more wood. Glancing down the hallway and through another open door, Nathan saw that Kathryn was inside of the main bedroom with Sandra, looking down at bottles of oils on the couple's bed.

Nathan decided that he didn't need to sleep yet, and with the thought of repairing his earlier comments to their new hosts, he trudged outside to find Sonny and help him to chop more logs. They found several smaller logs around the property and chopped wood in the relative dark as the snowflakes continued to fall and accumulate. The exercise actually invigorated both of them as they traded off between setting the two-foot logs for each other and splitting them with a very sharp axe. They spoke casually about their old professions, and Nathan told of his new one, careful to leave out the top-secret location, mentioning only that it was within the

United States, and that he had seen it more by video than anything else.

Sonny told Nathan of his work as an intelligence officer in the CIA. He gave astounding details of missions that were never revealed to the public. When Nathan asked why he was sharing this ultra-secret data, Sonny shrugged off the intimation of consequences stating the nation he had once worked for no longer truly existed. His efforts to protect America had been replaced with globalized leadership. They adjusted enemy lists that catalogued known terrorists along with harmless Christians. Such changes spawned a response from some people causing them to become ultra-nationalists as Sonny referred to them. He stressed just how dangerous a place the world had become and continued stating how many believers would be Harvested before the end of the world.

"My wife has used those terms as well – Harvest and end of the world. What do they mean?" Nathan asked, resting the axe he had been using as he listened to Sonny against the ground and not caring that his stillness allowed the snow to cover his hair.

"End of the world is a term explained in the book of Revelation and in other parts of the New Testament. It signifies there will be an end to the way this world operates. The term Harvest refers to the taking away of all those who convert to Christ before it is too late. Soon we believers, including your wife, will be taken away by God to be with Jesus. After that more people will choose to convert to Him as well.

"I did a word study on my iPad Bible. It indicated that many during this final timeframe, before the end of the world, there will be much martyrdom for Christians. The Scriptures are specific about this next phase, or the last three and a half years that are called the Great Tribulation."

"Why is it called that?" Nathan couldn't believe he was asking the question about something that he never wanted to hear from his wife, but he had to admit that hearing it from an ex-CIA agent enthralled him.

"Well, I don't know if I can do it full justice, because I have only studied it for a short time. I'm a Johnny-come-lately to all this," Sonny said as he picked up the axe Nathan had abandoned and began to chop, speaking between whacks while Nathan placed the next log for splitting. "There will be a lot of upheaval, because Satan will be cast out of heaven and restricted to this earth. He will literally enter into the *Anti-Christ*'s body. You see, he isn't allowed to do what he considers his primary job until then, which is to accuse the believers and kill them. He is gonna get so ticked off because he will know his time is short and he will do as much damage as he can. You don't wanna be here for that, Nathan!" he paused for a few seconds to emphasize the last sentence.

"I am sure I won't be," Nathan lied because he actually had no clue whether or not he believed all that he was hearing.

"We have had our struggles since first disappearances, haven't we?" Sonny asked.

"I guess we have."

"But nothing, and I mean nothing, compares to what it's gonna be," Sonny continued as if Nathan had not spoken. "Satan, in all his anger, will inhabit Cartiff the global leader and unleash his fury on Christians throughout the world. Even if someone is not a Christian, he will just consider their loss collateral damage. But, there is something you have to understand. God has already won the battle. No matter what Satan does, he cannot win," Sonny emphasized again as they finally decided to end their task and carry the wood they had cut into the cabin.

The conversation continued as two settled into the cozy fire lit room. "I don't know, Sonny. It is just hard to believe that things aren't going to get better. If you look historically at the markets, when 9/11 occurred, the stock market crashed. It went up and down for many years. However, by 2005, it was back up," Nathan tried to soothe himself from the scary predicament that Sonny was painting by focusing on the positives.

"Yeah, but it crashed again in 2008. But let me ask you what I was asking a few friends of mine: if the stock market is 7000, is God still on the throne, or, has He lost all his cattle on those thousand hills the Bible says belong to Him?" Sonny asked as he looked at the fire which shone as a sparkle in his eyes.

"I have no idea what you are talking about," replied Nathan, not having a clue what cattle had to do with God and the stock market.

"The answer is He hasn't lost a thing. His resources, wisdom and knowledge stand firm, no matter what is going on down here on earth. Truly, God has still seen all things that can happen and will happen. Did you know that Revelation was written with a perfect tense to its verbs?"

"I have no idea why that is meaningful," Nathan responded.

"What I mean is that Jesus was showing John this vision, who was writing down what he saw and it was as if he had been transported into the future to this timeframe. John was seeing the world we live in today from a heavenly perspective, as if it had already occurred and was occurring." At that moment, Sandra brought them both another mug of cocoa to help them thaw out as they sat by the fire.

Nathan spoke up, "Can I just tell you that I don't think it makes me less of a Christian if I really don't believe in the things you ascribe to? I think there are multiple interpretations to that book, and it's to the

239

reader to glean what they can from their own perspective. I totally respect your right to believe the way you do, but I am just unsure see it your way. You make it seem that you have got the meaning of the end all figured out, as if a book written 2000 years ago could understand the complexities of the time we live in and give you insight. That seems pretty far-fetched to me. No offense," Nathan concluded lamely.

"None taken," Sonny shot back quickly with a look that made Nathan realize the man somehow knew that Nathan's beliefs were shaky at best and non-existent at the worst. Nathan wondered just what Kathryn had been saying about him while he had slept that afternoon.

"What I have said is the truth. I can't promise you'll like it. I have given you the Scriptural perspective on it," the directness of Sonny's reply pleased Nathan even if the conclusions he had drawn made Nathan uncomfortable.

Deciding to end the conversation before he heard any more, Nathan changed the subject. "Hey, Sonny thanks for letting us stay. I promise I will pay you once I get back home. I think I am going to get a shower and go to bed. That wood chopping really wore me out."

"You don't owe us a dime. It's on the house as it were. Goodnight!" Sonny graciously did not pursue the former conversation, recognizing that he had planted some more seeds in Nathan's heart. Now it would be up to the Holy Spirit to be sure they were watered.

"Well, thank you very much. I will make it up to you someday...promise!" Nathan shook Sonny's hand before retiring to the bathroom for a very quick shower respecting the family's need to conserve energy and water.

Afterward he pulled on his robe and a pair of sweat bottoms that Kathryn had laid out for him and dropped easily into bed. "They are really nice people," he said thoughtfully surprising even himself with the admission.

"I know," Kathryn responded. "In spite of being mostly off the grid they make this home very comfortable and welcoming. It's like having a mini vacation in the mountains. I feel safe and that I am getting some rest. Oh, and thanks for chopping the wood. I know Sandra really appreciated you helping Sonny," Kathryn replied softly.

"Not a problem...goodnight," Nathan replied, cutting off more conversation with his implied *I am done talking for the night* tone of voice and abruptness. He felt like he couldn't take any more preaching or Scriptural references at this point, but he couldn't get the conversation with Sonny out of his head. He figured he needed time alone with his thoughts to process it all.

"Goodnight," Kathryn said. She quietly lay next to him sensing that he wasn't falling asleep. She stayed perfectly still so that she wouldn't disturb him and spent the time praying for Nathan that he would get a clue as to the existence of Jesus inside of this chaotic world. She was thankful that Nathan had spent time with Sonny through the evening and realized that Sonny was the best person for him to hear the truth from. Sandra had told her that Sonny was ex-CIA and from what Kathryn had heard, his way of communicating was effective and would likely draw the attention of most men – including Nathan.

Kathryn only wished that they had met this precious family a year ago to help break through the rock in Nathan's heart. She instantly put that thought out of her mind and asked for forgiveness. Before the initial Rapture, she would lament choices that she did or didn't make. But, since that fateful event, she realized the folly of that type of thinking. If she were to complain about anything, it would all funnel back to her lack of decision-making upon the only thing that really mattered - accepting Jesus as her Savior.

Meanwhile Nathan, invigorated by the exercise and shower, but also pretending to be asleep, silently contemplated the direction of his life. He thought of the different highs and the lows throughout his life. He confessed to himself that many of the low points related to his relationships with his son and Kathryn while a definite high point was this incredible job opportunity with Carmen, who was more friend than boss in some respects, even though they had had little personal contact. Nathan believed that he could easily share many of his marital issues that were occurring with this man who had his own history of break-ups. His mind wandered back to the conversation he just had with Sonny. He could not deny the wisdom that came from the mouth of the former CIA agent, but he could not accept it all either. He had no answer as to why he could not embrace the reasonings and beliefs of such an intelligent man as Sonny. Feeling somewhat restless and dissatisfied with his musings, Nathan sighed deeply and tried to put it all out of his mind. Solving the mess that was his life and the world around him would have to wait for another day.

CHAPTER 30

The next several days were spent in the same type of rhythm they had established with the Farrell's that first afternoon, while the snow continued to fall outside. Nathan had never actually experienced a blizzard from the perspective of the mountains before. He had briefly driven in bad conditions, but never lived through days of snowfall that even the Farrell's were calling a big one. Without the use of effective snowplows, which hadn't been available since before the disappearances, they were going to have to dig their way out of the almost four miles of driveway themselves.

After the first week of being snowbound, Nathan and Sonny were finally able to take off in his ancient Ford Bronco that graced his property in attempt to clear away some of the snow from the drive. The Bronco was mint green six cylinder with the strangest shifting abilities. *It's so retro*, Nathan thought. Nathan could not remember seeing one like this, other than in the movies. They attached the small snowplow up front and threw shovels in the back seat. The power of the vehicle was evident from the moment that they turned the engine over. Nathan wondered if a racecar had as much power as this souped-up vehicle.

They plowed for two hours, slowly progressing two miles down the driveway, repeatedly hitting drifts with some speed to break through, until one was so big it stopped them cold. The deep drift hid a creek bed which had developed ice as dense as marble. The Bronco could not gain enough traction to get over the creek and through the drift. They wrapped a winch cable around a nearby tree and hooked it on the back end of the vehicle to pull themselves out.

At this point, both of them exhausted from the effort of the day, Nathan hurt his back from trying to shovel a rather large clump of icy snow. He vowed to come back the next day as they drove back to the cabin. However, Sonny commented that only the sun would kill this one obstacle off in maybe a week or more.

The two limped into the cabin to concerned wives, Nathan being helped up the last few steps holding his left side and complaining of his back. After warming up by the fire to loosen the muscles, Sandra offered to work on both his and Sonny's backs. She easily raised Nathan's opinion of her by effectively manipulating his back, almost as well as any Doctor of Osteopathic (D.O.) manipulation techniques. Nathan had experience over the years. After a car accident, he tried several chiropractors who made some difference, but only one D.O. could give him any great measure of relief. He should have remembered that he could only stress it so much with chopping wood and snow shoveling exercises.

Sandra, however, expertly adjusted his shoulders and back in ways that he had rarely felt. "I worked for a D.O. who taught me some of his manipulation methods so that I could see a few overflow patients that had no insurance," Sandra explained while she performed a small miracle on Nathan's back. "We were trying to help people out, so I got my Nurse Practitioner's license. I have used it on the kids and Sonny many times, so he would be able to get out more firewood," she winked at Sonny with a twinkle in her eye.

"I'm going, I'm going..." Sonny laughingly replied as he swung his axe over his right shoulder, moving out toward the chopping block. The girls pulled on their boots to help out and play in the snow a little bit. Nathan could hear Sonny directing the kids to set up the next log on the tree stump, but the confinement of the days had caused a surplus of energy to build up and they just had to play between each directive. Each time Sonny addressed the girls his commands were firm but loving. Something that Nathan realized he had never attained with Samuel when he was a boy. There was always harshness in Nathan's interactions with Samuel when he was younger which lead to a distance between him and his cherished and only son. This bothered him to the day that his son left the earth. Most days, he attributed it to his need to discipline a young boy into an effective young man.

Watching the interaction between Sonny and his daughters, he saw the truth that he had allowed work disappointment and a mid-life crisis, to blind him and separate him from Samuel. He hadn't been a good father to the only son he thought he would ever have. At his age he would have had no way to rectify that error, even if Samuel had not gone missing. He pondered what his son would have become in life, perhaps working in Nathan's own architecture practice one day. Nathan considered that if he had been a better father, then maybe his son would not have chosen a career in the church, but instead a career with promise. The thoughts brought tears to his eyes and he realized that although several years had passed, the pain was still raw.

After Sandra's treatment and adjustment of him, Nathan felt totally relaxed. She added the final touch of essential oil aroma therapy, sending him to dreamland. He found his eyes closing, his body loose to the point he didn't care that he was still lying on the floor. Sandra was busily explaining to Kathryn about the properties of the essential oils she was using, but Nathan could barely hear the words, much less comprehend the complicated names that were beyond the ability of his numbing mind to grasp. Almost instantly, Nathan dropped into a dream:

He walked from room to room in a house with which he was unfamiliar. Each room had more closets than he had seen before in any house he had ever thought of designing. There was an intricacy to the house that only a few builders he knew would even tackle due to the ornately carved wood and sparsely painted, built-in white drawers which allowed the old wood to dully show through. A closer inspection of the closets and some of the sparse furniture within the rooms caused him to wonder why the final paint job was so shoddily completed. It was utterly incompatible to the wood or the closet spaces that were created. But what struck him most was that each room was stuffed with rotting meats and spoiled food on the floors. The smell invaded the landscape of his dream deeply until he reluctantly opened another bedroom door.

He knew not for what he was searching. He just felt strongly that he needed to find anyone who might occupy the home. The hallways became longer while the lights glowed increasingly dim in each room he came to. The furniture now looked better, but he knew that it was an illusion because the illumination had been reduced. Where was he going in this house? At that last question, he stepped toward a doorway that terminated in a very large room. All of the chandeliers were expensive and very dusty. It was as if the owner of this structure had not cleaned in years.

Nathan began to call out for someone who might live in this lonely house but only heard silence when he should have at least heard the echoes of his own voice. Looking around once more he saw that there were many cubby holes for materials to be stored. Perhaps for foodstuffs, such as in a pantry type closet space, or shoes in walk-in closets, but they were all empty. At the last room, he stopped when he saw movement and then realized he was seeing his own visage in a series of mirrors. The reflection, however, was of himself looking not much older than he was, but scarred and bruised as well as emaciated. While his jowl lines looked more pleasing to him, nothing else *about the reflection looked healthy. Even the shoes didn't match his belt, nor his socks to his pants. He noted that his shirt was rumpled and not tucked in.*

It was hardly the professional image he portrayed on a daily basis even when he just kicked around the house watching a ballgame. The man in the mirror had seen trials that were beyond comprehension. Nathan had never experienced what the man in the mirror portrayed. As he stared in gross fascination at the image, the truth of it hit him. He knew with certainty, he was staring at an unpleasant future of himself.

He began to look for a way of escape from the horror looking back at him. He yelled and kicked at the furnishings and pounded on the walls. Nothing he did made a noise, because sound was not allowed in this house. A house he had built. A house he had built that trapped him and left him with nothing.

Nathan awoke slowly, the remnants of the dream fading away. The ominous feeling of doom was gradually shaken off by the sense that his back seemed to be significantly better. Nathan slowly clambered to his feet and perched himself on the couch in the living room wrapping one of the numerous afghans around himself to ward off the chill that seemed to have invaded the cabin. After a few minutes of reorienting his subconscious into awareness, he realized that he could hear worship music playing and water running. The fire, for the first time in the almost one week that they had been there, was beginning to die. It appeared that no one had stoked the flames for some time. Kathryn or Sandra, he surmised, must have placed the afghan around him when he lay upon the floor for those many hours of deep sleep. After throwing a new log on the fire as well as turning the mass of embers over, the flames rose to life again. The familiar crackling almost overtook the music from the kitchen and had also drowned out the sound of the running water.

Maybe they were finishing with the dishes? He really liked how this family operated around him. They brought peace around him for long periods of time. He had been surprised through the week to find that the peace suited him.

In the quiet of the cabin, his recent dream came flooding back. He tried to consider the meaning of the dream. If he were more religious he might almost call it a vision because this one didn't feel like a normal night-time dream. He only remembered one other dream in his life from when he was ten years old that had been like this, and it had displayed in his mind like a Broadway play night after night. He suddenly realized that he hadn't remembered any other dream since that time until now.

That was the strangest dream, he thought as he threw the afghan off of himself and onto the couch and moved toward the sound of running water. As he walked into the kitchen, he noted that the water was running into one side of the double sink with bubbles visible around the drain on the other side, but not one person occupied the kitchen. He wondered if they may have left it going unintentionally as they ran for cover from a car that was coming up the drive that caught them all off guard.

He turned off the water and found the iPod that was playing that infernal worship music that these people loved so much and killed that sound as well. He stood in the relative silence, listening with all of his might for the potential sound of crunching tires against snow that would signal the alert, but he heard nothing. With a shudder he realized the silence was similar to the lack of sound within his dream.

Setting his mouth in a sneer so he wouldn't have to admit to the unease that was trying to creep over him, and telling himself that the whole family and his wife were messing with him, he traipsed from room to room, blowing out a candle if there was one burning unattended and searching for a potential occupant. Just so he didn't have to back track, after each room was thoroughly searched, he shut the door to remind him that it was cleared. But as he systematically eliminated the upstairs, downstairs, and the basement rooms, he came slowly back to the kitchen having found no one.

He stepped outside with his hands slipping into the sleeves of his cardigan sweater trying to call out as quietly as he could for Sonny, but even he could hear the edge of desperation in his voice. Over half an hour later, after he had foraged through the wooded areas searching for footprints, but finding none, he sat on the back-porch step in the pool of light created by the single bulb above the kitchen sink shining through the window. He shivered in fear and cold at the same time.

"Where is everyone?" He asked aloud. Then he realized that they might have gotten out of the driveway and gone to get some supplies. He used his phone hooked to the Wi-Fi to call Kathryn's cell, and he heard it ringing from where it sat on the countertop by her purse which she had evidently not taken with her, wherever she had gone. Frantically, he reached for his car keys to head down their driveway, when he saw Sonny's keys for the Bronco hung on the old style key hook like the one that he grew up with in his parent's home. He took the Bronco on the trek down, knowing the four wheel drive would perform better than his luxury car. He drove as far as the same pile and ice and snow that had stopped them earlier when his back went out. From there he trudged out into the bone chilling temperatures, remembering his coat this time. He made it all the way to the road but realized that he had encountered no footprints in the snow down the path he had taken.

"I can't believe they left me here. What good Christians are they anyway!?" he exclaimed into the wintery sky as he returned to the cabin, worried and concerned, but unable to shake the rising panic in his soul. Pieces of conversations he had had with Sonny over the last week came back to him, as did portions of the things that Kathryn had constantly tried to tell him over the last several years. They began to fill his mind with more questions than could be answered in one night, if at all. As he looked around at the empty cabin once more, he was afraid he would be finding those answers on his own. Alone.

End of ForeTold Book One.

ForeTold Book Two follows Nathan's life and others as they experience the Great Tribulation, the Glorious Appearance of Jesus and the return of Jesus to the earth.

ABOUT THE AUTHORS

JEFF SWANSON

Jeff Swanson has a passion to empower others with understanding of the life-giving one-hope found in Scripture. His talents as a speaker and teacher have led him to 'Share the Word' with thousands of people at churches, commencements, & conferences. He has been interviewed on Fox News Live, numerous Christian television shows, and on radio internationally.

His message is based on a thirty-year work that was published by *The Plan Bible*™ in 2010. The work is a Bible, reordered by time, taking the reader on a journey though the Past, Present and Future. It demonstrates the Bible's divine origin by color-coding & hyperlinking prophecy. His work has been endorsed by Dr. Tim LaHaye and Dr. Hilton Sutton.

Jeff graduated from ORU with a degree in business management, and later was awarded the distinguished CLU designation. In his financial services career, he was instrumental in leading teams to develop a new banking system, which successfully authenticated, validated and transferred billions of dollars.

Jeff and his wife Pam of more than 25 years reside in the Tulsa area, along with their three children and son-in-law. More information can be found at www.PlanBible.com.

DR. SCOTT YOUNG

Dr. Scott Young has his clinical doctorate in Audiology. He has worked with private practices, ear nose and throat Physicians, and hearing device manufacturers, fitting more than 20,000 patients successfully with hearing aids. Having taught hearing aid dispensers and audiologists how to complete good patient care effectively, he was also an integral part of manufacturing hearing aids of all types. Dr. Young started Hearing Solution Centers in Tulsa in 2005 (www.HearTulsa.com) and is happily married to Wendy since 1993, with his son in college at Oral Robert's University.

Besides being a published author, he is also a singer and a songwriter. His first book, *The Violin's Secret,* is a WWII novel about a family's struggle to escape the Nazi torture of life as they rescue a Jewish family from death. *Singing in the Mind* is a non-fictional study of how singing occurs in the brain. It focuses on how worship can change the life of the singer, as well as how music interacts with culture from a Biblical and scientific standpoint. His third book, *The Professor in History,* places an atheist professor in the past to interface with the historical Jesus and discover what he knows about his own life, not to mention the lies he has believed about the Biblical Jesus. Dr. Young's passion is writing and teaching the Biblical truths in unique ways.

Scott testifies that Jeff's PlanBible.com helped him write the book *Singing in the Mind*, finding passages that he never saw in Scripture before. He has read the Bible cover to cover more than ten times, but sometimes it is hard to locate passages in Chronicles and Leviticus because of the difficulties in reading those books. The Plan Bible gives the reader insight as to when the chronology is placed. He supports Jeff's ministry, and they have integrally tied their families together.

Scott's other works can be found on www.DrScottYoung.com, as well as finding his ministry and audiology videos on YouTube and Facebook.

More Titles Available at
www.PlanBible.com

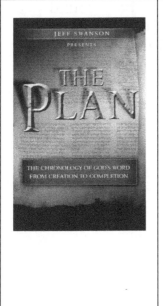

The Plan:
The Chronology of God's Word from
Creation to Completion in eBook
(NIV & KJV)

The Plan is a complete Bible rearranged chronologically (Event order by Time). Some call it 'The roadmap of world history' because it reveals not only where humanity has been, but also where we are going. It establishes truth by placing all witnesses (Authors) together for each event. It demonstrates the divine origin of the Bible by linking biblical prophecies to their fulfillments in 950 threads that span all time. They are color coded for clear understanding.

ForeTold II

Experience the trials of unbelievers. This fiction novel is based on the 2,500 biblical prophesies promised that will come to pass in the soon future.

The saga continues. Follow the survivors that endure the Great Tribulation period. Their powerful testimonies give glory to God as they make their way through ever-increasing natural disaster, supernatural events and political upheaval, as they come to know Jesus Christ as Lord and enter the Kingdom to come.

The Plan's Second Witness:
The Chronology of Enoch I & II and the
Book of Jashar from Creation to
Completion in eBook

The Bible is the first and foremost authority for truth. *The Second Witness* gives testimony to God's entire plan that has been known from antiquity. This book builds faith in God's word as supporting documents to Bible. These books are mentioned by name or quoted directly or indirectly in the Bible. The language has been modernized into a New English Version for easy understanding. It follows the same format of The Plan with 14 C's of history and prophecies linked and color-coded.

	God's Co-Creation Process This nonfiction helps you walk out God's plan for your life. This practical tool empowers you to identify and navigate the good things God has given for you to do to fulfill your purpose on this earth. It takes you on a journey through your soul. The journey starts with God planting His ideas as seeds deep in your spirit, then growing those seeds as your head gets understanding, and finally, manifesting those ideas into a real harvest.
	The Plan Outline Book This 63-page paperback is a helpful world history outline taken from The Plan: The Chronology of God's Word from Creation to Completion. The 14 C's of history with all the major events starting with Creation and ending with Completion of prophecies yet to be fulfilled. It displays the 440 biblical dates along with over 800 world history dates.
	Many more resources including teaching series in various formats can be obtained at the website. **Also The Plan Bible app is on the way stay tuned!** **www. PlanBible.com**

CPSIA information can be obtained
at www.ICGtesting.com
Printed in the USA
LVHW080617140320
650069LV00039B/1606

9 780983 084457